MURDER RUN

JOHN HUNT

Black Rose Writing | Texas

ISBN: 978-1-68433-730-9
PUBLISHED BY BLACK ROSE WRITING
www.blackrosewriting.com

Printed in the United States of America
Suggested Retail Price (SRP) $19.95

Murder Run is printed in Garamond

*As a planet-friendly publisher, Black Rose Writing does its best to eliminate unnecessary waste to reduce paper usage and energy costs, while never compromising the reading experience. As a result, the final word count vs. page count may not meet common expectations.

DEDICATION

This book, like all the others, is dedicated to Louise.

SPECIAL THANKS

To my beta readers, Ethan Hunt and podcast co-host Kyle Grant, thanks! As usual, you saw points I missed and made this book better.

Thanks to Jaime Groff, who went through my manuscript and cleaned up the messes with deadly efficiency. Because of her, this book reads as smooth as a lake on a windless day. If it is ever rocky, that would be my fault.

To my growing reading audience, of course, thank you for talking about me and my work. As you know, that is the best way for an unknown author to step out from behind the curtain and appear onstage. Let's keep it going shall we?

PRAISE FOR AUTHOR JOHN HUNT

Doll House

"Olivia. She's a brilliant character, broken, but trying to survive on her terms."
–Ginger Nuts of Horror

"The female lead, Olivia, is a great character. She reminded me of Jamie Lee Curtis." **–Cedar Hollow Horror Reviews**

"It is certainly shocking and gruesome, but John Hunt manages it quite impressively." **–The Novel Pursuit**

"I was engaged from the very first to the very end." **–Strong Book Reviews**

"*Doll House* is a deeply felt and admirably realized tale of an unending real-life nightmare." **–Mallory Heart Reviews**

"My head is spinning... I was clenching my hands and biting my nails the WHOLE time." **–After the Pages**

"I absolutely loved this book." **–Bolton Library**

"If you want a 'scare your pants off' type horror thriller, then look no further."
–Clues and Reviews

"*Doll House* was one heck of a psychological thrill ride!"
–Butterfly's Booknerdia Blog

"...the author has created a masterpiece thriller." **–Gothic Moms**

"Superb book in a gruesome way." **–Love Books 'n' Family**

"A book of the year!" **–Buried in a Book**

The Tracker

Off The Grid

Balance

"John Hunt is my favorite author. Scaring the "oh my god" out of me with every line I read. All of the insect facts bothered me almost more than the story did…." **–RHB, *Amazon* review**

Four Shots of Horror

"Hunt has thought up some clever scenarios in these stories, and they don't always play out quite the way readers might expect. Along the way, there are some definitely uncomfortable moments. *Four Shots of Horror* will prove quite intoxicating for fans of the genre." **–*Silver Screen Videos***

MURDER
RUN

-1-

Kyle sat in his pickup truck smoking a cigarette and watching the front door of Rachel's Watering Hole, thinking about his big brother and how much it would piss him off to know Kyle was at this very moment parked outside a bar. Kyle stopped at this small-town bar because he liked the bright pink neon sign. He saw the sign from the highway. It drew him to the bar like a patio light does a moth. The 'H' in 'Hole' blinked, stuttered, and fluttered like a candle about to be blown out by an errant breeze. If the light in the letter extinguished, the sign would read Rachel's Watering ole. Kyle smiled and exhaled a plume of smoke through his nostrils. He spun the cap off the Wild Turkey whiskey bottle he held between his thighs and took a swig. Kyle grimaced, twisted the cap back on and sighed as the warmth oozed into his middle, spreading fingers of pleasure throughout his body. He followed the drink with a drag from his cigarette. Booze and nicotine. In Kyle's mind, no better combination on this planet existed.

Kyle wanted to go inside. He wanted to hear music, and he wanted to see real people. Regular people in a regular bar enjoying each other's company, and maybe even talking about the continually disappointing Blue Jays baseball team. He wanted the bubbly taste of beer on his lips. Maybe one of those heavy tasting IPA beers that would make him gasp after draining half of a bottle. No, not a bottle. A pint glass. A clear one so he could see the circle of white foam on top after the bartender slid the glass across the bar and into his hand as though pulled by a magnet. Only his brother told him to come straight home and his brother, Kyle knew, always tried to do the best he could for Kyle. Kyle was a person best characterized as a fuck-up. Kyle knew it. His brother Steven sure knew it and because of this fact, Steven only wanted to protect Kyle from himself, right? As the last few years attested to, Kyle did need such protection. Maybe he should listen to Steven this time and get his ass home in record time. Actually surprise Steven with how fast he had gotten himself home without a fuck-up to his name.

Not a recent one, anyway. Kyle's eyes zeroed in on the pink sign. Decisions, decisions. One beer wouldn't hurt though, would it?

Kyle sucked another lungful of smoke and said, "It's never just one beer. Don't go kidding yourself."

He reached for the keys in the ignition to start the truck and get the hell away from the place, but his hand hesitated over the key ring.

"Fuck it," Kyle said. He removed the keys from the ignition and flicked his cigarette out into the night. Red sparks flickered and then disappeared. He opened the door, paused and glanced at the screen of his cell phone on the seat beside him. He picked it up and a message from his older brother flashed on the lock screen. It read: *Get down here. Don't stop. Don't pass Go. I'm waiting for you little bro.* Holding the phone in his hand, he grimaced. Kyle knew what the message meant. It meant don't stop at any place… period. It wasn't in the typed message, but it certainly meant that Kyle was not to even go near a bar or any establishment with alcohol prominent on the menu. It meant, listen to your older brother, you little bitch. Even if the advice, no, the command, was coming from a good place, it was still a command and Kyle never responded well to commands and after all that he had been through, he wanted a damn beer. He deserved that beer. He'd earned it.

Kyle muttered, "Fucking Steven," and stepped out of the truck. He didn't need a babysitter. He tossed the phone onto the passenger seat. Kyle stretched across the driver side seat and put the bottle of Wild Turkey back into the glove box. There was money burning a hole in his pocket and he didn't want any texts or calls from his brother to mess up what could be a fine evening. One beer. That's all. One beer and he'd be back on the road to home.

He stuffed the truck keys into his pocket and popped a piece of gum into his mouth to get rid of the smokey taste on his tongue. He combed his hair with his fingers and smiled. He crossed the lot to the door, feeling good with a little whiskey buzz in his belly. He pulled open the door and walked inside. Later, much later, he thought it would have been better for everyone if he had just listened to his brother and drove on by.

•　　•　　•

Kyle stopped inside the door and inhaled the scent of beer and peanuts. He nodded to himself. Coming in here was the right decision. Budweiser, Coors

Light, Busch Light, and Old Milwaukee signs shone and twinkled from above the dark wood bar. Kyle had to stop himself from licking his lips. It'd been so long since he'd had a beer. It wasn't something they allowed him to have where he'd been.

Kyle's boots clonked on the wooden boards as he strode to the bar. Rick Springfield was singing *Jesse's Girl* from speakers mounted in the corners of the bar near the ceiling. A woman, presumably the same Rachel named on the bright sign outside, leaned on the bar in-side profile to Kyle, talking to another woman sitting on the customer side of the bar with her elbows on the shiny wooden top with a glass of beer between them. Rachel smiled and moved her hips from side to side. Kyle could see she was trying to pick the other woman up. Judging by the return smile, he thought the presumed-to-be Rachel had a good shot of being successful. Kyle waited for a second or so, and because he wanted a beer so bad and was defying his brother and his own good sense to get said beer, he interrupted them. Romance could wait, his thirst could not.

"Excuse me! A pitcher of your finest Budweiser!"

He meant to say pint, but pitcher came out instead. He didn't change his order. A pitcher sounded just about right to Kyle. Hell, it sounded perfect.

The bartender turned to Kyle. On her shirt and above her left breast, Kyle read the name tag: Hannah. Huh. Not Rachel. He smiled, and she didn't return it. If Hannah's eyes were guns, Kyle's body would be bullet riddled right now.

To the other woman Hannah said, "I'll be back."

She poured the pitcher of beer and placed the jug and a clean glass in front of Kyle.

She said, "$15.00."

Kyle placed a twenty-dollar bill on the bar and said, "Here you go."

Hannah pocketed the money and returned to the other woman and leaning on the bar, she continued flirting. Kyle poured a glass, drank half of it and filled it back up. He said, "Can I have my change?"

The song changed to a Bruce Springsteen one. Kyle didn't know the song, but he knew the boss's voice.

Hannah straightened and with a frown so deep it dug lines into her cheeks she walked over to Kyle. She slapped two toonies and one loonie on the bar. Smiling, Kyle scooped them up and put them in his pocket. No way was he giving her a tip. Not with that attitude.

Hannah waited a beat, sighed and returned her focus to the other woman. Kyle, with his drink in hand, spun around on the stool to take in the rest of the bar. He leaned back so his elbows rested on the bar. To the left of the entrance was a dance floor with a raised seating area by the bay windows at the front of the bar. The walls were an ugly beige wood paneling, but ugly though they were, Kyle thought they suited the bar. Black Jack gum, Enjoy Coca-Cola and posters with cigarettes being hawked by cartoon women with exaggerated cartoon hourglass figures decorated the walls in shiny, dark wooden frames. Hanging from the center of the dance floor was a disco ball with bull horns attached to them. On three sides of the dance floor were tables and chairs, raised for people to have a view of the people moving and dancing. A group of men in Boston Red Sox jerseys had their heads cranked to watch a TV bolted to the wall above them. Pitchers of beer and glasses littered the table. Some were empty, some full and some not quite either.

Further down from the men, three women occupied another table. One woman was looking at Kyle while the other two chattered happily beside her. He returned the woman's look and thought beer wasn't the only thing he hadn't had in a while.

• • •

Grace DeBoers saw the man when he walked into the bar and the conversation volume of her two friends beside her went from an eight to a one. His wavy hair, or hockey hair, the kind that would curl out from under the back of a baseball cap, had caught her attention. The more she studied him, the more she liked. The man moved with confidence. A swagger that drew her eyes. He had an air of danger about him too, a cloud of it, that he disguised with a young man's smile. She saw through his smile to the animal underneath and it made her heart thrum. She watched him get his beer, drink some of it and spin around on the stool. He noticed her looking at him and he returned the look. She felt a thrill inside. A tingle in her stomach and a bit of heat between her thighs. In her group of friends, men typically noticed her last. She was the alternative. The drunk pick-up at the end of the night when all the other, better looking options, were taken. She was the chubbier one of her group of friends. Her role was usually that of the wingman. Her job had been to support her friends when they were being hit on, and when they were doing the hitting on. Tonight, it looked like it would be her turn. She smiled. A nervous shiver shook her hands. It was never her turn.

The man left his stool and walked toward her carrying a beer glass and pitcher. Looking up at her from the dance floor, he smiled and said, "Hello. I'm Kyle."

"I'm Grace."

Holding up the pitcher and smiling he said, "Care to join me for a drink?"

"I'd love to."

•   •   •

Grace left her friends and joined Kyle at another table. They smiled encouragement at her, but didn't Grace see Rhonda's smile turn to a frown? As though she should have been the one Kyle approached? Wasn't this man making a mistake approaching Grace? A typical night would see Rhonda being assailed by all the good-looking men and then, only if Rhonda didn't choose them, would they turn their attention to Grace. She had always been the "she's better than nothing" alternative. That didn't happen tonight. Not at all. Kyle walked straight up to Grace and even when his eyes fell on Rhonda, all he did was nod at her before turning his attention to Grace. Grace loved that because that never happened to her. Was Rhonda annoyed by that? Grace didn't know, and even though she shouldn't feel anything about that little tidbit of information, she did. For once, Grace felt like the pretty one. She felt like the chosen one in the group. For once, she was getting a taste of what it is like to be chosen first. And Kyle was really good-looking. For those reasons Grace missed the cues she would have normally been dialed in on. He smiled, but his eyes stayed flat as a black, still pond. His predatory gaze lingered a little too long. She saw him look at her breasts and lick his lips and that, in other instances, would have been a deal breaker. Except Kyle was handsome and he had chosen her over Rhonda. And the alcohol he continued to feed her did not help her judgment at all. She loved to watch the muscles of his forearms ripple as he manipulated the glass of beer in his hand. He could handle her with those strong hands. Pick up a heavy girl like her with ease. She loved that his eyes were a bright beautiful green, similar to the green grass on the rolling hills of a plantation in some Hollywood movie. Calling them emerald didn't do them justice. Almost insulting to those otherworldly orbs, when she thought about it. Wait. Why was he looking at her like that? Had he asked her something? What had he said? Why had she drunk so much?

She said, "What was that?" Only it came out like 'what-wuz-tha?'

Smiling his green-eyed smile, he said, "You wanna get outta here?"

She blinked and inhaled a deep breath, trying to force a moment of sobriety. She glanced at her friends. They were now talking to the guys in the Boston Red Sox jerseys. They had put their tables together and were laughing and sharing what looked like chicken wings but could very well be ribs. They were licking their fingers and building an impressive pile of red-stained napkins. She couldn't see from here, but if she had her choice, they would be ribs. She loved ribs.

Smiling at Kyle, she said, "Sure."

Kyle said, "Well, all right," and lifting his glass of beer, he finished what remained in two gulps. He grabbed her hand across the table and gave it a gentle squeeze. He stood and looked down at her, smiling except the smile looked drawn on, like that was how Kyle thought a smile should look like but didn't quite know how to pull one off. A line of ice traveled down her spine and she pulled her hand back and started shaking her head and then he touched her chin with his index finger and middle finger. A gentle touch, a soft touch, and she lifted her eyes to his. A touch such as that, what was she afraid of? She stood and said with a bit of a slur, "Let's go."

Her friends didn't see her leave.

-2-

Sunlight filtered red through the skin of Kyle's eyelids. He noticed the sensation of heat burning his chest and his left arm. Something heavy was on his lap. His breath warmed his nostrils. His neck hurt and a sharp pain on the left side throbbed electric through the muscles of his trapezoids. These combining sensations nudged him closer and closer to consciousness. He coughed, tasted beer and cigarettes on his tongue and coughed more until something large jumped into the back of his throat.

Kyle said, "Agh!"

He turned his head to the left and spat what was in his mouth out the window. He cracked open an eye and saw that he was in his truck, sitting upright with his window open. He coughed and gathered more salty substance in his mouth. With a hearty throat-clearing, he spat the contents out of the window and onto the side of the road. He grimaced. It had some weight to it. He'd heard it hit.

He groaned squinting at the day's brightness. His brain felt small and dry in his skull. He blinked more, clearing the film of sleep from his eyes.

Kyle's voice croaked, "Where the hell am I?"

Using the back of his hand, he wiped the remnants of spit from the corner of his mouth. The skin of his hand felt sticky, almost tacky. He looked at his hand and saw a dark red coat on the skin. He looked at his other hand. Also red. He knew what it was, and it confused him. How? What? And then he looked down into his lap where he felt the heaviness. Grace's head sat in his lap with her mouth turned toward his groin.

"What the fuck!"

Beside him, in the passenger seat sat her headless body. She was topless and slumped away from him, so the stump of her neck pressed against the closed passenger window. Her torso had red gaping mouths in it. Kyle knew what those were. Stab wounds. Her blood coated the inside of his truck.

Kyle groaned and pressed the palms of his hands into his eyes.

"Why do I do this? Why? Why? Why? Fuck me…"

• • •

Flashes of the previous night, like snapshots on the camera roll of a cell phone, pulsed through his brain until they coalesced into a running nightmare. When they left the bar, Grace had been drunk. Real drunk. They drove away and she directed him to a secluded wooded spot where she said she used to make out with high school boys when she was younger. She sometimes let them slip a hand up her top. She smiled when she told him that, eyes hazy with remembrance. He remembered thinking how sexy that simple admission had been. A shy girl admitting to something naughty. The interior green lighting of the radio screen made her red lip-sticked smile appear black and he liked that too. He lit a cigarette, and she took it from his mouth and inhaled. She gave him the cigarette back, reached into the tight pocket of her pants and pulled her hand out. In her palm, like eggs nestled in a nest, were two blue pills. MDMA. She offered him one. Slurring, she said, "You ever fuck on X?" He never had. And he sure would like to try.

They swallowed the pills at the same time. She giggled while covering her mouth with one hand. He leaned over to kiss her, his groin pleasantly full of blood and she mashed her lips against his mouth with such force he felt her teeth click against his. In that moment, Kyle was glad he had stopped in that bar for a beer. Fuck his brothers worrying. Here he was, making out with this sexy woman in his pickup truck at the local make-out spot in a town he didn't even know the name of. And now he was going to get lucky. Yeah, Kyle was glad he ignored his brother and went into Rachel's Watering Hole. Best idea he'd had in, well, at that moment in time it was the best decision he had ever made. Period. Kyle maneuvered his hand under her top and was sliding it up to her breast, just like those high school kids had back-in-the-day. Grace cupped his groin with her hand, he moaned, and then really drunk Grace puked in his mouth and promptly passed out. Stunned, he watched her limp body slide away from him. Puke is one hell of a mood killer.

"Fucking bitch!"

The smell, the taste, the chunks of what-in-the-hell-is-that in his mouth? French fries? The acidic taste of her vomit burned his tongue and feeling a clench in his guts, like someone opening and closing their hand inside him. Before he could dredge up the will power to stop himself, he spilled the contents of his stomach across the prone body of Grace. It splashed across her chest. Some of it hit her cheek and droplets spattered her chin. She flinched but didn't wake up. And sitting on the skin of her chest, peeking at him from between the mounds of her breasts was the little blue pill he had swallowed.

"Goddamnit!"

The interior of the truck stank with the sharp aroma of vomit. Bile covered his shirt and face and to top it off, he wouldn't be getting laid and if he let it, the buzz he had worked so hard to cultivate would fade away and then what would he have? Less than nothing. A big handful of fuck-all.

"To hell with that!" Kyle reached past her and unlocked the glove box. His grasping hand closed on the bottle of Wild Turkey. He held the bottle up, saw over half of the liquid remained, and with an angry twist, he removed the top and tipped the bottle to his mouth. The liquid burned his throat as it went down. Tears sprung to his eyes. The smell inside the truck hit him again. He compressed his lips and scrambled out of the truck and away before he puked out the recently consumed alcohol.

He walked away from the truck and sucked in the clear night air. His stomach settled enough for him to continue drinking and so that's what he did. He paced and drank, paced and drank, muttering to himself, while eyeing Grace sprawled out in his truck. Kyle's buzz returned and his inhibitions, which, to be honest, weren't very strong to begin with, melted under the gulps of alcohol pouring past his lips. He peered into the truck. Grace's head was canted at what Kyle thought to be an uncomfortable angle. A real neck-crinker. A string of yellow drool ran from her mouth to her shoulder. It shuddered with her breath. The shiny filament made Kyle think of a spider web. The little blue pill he had puked on her chest rose and fell. He reached in and plucked the pill off her skin and stuck it in his mouth. He swallowed a generous amount of Wild Turkey to chase the pill down and continued pacing.

Every so often, his gaze would return to the rise and fall of her chest. He wondered what her breasts would look like. Would they have big nipples or little ones? He was partial to the little ones. The kind with a nipple that looked like the eraser on the end of a number two pencil. Who was he kidding? He liked all boobs. It's not like he'd turn away from a pair flashed at him.

Grace's pale skin appeared ghostly green under the glow from the dashboard and he imagined her nipples would be dark, dark like her lip stick had been. He licked his lips. Would it hurt to look? To see what they looked like? No, probably not. She'd never know, would she? Not passed out like that. In no time at all, Kyle talked himself into pulling the top of her shirt down.

The next step was easier after that. His eyes grew seeing her shiny bra. Sheen, reflective and he spotted a circular shadow where her nipple would be. He didn't realize it, but he whispered, "Oh man," as he reached for one of her bra straps. He slid one strap down her shoulder and revealed one breast. Pencil erasers. Perfect. He brushed her nipple with his finger, and it puckered and stood up. Before he knew it, he had her shirt off, her pants off, her underwear down a bit and he was getting ready to take his pants off, his penis throbbing pleasantly against the zipper of his jeans. He had his belt loose and the top button on his jeans undone when Grace woke up. Groggy and still drunk she peered at him with her mouth half open. Her eyes bulged as she realized she was almost naked, and Kyle was in the process of taking his pants off. She blinked, said, "What?" She saw her shirt in the crease of the chair, and she snatched it and used it to cover her naked flesh. Kyle, shaking his head, said, "No, no, no, no," and yanked the shirt from her grip and threw it into the darkness. She didn't like that. Not one bit. The fight was on.

She hit him with ineffectual slaps to his face, his shoulder, and his chest and she called him a bastard. He grabbed at her wrists, but her skin was slick with vomit and she slipped his grasp and kept hitting him. One of her fingers went in his nostril and a sharp pain watered his eyes. "Fuck!"

Enough of this. He punched her in the nose. He felt the cartilage crunch under his knuckles. It was a good hit. A real corker, as his brother would say. Her eyes rolled back. He leaned over top of her planning to pin her arms above her head with one hand so he could get his penis out and put it to some use. That had been the plan anyway. Right up until the moment she kicked him and nailed him with the perfect hit on the end of his dick. The heel of her foot pushed his hard-on into his own body. He squealed and let go of her. The pain crossed his eyes and he bit into his tongue. Salty blood filled his open mouth. His stomach clenched again, but in the deeper part, the cabinet of pain reserved especially for testicular beatings produced a distinct nausea.

The passenger door opened with a squeal. It was a moonless night. She knew the area and Kyle didn't. If she slipped away into the darkness, if he lost her, he'd be done for. He'd have to go back to that *place*. He couldn't go back there. Not ever again.

He had to stop her but the pain resonating deep in his guts stole the strength from him. Agony flaring out from his centre reached out to tremble his legs and palsy his knees. It made it hard for him to move, to breathe even, but he knew the danger of letting her escape. His anger rose, a behemoth of unreasoning consuming any self-control he might have had left. Kick him and try to run from him, huh? No, no, no. They were just starting to have fun. They were getting to know each other really well out here, right?

He grabbed her retreating calf and pulled her to him with his left hand and when she got close enough, he punched her with his right hand and kept hitting her. She screamed and squirmed, and he hit her in the thigh, the hip, the arm and her voice rose, hitting the panic pitch, and his fist sunk into her middle stopping all her ear-piercing god-awful noise. He dragged her closer to him and her mouth was a cavern of blackness, trying to drag in the air his fist had stolen from her. He punched her in the face and her arms flailed out to her side. Her eyelids fluttered.

Kyle said, "Fuckin' right! Goddamn cock-tease!"

He hammer-fisted the side of her head, because why not, and he crushed his own pinky against her cheekbone.

"Goddamnit!"

He hopped out of the truck and spun in a circle outside the open door holding his injured hand tight to his side. She kept fucking hurting him!

Kyle reached under the passenger seat, fumbled around with his uninjured hand while Grace moaned. His hand closed on what he had been searching for and with a face-splitting grin, he pulled out his knife. He first saw it at a flea market and knew he had to have it. It looked like the knife Rambo always carried around with him in every movie. The one with the compass and matches concealed in the handle. Kyle said that information to the vendor, excited, his eyes eating up the dark blade with the metal teeth running along the spine. The vendor grinned, nodded, and invited Kyle to twist off the knob at the end of the handle. He did and there was a compass and honest-to-god matches in the handle. Sold!

Grace said, "Whuh... ack."

"Shut up."

Kyle unsnapped the button on the sheath and took it off the blade. Once the blade was free, he sunk the knife in between Grace's ribs. It went in easy and the sensation was so satisfying that Kyle shuddered and spent himself in his pants. Pleasure and pain. What a ride. A part of him cringed from himself. Only a monster would get off on sticking a blade in a person. And like any monster, Kyle didn't like being confronted by his own evil. Much better to turn away from a self-revelation of that nature than to confront it. Grace cried out. A high-pitched guitar squealing noise and Kyle smiled, and all introspective thoughts fled from his mind. He struggled to get the knife out of her side. He had stuck it in her deep. He had to twist the blade and pull on it to release it from her flesh. After that, once he learned the trick of freeing metal from flesh, he ripped her apart. The scary part was, he didn't remember doing most of it. He enjoyed it, though. He remembered that for sure. Because he felt guilty about it. The feeling good about it, not the actual killing.

He dropped his hands from his eyes and whispered, "Why did I cut off her head?" And then, "What the fuck is wrong with me?"

He picked her head up from his lap by her hair and dropped it on her torso. It rolled off and fell to the floor of the truck with a thump. Kyle closed his eyes. Don't think about it. Don't think about her. What's done is done. He opened his eyes and saw a pack of cigarettes in between his legs. Her head had hidden this bit of treasure. He picked the pack up. The pack was beaten up a bit, crumpled and damp with blood. He hoped the smokes weren't too damp to light.

Opening it up, looking at the picture of the woman with yellow, broken teeth on the cover (like that horrid picture would somehow curb his nicotine addiction) he hoped there'd be some smokable smokes inside. The first one he pulled out had a crack halfway down. A short smoke, but still, a short smoke was better than no smoke. But there might be better ones inside. Kyle shook the pack and spilled the contents onto his lap. There were three unbroken and unbloodied cigarettes left. He smiled, picked one up and flipped it into his mouth. He patted his pockets, felt the lump in the left one, and reached in and pulled out his pink Bic lighter. He lit the cigarette, sucked in the delightful poison and tried to calm his running mind and think. How to get out of this? He'd have to get rid of the body, and somehow clean the truck, which made him laugh. It was filthy with blood and gore. It made him think of *Pulp Fiction*. He expelled smoke from his mouth in a dense cloud. Clean this up? Yeah, right. Shaking his head, he heard tires on gravel. Frowning, he looked into the review mirror and saw the roof lights of a police cruiser.

Dropping his cigarette from frozen fingers, he said, "Fuck."

-3-

Officer Ruby Wilson, 'Rubes' to her friends, picked up her coffee cup and sipped on the bitter drink with one hand. No milk and sugar for her. Dark, hot and bitter described her coffee of choice. She was using her other hand to type a message on the laptop computer to another officer. She was trying to arrange social drinks after work with her shift at Rachel's Watering Hole while steering the police cruiser with the inside of her left thigh and the top part of her knee. She was driving toward the town's lover's lane dead end to write speeding ticket notes. She was one of ten officers in the small town of Leonard, but even though the town was small and therefore, the crimes were small, and the criminals known (some of them even neighbors), she still had to hand out tickets. Even though there wasn't an official monthly quota, there was an expectation to produce a measurable representation of work for every officer. It was more like an accounting of your time at the end of the month while being paid by the taxes of the good citizens of Leonard. She had learned two things early on the job: ten tickets a month kept the bosses happy and as long as she gave those tickets to out-of-towners, the taxpaying citizens were also happy. Less headaches for her all around and that counted as a win in Rubes' book.

On this particular early morning, she had caught two such out-of-towners speeding on a road that went from eighty kilometers an hour to fifty kilometers an hour and then back up to eighty within a short kilometer long stretch. It was a cheap ticket because it was a sneaky sign placement. She suspected the town council had voted to set up this diabolical speed trap. Tickets did generate revenue after all. But she still needed her ten tags and monitoring that speed trap was the easiest way to get them so, to hell with the out-of-towners. She didn't know any of them anyway.

Driving down the gravel road to her spot, she wasn't expecting to see anyone parked there. That was a weekend or evening thing to find teens parked at the dead end, drinking and smoking and making out in their parents' cars. And because of that, she wasn't looking through the windshield ahead of her. She wasn't even watching the road. She was tapping on the keyboard while driving with her leg. When she looked up and she noticed the truck, she stepped on the brake. Confusion creased a line between her brows. And when a man ran from the open door of the truck away from her and into the tree-line like someone had set his ass on fire, she flinched hot coffee onto her hand.

"Damnit!"

She placed the coffee in the holder and wiped her hand on her pants. Good thing her uniform pants were dark. Ideal for hiding stains. When she lifted her head, she saw the back of the man disappearing into the thick low-hanging leaves.

"What the?"

Rubes glanced at the radio microphone beside her, frowned, and peered at where the man had disappeared to in the trees. She didn't know what to do. Was the car stolen? Was that why he ran? In the five years she'd been on the job, no one had ever run from her before. There had never been a reason to. A brief thought of chasing him entered her mind, but she had no idea why she would chase him. Because he was running? Was that an actual reason to chase after someone? Suspicious running? Maybe. Because when she thought about it, he was definitely running because of her. The big white police car with roof lights had lit his particular ass-fire, that's for sure. And why do people run from the police? Because they messed up in some way. Taking the steering wheel in her hands she navigated closer to the truck. She parked the cruiser and, leaving it running, stepped out and studied where the man had run to. She couldn't see him anymore. Didn't even hear him or the crashing sounds of a person running in the brush. Was he hunkered down watching her right now? A chill ran down her spine on this hot day. She patted the gun in her holster on her right hip and approached the abandoned truck.

She noticed the smell first. Ruby once investigated a fatal car accident in which a gravel truck crushed a Mini-Cooper against a light pole. The car looked like a person had stepped on a pop can and crumpled the weak metal under their foot. Ruby saw blood running from the bottom of the mangled metal door while approaching the accident. Not dripping. Not like a pit-pat from a broken faucet, no, the blood poured from the seam of the door. As she got closer, she wrinkled her nose. She smelled meat. Like steak left to thaw on a counter. A strong, metallic smell of death. Recognizing the same smell from that nightmare day was emanating from the open door of the pickup truck, she paused in her step. She didn't realize it, but she sniffed at the air, lifting her nose into the breeze. She stopped walking. She didn't want to get closer to the truck.

Her mind flashed to the man running from the truck like a man electrified by the most terrific guilt. What had he left behind? She didn't want to see what was inside that truck. But she was a cop. And like so many things in life, what you want and what you get are so often very different things. Ruby exhaled. Her boots scattered bits of gravel. She saw dark stripes marring the tan interior on the inside of the open driver side door. Like someone had thrown dark paint onto a light colored wall. Her eyes followed the streaks to the thickening darkness leading into the truck and she blinked. Ruby didn't understand what she was seeing. It was too strange. Too unreal to be real. Rubes' gaze settled on a pale body pushed against the passenger door. A body with a stump where a head should have been. Her eyes found the head of Grace DeBoers. A woman she knew. From a family she knew well.

She turned from the truck and fast-walked back to the cruiser, sucking in big gulps of air, concentrating on calming her heaving stomach and thinking, don't puke at a crime scene, don't you dare puke at a crime scene!

She called the dispatcher from the portable microphone at her shoulder while scanning the tree-line where the running man had vanished. Her voice trembled and shook. She stopped mid-sentence a few times, having lost her train of thought, but at least she hadn't puked.

-4-

"You did a good job."

Nodding, she said, "Thanks, Chief."

"You feeling okay, though? You look a little… unwell."

"I'm all right. It's just…"

"Yeah?"

"I knew her. I didn't expect… I don't know what I expected."

"Yeah. We all knew her. And this is not something anyone could expect. I mean, we're small-town cops. Break up a domestic argument now and then, a bar fight, see the occasional bad accident, but this?" He turned his face to the sun, sighed and said, "No one could have expected this."

"Yeah. I guess. That guy ran though. What if I chased him? I could have caught him. Maybe. I am in good shape. Why didn't I chase him?"

"You didn't know what you had, so why would you chase him? Look, you did right Rubes. You'll think you didn't for a while and that's ok. That's normal. But you did right. Tell you what, I'll have Tracy come and relieve you here, get you home, so you can lunch with Rick, kiss your little one on the head, and you know, be normal. Tracy can wait for the crime scene crew."

"No, no. She's busy out searching for this guy like the rest of our guys. I can wait. This is my responsibility. I'm fine, Chief. Really."

The Chief, whose real name was Craig, but since everyone in the town called him Chief, even his wife, he thought of himself in his own head as Chief, pulled off his hat and scratched at the thinning spot on the crown of his head. The itched reminded him that his hair was deserting him, and he didn't know how to feel about that. Getting older, was all. Happens to everyone.

He put his hat back on and squinting one eye at Ruby said, "If you're saying you're all good and you can stand guard for when the crime scene crew gets here, that's fine by me. But you need to be honest about it." Pointing to the truck, he said, "That's a terrible thing for anyone to see. You'll never un-see something like that. And sometimes, after seeing something like that, it's best to surround yourself with people you love."

"Yeah. I get it. I'm not feeling the best about it, that's for sure, but I can still do my job. I'll wait for the crime scene crew."

"All right then. You need anything give me a shout. On the radio or on my phone."

"For sure, Chief. Uh, you going to go tell him?"

"Yeah."

"Be careful. You should probably take someone with you. He's not the best to deal with on good days. And this is not going to be a good day for him."

"I should be all right. You know, I'd be surprised if he didn't already know."

"Wouldn't he have called you if he did?" The Chief pulled his hat off and scratched at his thinning crown again. He grimaced. He might have scratched a little too hard. He said, "I don't know about that. I suspect he's on the phone to a lot of people right now. There's a man in the woods he and his crew will be hunting him sooner or later and he's probably busy getting them all together to do that. I think, all in all, it'd be better for that man if we find him first."

Ruby peered at the Chief with hard eyes. "I hope they do find him first."

He studied Ruby, sighed and said, "After the crime scene people finish here, go home and get some rest. I'll need you fresh for tomorrow."

Ruby's cheeks flushed. She said, "Yes, Chief."

-5-

The Chief sat in his SUV with the portable chirping and the air conditioning fan whirring as he waited for Inspector Theresa Greaves of the Ontario Provincial Police to return his call. He'd already spoken to her and had solicited the help of the OPP's crime scene crew. The town of Leonard did not have their own crime scene unit. They had officers trained to take photographs, collect fingerprints and DNA evidence for minor offences like petty thefts and not-so-serious assaults. A murder was a completely different game though, and the officers of Leonard lacked the experience and the sophisticated equipment to process the evidence for such a high-profile crime. The Chief reached out to the OPP, specifically Inspector Greaves, and she had been more than happy to help. He had to call her back because the town of Leonard also lacked a K-9 unit. He had to think about every potential criticism of the investigation when they caught the bad guy and brought him to trial and the real circus began. Or worse, if the grieving father caught the bad guy and he had just vanished. There would be a lot of questions the Chief wouldn't have any answers for. Bringing in K-9 to start a search for the bad guy would be one less criticism he would have to face.

"Hello?"

The Chief said, "Inspector?"

•　　　•　　　•

The Chief turned off one gravel road and onto another. The chassis dipped hard one way spilling the Chief's coffee from the small drink opening and splashing onto his radio microphone. He muttered, "Crap," and wiping the radio microphone with a napkin from his leftover McDonald's meal while driving on the pitted road, he stopped outside a gate attached to a chain-link fence surrounding a large open property. The silver chain squares of the fence reflecting the sun blinked at him intermittently as he peered through. A small house on a neatly trimmed lawn the size of a football field sat a good hundred feet away from the fence. Behind the house was a steel, prefab shed glinted in the sun and cast a fat shadow on the house, partially covering it in darkness.

On top of one fence post sat a camera. The rumor was that it was a fake camera and posted there to keep the cops from trespassing as though that was something police officers did on a regular basis or something. The fence encircling the property belonged to Hank DeBoers, the President of the local Outlaw Motorcycle Gang (OMG) Satan's Soldier's, a not so clever homage to Hitler's Germany SS soldiers.

The Chief parked the cruiser and stared at the closed gate thinking maybe Ruby had a point and he should have brought another officer with him to this place. That big goon they had hired, the new recruit, would have done the trick. What's his name? Raymond. The six-foot-five Ontario Hockey League defenseman. Yeah. He'd have been a good pick to bring along. Hank was not going to be a happy man right now and he wasn't a nice man to begin with. The size of Raymond might make Hank think twice before allowing his anger and grief to turn into violence. The Chief should turn around, go back to the main road and call Raymond to come with him to talk to Hank. That's the smart thing to do. The Chief wrapped his fingers around the shifter and depressed the brake to put the cruiser into reverse when the gate swung open. Huh. The Chief guessed maybe the camera wasn't a fake after all.

The Chief drove toward the little house in the distance. In the front yard were rusting skeletal hulks of cars, trucks, and motorcycles. With his window rolled down, the Chief could hear the clanking of metal and the music of Creedence Clearwater Revival playing from a speaker coming from the steel prefab shed. The Chief heard the music, was aware of it the way a person is of elevator music, but his attention was focused on the man standing on the porch of the house. Muscles rippling from a lifetime of hard work and suspected generous injections of steroids, Hank waited for the Chief with his arms crossed and tear-tracked cheeks.

• • •

Hank handed the Chief a cold, sweaty can of Coke. Hank held a bottle of beer in his giant fist. He sat in a wooden chair beside the Chief. It creaked with his settling weight. Tears trailed down Hank's cheeks. He wasn't crying per se. When he spoke, his voice didn't shake or quiver, but the tears kept flowing from his eyes. His jaw bulged and relaxed, bulged and relaxed. Hank's mouth was a tight line in his face.

Hank said, "I appreciate you coming out here in person to see me, but I already know what you're here to tell me. I also know one of your officers let the fuckin' bastard get away."

"It wasn't like that…"

Hank turned his gaze on the Chief and through clenched teeth said, "It was exactly like that." Hank exhaled and forced a smile. It was an odd sight with the wet cheeks and shiny eyes. "But that will probably turn out to be a good thing… for me."

The Chief dropped his eyes to the can of Coke in his hand and lifted it to his lips for a sip.

Hank said, "You know who he is yet?"

"We're working on it."

"Would you tell me if you did?"

"No."

Hank frowning, said, "No matter. I'll find out my way."

"Look, Hank, you should let the police handle this…"

"Fuck that! It was you fucks that let him run off into the woods in the first place!" Hank leaned towards the Chief, getting into his space. He said, "Grace was a good kid. No, she was a fucking great kid. She was a better person than I ever was or could be. What happened to her…" Hank shook his head and looked away. He said, "That shouldn't have happened to her. Not to her. Grace was the best person I knew. Better than anyone on this filthy planet. This isn't right."

"And we'll get him, Hank. We'll get him."

"Oh yeah? And then what? Three squares a day and a cot for the rest of his life? Your courts are a joke."

"That might be true. Or it might be it's the best we got." The Chief stood, stretched, and looked down at Hank. He said, "I know you're hurting Hank and I feel for you, I really do. I knew Grace and I agree with you, she was a good person. No doubt about that. But if you or any of your pals get in my way, I will arrest you. And that's a fact. The police will bring this guy in."

Staring at the Chief, evaluating him, Hank said, "I guess I'll just have to leave this matter in your capable hands."

"Why is it that I don't believe you when you say that?"

Hank said, "I don't care what you believe. Now get off my porch."

-6-

Tree branches scratched him. Roots tripped him. His feet slipped over rocks. Breathing hard, Kyle's lungs felt empty and hollowed out. He could smell himself and it wasn't pleasant. Sweat layered his skin. Grace's blood on his body became slick and tacky. The scratches on his face and arms stung. His hungover brain was cooking inside his skull on this hot day. He dreamed of water. Images of kids in front of an open fire hydrant teased him. This was turning into the worst day of his life and that was saying a lot. All because he wanted a beer. A stupid beer!

A branch raked his cheek under his left eye.

"Fuck!"

He stopped running. He put his hands on his knees and tried inhaling the air of the entire world into his empty lungs. He attempted to spit but had no saliva to spit with. His ribs hurt from expanding continuously and rapidly. And the years of smoking wasn't helping his endurance any. Kyle straightened and leaning his head back, he looked up into the sky through the trees. The sun was climbing through the screen of trees. He shook his head and slowed his breathing. His heart wouldn't slow down, content to be dancing an erratic jig in his chest. Kyle flinched from a pain spike on the left side of his body right under his left nipple. That scared him. Would he have a heart attack out here? Wouldn't that be something? To die while running from the people who were paid to help other people. And arrest people, let's not forget that. No, no. Can't forget that undeniable fact. Still, it would be a stupid end to a stupid day. He closed his eyes and put his left hand over his heart. He willed it to slow, to return to a normal rhythm. His heart stopped sprinting. It slowed to a challenging run, like a man running with a limp. He examined his surroundings. Trees, bugs, and guess what? More trees.

"Where the hell am I?"

A small laugh slipped out and it morphed into a sob. He didn't even know what town he was in. He hadn't seen any town signs. The bar's neon announcement had lured him in, sure, but he didn't know what town he had stopped in. That damn Rachel's Watering Hole sign had fucked him. Like a pedophile luring kids with a puppy, the promise of beer, people and music pulled him in and now look where he was at! What was he to do now?

He had to keep moving and hopefully not run right into the arms of any waiting police officer. Running panicked through the woods without any idea of where he was or where he was heading to, for all he knew Kyle might have circled back around and any second now a police officer would pop out from behind a tree with a gun pointing at his face. And in the woods, with no people and no cameras, who knew what the police might do to him? He had cut off someone's head. Don't think about it. Let it go. Get going.

Kyle glanced behind him, holding his breath, listening with his head canted to the left. No police. He exhaled. He might have gotten away for now.

A dog barked. Kyle extended his neck and stood on his toes, glancing to where he thought the dog's bark had issued from. Hard to tell the origin of a bark in the woods. The brush and hills distorted sounds. It was almost impossible to pinpoint a direction until the animal was right on top of you.

Bark-bark!

"Oh, no…"

Kyle didn't see the dog but knew following behind that dog was a police officer with a gun. It was possible someone was walking their dog out here, but not likely. He just ran from a truck with a dead body in it. Either way, it was safer to believe it is a cop than not. So, it is a cop. He didn't know which animal he was more afraid of. The dog or the cop. He didn't want to get bitten by a dog. He'd seen them at work on those cop shows, ripping and tearing at a screaming suspect while some overweight cop arrived all sweaty and out of breath. It didn't look like a fun time. He also didn't want to get shot. Either choice sucked.

He shook his head. Who would win Kyle's fear award didn't matter right now. Time to get a move on and dance his ass right out of this town. His right thigh muscle twitched. A stitch stabbed his side.

"Why me? Why does this crap always happen to me?"

With one last look behind him, Kyle ran from the barking dog.

-7-

The woods play with sounds. The trees can amplify them, muffle them, or make them echo. Because of that, the source of the sounds was hard to pinpoint. The barking dog was a police dog. Kyle had that right. The dog's name was Julius, as in Caesar. Constable Miles Granger was the handler and named him Julius because he is a Roman Empire history nerd and thought Julius Caesar had been the most capable Roman general in a long line of capable Roman generals. Miles and Julius arrived at the scene of the homicide two hours and forty-three minutes after the discovery of Grace. Pointed in the direction Kyle had gone by Rubes, Constable Granger and Julius ran off in pursuit. Julius had proven to be a great tracking dog within the confines of a city. He'd find the scent and follow it until it led him to the criminal they were pursuing. He never quit. Hiding under a car or hiding in a garbage can, it didn't matter, because if the bad guy was in an urban environment, Julius would find them. He always did. The city contained man scents, garbage scents, machinery scents and not much else. Julius knew them all and was not tempted to follow anything other than the scent Miles selected for him to follow. There were fewer organic distractions for the nose of Julius.

Tracking a man through the woods was a different story and not something Julius had been exposed to. Julius and Miles trained together primarily in cities and warehouses. Drug-sniffing and bomb-sniffing suitcases at airports and appearing at public events for the kids to ooh and ahh at took up most of their time. Real nature, not the man-made cities, was doing a number on Julius and Miles noticed the change at the beginning. There were so many interesting smells Julius wanted to investigate. Julius knew he should follow the commands of his human only his brain wouldn't acknowledge those orders that had been so diligently drilled into his doggy mind. Not with so many new scents to pursue, analyze and enjoy. Julius found the trail of Kyle and followed it, loving the hunt and running with his human outside. Shortly into the pursuit, another scent demanded Julius' attention. A scent that bopped him on the nose demanding, 'Hey! Follow me!' Julius felt compelled to comply.

Julius had found the trail of a rabbit and his quivering nose chased the most delicious rabbity smell until said rabbit exploded from a bed of leaves. It ran from Julius through bushes and over a narrow, meandering river. What fun! When Julius barked with excitement, Kyle was maybe a kilometer away. Kyle hadn't been running in circles. He ran in a line in the shape of a long crescent moon and eventually, he would have circled back toward the police. Julius' bark scared Kyle off this route and in another safer direction away from the police and toward a cottage where a family of three were spending the summer.

Julius never made it past the rabbit warren the frightened creature had fled into. It took some time for the cursing and red-faced Miles to drag Julius away from the hole in the earth. And when he got him away from the wonderful smelling hole and placed Julius back in the police cruiser, Julius didn't understand why his human was calling him a bad dog. He almost caught a rabbit, didn't he? That wasn't bad. Catching a rabbit was good. Julius thought he was a good dog. He whined in protest.

-8-

Hank watched the Chief's retreating SUV kick up dust as he drove off Hank's property. Once the vehicle passed the gate, Hank stood and walked inside the front door and put his empty beer bottle on a side table beside key rings and a bowl of change. Christine sat on a brown plaid-patterned chair waiting for him. Black mascara tracks marred her cheeks. Her upper lip shone from the sunlight creeping in the window beside her and a cigarette smoldered in her right hand. On the table beside her was a glass filled with clear liquid and ice. Knowing Christine, Hank suspected the glass to be full of vodka.

"You gonna let that cop get him?" Her voice was thick and croaky.

Christine was Grace's mother. She and Hank hadn't been a couple for a long time. When they split up, Hank bought her a place on the other side of town as far away from him as possible and Grace had lived with her for the past eleven years. Christine hated Hank and she didn't keep her feelings a secret. That was fine with Hank. He hated her too. He worried about her when they were first splitting up. She knew too much about him, his business and where his hidden skeletons were that he preferred remained hidden. He worried he might have to make her disappear. Getting rid of an ex-girlfriend was always a messy affair. Because he was a criminal, the cops would never stop looking for her, alive or dead, and they would never stop looking at him as the person who made her disappear. And when Grace got older and learned who her father was, she too would wonder if her old man had killed her mom. He wouldn't want that. It was Christine who offered a solution to his problem. She told him that if he bought her a place, paid all the bills and let her take Grace then she'd forget everything she ever knew about him. Hell, she wanted to forget him anyway so the task wouldn't be hard at all. And she'd even let him see Grace on a more or less regular basis. A good deal considering the alternative.

What Christine forgot to mention was that she planned to poison Grace against him. She had been so good at it that eventually Grace refused to see him. And what could he do about it? Nothing. He'd underestimated Christine. She was a harder bitch than she pretended to be. And that hardness was showing today. She had raced over to his house once she learned about Grace and before she could get into it with Hank; the Chief had driven up his driveway. She waited patiently for the Chief to leave before she could go after what she wanted from Hank. Crazy thing was, she must think he cared about what she wanted. The only thing he had ever wanted from Christine was to see Grace and Grace is no more. Hank didn't give a crap about Christine or what she wanted. To him, she was the turd that wouldn't stay flushed.

He said, "Whatever I do or don't do, I'm not going to tell you about it."

Hank continued past her to the back door. She yelled, "You get him, Hank! You get that bastard and bring him to me on his knees! On his goddamn knees, you hear me!"

Hank pushed out the back door and walked to the garage. Four of his crew were there and when Hank's shadow crossed the garage door threshold, they looked up from their work. Hank ran a mechanic shop out here and mostly employed other bikers. The shop served as a convenient way to launder his drug money and a nice little bonus was that he could write off the tools as a business expense. He had been pushing meth for a few years and before that, heroin and cocaine. But now that Fentanyl was becoming a thing he decided to get in on the action early. Better to be early than late in the drug dealing world. Today, they were actually working on cars for real customers and not packaging and sorting their latest drug supply.

Hank said, "You hear from the other clubhouse yet, Jimmy?"

"Yeah."

"Are they in?"

"Oh yeah. All in and on their way."

Hank nodded. He said, "Ok. Let's go."

-9-

After leaving Hank's home, the Chief was heading back to the crime scene when Rubes called him. She told him the interesting spectacle of the K-9 track and although a little disappointed; he wasn't too surprised. The track had started two hours after Rubes had seen the running man. With the wind, other animals and environmental factors, that's a long time for a scent to hang around for a dog to pick up on. But at least he could check that off his to-do list.

"What about the crime scene unit? Are they there yet?"

"Yeah. They're just waiting for the coroner. Apparently, she was having brunch with some friends and said she'd be awhile."

Smiling, the Chief said, "I bet they liked that."

"They didn't seem to care. The one crime scene tech said it would give them time to take a cursory look at the scene and plan how to process it."

"Oh. I guess that's good, then. If you need anything, like coffee or a breakfast sandwich, whatever, give me a shout."

"You got it, Chief."

The Chief had pulled over to the side of the road to talk to Rubes. She didn't sound like herself and that worried him. She should be the first one to go home once they caught the guy. Maybe even before that if he arranged for another officer to relieve her. He would have to keep that in the back of his mind for later. Now, after her call, he was considering what to do next.

As he saw it, he had three problems. They don't know who the bad guy was. They don't know where he is and the third problem was Hank and his boys. They would start their own hunt soon enough. All were challenging problems to have. He needed to prioritize. What is the most important problem to deal with? Finding out who killed Grace, right? Maybe. Maybe not. The Chief worked through the problem by writing his ideas down in his notebook.

The truck wasn't the bad guy's or at least it didn't seem to be. It was registered to an eighty-nine-year-old man from up north and from what Rubes had said; she hadn't seen an elderly man running from her and into the woods. The Chief had his dispatch send a message to the police service responsible for the area where the old man lived and asked them to send an officer out to his place to find out who had his truck. The truck wasn't on the police database as reported stolen, but that didn't mean it wasn't stolen. Some people went away on vacation and returned to find their home broken into and their car stolen from their driveway. The truck might have been parked in a garage somewhere and maybe the old guy hasn't noticed it missing yet. Or it could be as simple as the old man selling the truck to the runner and he hadn't reported the sale to the Ministry of Transportation yet. Hell, the old man could have this guy's name, address and phone number for all the Chief knew. But was that the most pressing problem to solve? No. This bad guy had run from a pickup after decapitating a young woman. Catching him before he runs into someone else is priority one.

Sure, Hank is a problem but for now, he is really only a problem to the bad guy. He is not a problem to any innocent civilian of Leonard. He'd only be the Chief's problem if he got in his way. For the safety of the public and the safety of the bad guy, the police had to catch the mystery man first. How could he accomplish that? How could he keep the people of his town safe? Not everyone knew that this guy was out there running around tired and afraid. A dangerous combination. Who knew what he might do if cornered? And it isn't like the Chief could start phoning everyone in town. Huh. He couldn't but...

He phoned dispatch. "Hey, Marjorie. Quick question for you. If you wanted to spread news and spread it quick, who would you tell? What I mean is, who are the biggest gossips in town?"

"Oh. Huh. Let me talk to the others in here. We'll come up with a list."

"Could you do one better?"

"Sure."

"After you make that list, could you all phone them, give them a description of this guy and have them phone everyone they can and have those people phone everyone they can and so on and so forth? And have them write down the name of everyone they call and to pass that on too so there is some kind of record somewhere of who is called. Make sure to tell everyone to not, under any circumstances approach the suspect. You need to make that very clear."

"Yeah. We can absolutely do that. On a side note, no one says so on and so forth anymore."

"What? Oh, and if someone can't get a hold of someone that they think they should be able to get a hold of, send two officers out to check, ok? Two officers every time."

"You bet. But Chief, aren't you nervous?"

"About what?"

"About every farmer and hunter out there with a gun shooting first and asking questions later."

"I am a little worried about that, but not as worried about that as I am about not spreading the word and having this guy kill someone else, you know? Still, I don't want anyone shooting anybody so be sure to tell everyone to be careful. If they spot him, get to safety first and then call us. No heroics from anyone. And especially no shooting."

"After what he did to Grace, I wouldn't lose any sleep over him getting killed, to tell you the truth."

"Maybe you wouldn't, but it's not you who has to answers questions if he does and we didn't try to prevent it. I don't want anyone getting shot or killed. Hey, Marjorie? How many of our officers did you get a hold of?"

"All of them."

"All of them? Good. That's good. Say, can you look at a map and assign areas for them to patrol? I don't want this guy getting out of town. And you know what? Since they are all in, have them double up in one car. I don't think we have enough cruisers for every single officer, so, that'd help and it's just safer."

"Got it."

"Did you get any info back from the owner of that pickup?"

"Not yet."

"Let me know as soon as you do."

"Sure. Oh, have you released anything to the media? I'm getting calls like every five minutes in here."

"Oh, yeah?"

"Yeah. Maybe give Bobby Roberts a call? At least he's our media guy and he can get it on our local radio station."

"Good call. I'll do that."

"And I'm serious. We're getting calls from the outside media like crazy in here. Prepare yourself."

"For what?"

"Pardon my French Chief, but the media shitstorm. It's coming, and it will be a doozy!"

-10-

Sunlight poked through the overhead leaves and golden motes flickered in the air. Birds chirped. Animals rustled. Emerald greens, dull browns, colorful flowers and blossoms created beautiful scenery. And Kyle hated all of it. Give him the grey bricks of a city, the sound of cars and the scent of exhaust any day of the week over this… natural easy-to-get-lost-in world.

He hadn't heard a dog for some time and now he shuffle-stepped through the woods, sweaty, exhausted and hopeful he wasn't being tracked, but afraid to stop moving. He was lost. He was tired. He was thirsty. So thirsty he considered chewing on leaves thinking there must be moisture in them, right? A tree lived off sunlight and water, so there should be water in the damn leaves, shouldn't there? He stumbled over a root, swore, cried a bit, called himself a pansy for crying and continued on. Kyle toyed with the idea of giving in and calling his brother. If he looked at the maps app, it would show where he was and in what town. He could have his brother come and pick him up. He didn't know what he would tell him as to why he needed a lift considering it had been his brother who had sent him the money to buy the truck. His brother had sent him the money for a cheap phone too, but that was only so his brother could try to control him by calling him and texting him and bugging, bugging, bugging. Kyle would just have to call him and tell his brother to come and pick him up and to hell with his questions. He was dying of thirst in some unknown woods in some unknown town being chased by the cops for something he barely remembered doing and so his brother would have to wait for the answers to his unimportant questions, wouldn't he? Just thinking about how unfair his brother will be and how many questions he'll ask made Kyle angry. Why did his brother have to be so hard? It isn't like all of this is his fault, right? If his brother was so concerned about him screwing up, he should have driven up to get him. If his brother had picked him up from that place he wouldn't be in this mess, would he? He wouldn't have stopped at that bar, that's for damn sure. And that girl would still have a head attached to her neck and no cops would be chasing after him through these goddamn woods. Getting angry thinking about it, how this mess was as much his brother's fault as his own, he reached into his pocket for his phone. It wasn't there. Must be in his other pocket. He checked. It wasn't. He had lost his one lifeline out of this mess. He must have left it behind. Either in the truck or near it.

Heart pounding as hard as when he had been running from the barking dog, Kyle stopped walking, held his head in his hands and said, "Fuck!"

-11-

Sitting in her cruiser and reading a book, Rubes was doing whatever she could to keep her mind occupied. Grace's headless body kept popping up in her head, right behind her eyes, forcing her to see it again and again. No matter what she did to try to distract herself, the image would reappear. She couldn't force it to stop because she had no idea when it would knock on the door of her brain. It didn't announce itself. It didn't say, get ready, here I come. It showed up as unwelcome as a door-to-door flasher or a Jehovah's witness trying to sell salvation. At first, Rubes tried listening to a podcast. When that didn't work, she stepped out of her cruiser and walked along the inside of the police tape she'd strung up on the trees and did her best to keep her eyes averted from the truck with Grace's pale bloodless body inside. The image of Grace as she'd last seen her became more insistent the closer she got to the vehicle. She saw it floating in the air in front of her, superimposed over the pastoral scenery. That had been too much for her and she retreated to her cruiser.

When the K-9 guy and his dog showed up, they had proven to be an effective distraction for a time. The positive energy the handler, Miles, had when she pointed out the last area she had seen the man running made her think maybe, just maybe, they might catch the guy. Maybe that would stop the replay of death in her head. Rubes had heard the dog's barking intermingling with the handler's cursing. Then she saw them both exit the woods. The handler's face was anything but positive. Miles face was a stop sign shade of red. His frown was so pronounced Rubes thought it might snap his jaw. He saw her looking at him and said, "Nothing. We found nothing!"

Before she could even think of asking follow-up questions, he sped off in his cruiser, white-knuckling the steering wheel.

After that, she turned on her tablet and read a book on her Kindle app. On the first page, she saw Grace's head and her open-eyed stare. The skin so white it didn't seem real. She closed her eyes and held her breath until she had to either inhale or pass out. It scared Rubes thinking she might go through the rest of her life seeing Grace's headless body. It could happen to her anywhere. She could be in the grocery store, pick up a cabbage and boom! Grace's head. Or at the swimming pool with her husband and their son, and yeah, look at that, Grace's headless corpse sliding through the clear, eye-burning chlorine filled water. She might never be free from this day.

She closed her eyes and tried to breathe through the fear. Thankfully, distractions arrived to help her tuck the problem away to the 'don't worry about it now' place in her mind. The crime scene unit arrived and while they were pulling up outside the crime scene tape, the coroner called her back. After she spoke to the coroner and the crime scene guys started setting up to process the scene, she called the Chief. Those brief, busy moments kept the images at bay. She watched the crime scene crew do their thing. They were walking a wide circle around the truck and staring intently at the ground. Rubes wanted to talk to them not because she was a sociable person, but because she knew she needed to distract her brain to keep the Grace images away. But they were too close to the truck, too close to Grace. She felt that it would be physically impossible for her to go over there and start chatting them up. If she had been able to be near the truck, she might have heard the beeping from Kyle's phone long before the crime scene unit had shown up. Instead, it had been the crime scene guys who heard the phone ringing.

Cst. Brandy Campbell heard the phone ringing. Her first instinct was to pull out her own phone and check it but no, her pocket wasn't buzzing so, it wasn't her phone ringing. She turned to the sound. She saw the phone behind the front tire on the driver side. She turned to her partner, Ralph, and said, "You think that's the victim's phone or the bad guy's?"

He shrugged and said, "How would I know? Should we answer it?"

She said, "I don't know. Let's ask scene security. What's her name again?"

"Constable?"

"You're a lot of help."

• • •

Peripheral movement caught Rubes' attention. The tall crime scene man waved at her. She put her tablet down beside her and stepped out of the cruiser. He motioned for her to come closer to the truck. Her stomach tightened. The thought of walking closer to the pickup made a thin sheen of sweat ooze from her skin. She could feel it all over her body. Her breath quickened. She took a few steps and shaking her head from side to side, she stopped.

●   ●   ●

Ralph said, "What's she doing?"

"It looks like she's not coming over here?" Brandy's voice lilted at the end, making the statement a question.

"The phone stopped ringing."

"Go tell her what happened in case it rings again."

"All right."

Walking towards the Constable with the sun hot on his back, Ralph noticed how beautiful the day was turning out to be even though he had been doing this job for years now, and knew terrible crimes paid no attention to the weather. Murder happened in the sun, the rain, the cold and in the snow. Knowing that, Ralph still thought such things are worse when they happened on a nice day. It was as though the day was lying to the world, covering up horrid happenings with sunshine and a perfect light breeze while wearing a pleasant face and holding a bloody knife behind its back. Ralph sighed. It doesn't matter now how nice the day was turning out to be. Ralph will be working this scene for a while yet. His day was shot. Hell, depending on how the processing went, his week could be shot. No weekend fishing for him. But then, that girl in the truck, her day was more than shot. Her day had ended in the most permanent way. The best thing he could do for her was to do his job and do it well. The Constable was leaning back against the door of her car. She stood with her arms crossed and although she was wearing sunglasses, Ralph got the impression that she was uncomfortable.

"Hey, uh, there's a phone by the front tire. It's ringing. We were wondering what you want us to do."

"Is it… Grace's?"

"The victim? I don't know. It could be hers. But it could belong to the guy who ran off."

"Oh."

"Yeah. You want to come look? We can take photos of it, document it, then if it rings again, you can safely answer it."

"I can't."

"Can't what?"

"I knew her. I found her. Sorry, but I can't go any closer."

"Oh. Ok. Um, you might want to call your boss then, to see what he wants us to do."

"I can do that."

-12-

The Chief used the ever-handy Google Maps for a top-down view of the town. Free and easy enough to use for even the technologically challenged. Manipulating the map with his fingers, the Chief wondered what he'd do if he happened to be a murdering runner? If the bad guy kept running the one way, that would take him southwest, through lots of forest and unforgiving terrain before running into the Benson's farm. That's only if he was running in a straight line. To expect he'd run in such a straight line through the brush would be unrealistic. The woods aren't all smooth and clear of obstacles like roads are. The Chief grunted. If he had enough people, ideally, he'd place them all around this wooded area at all the compass points. All of his people weren't in yet and even if they were, he didn't have enough staff so, no point in wishing for the impossible. Wait. There.

The Chief pinched the screen to zoom in on a house. If the bad guy angled off to head directly west, he'd end up near the old Grayson house. That was a different place with quite a different family. Different didn't cover half of what he'd heard about the house and the family. If the rumors were true, the Grayson's were the first family to settle in Leonard and they built the first house within the town limits. And it would also be the last place anyone would want to run into. The Grayson house was far enough away still and the Chief shouldn't be distracted by that what-if scenario. Not yet anyway. Finding that place in this giant dense forest would be like finding the proverbial needle in that haystack everyone was always talking about. So, ok Chief, focus.

He moved the map around with his finger. If this guy went more south, he'd run into the cabin owned by that big city family. The wife was a doctor and the husband, a banker or investor? Something to do with money. They had a young one, too. A ten-year-old boy. What is his name? David? No. Devon. The Chief had met the family once. The kid seemed bright. The young boy always had a book either in his hand or stuffed into his back pocket. The Chief wondered if they would be up at their cabin right now. It was summer, so, maybe. He made a note to have someone in dispatch call the cabin directly. He doubted any of the townsfolk had their number. Maybe the closest neighbor did, but that was a big maybe. As he added that to his growing to-do list, his phone rang.

"Chief here."

Rubes told him what the crime scene guys had found. He stomped on the gas and white-knuckled the steering wheel. He wanted to be at the crime scene in case the mysterious tire-phone rang again. He forgot about arranging for dispatch to call the city folks' cabin to warn them.

-13-

Kyle saw the cabin through the trees, blinked a few times to make sure it was real and not a hope-mirage, and since it didn't disappear, he crouched-walked and forced himself to move slowly. If there were people inside, he didn't want them to hear him barreling through the woods running toward them. It was difficult for him to move slow. Kyle thought about all the food and water in there and his stomach growled. He wanted to run in there, roll around in the pile of food he imagined being in there and suck out all the water from the taps. Then, if no one was home, maybe even take a twenty-minute power nap and think about what to do next.

The cabin might even have a phone. That might be pushing his luck. Most people didn't have home phones nowadays. They just used their cell phone, but still, it was a possibility there was a home phone inside because it was a house in the woods. Then he could call his brother and have him come get him out of this goddamn hellhole of a town. Man. His brother was going to be pissed.

Parting branches with his hands while crouching low, Kyle circled the cabin from within the trees. There isn't a car in the driveway. That's usually a good sign no one's home right now. Could be a summer place or something. That'd be amazing if no one was home. He watched. He waited. His stomach gurgled. He tried swallowing but his mouth was too dry.

Kyle left the safety of the trees and paused, his eyes roving everywhere, his body tense and expectant. Nothing. No cops popping out of bushes and no men in black masks with assault rifles rappelling down from above.

Kyle tried the front door and checked all the windows. All locked. Didn't matter. He wasn't leaving here without drinking water at the very least. He broke a window in the back figuring someone would have to walk around the back of the cabin to see it. He stepped inside and said, "Hello?"

No answer. Smiling, he walked into the kitchen, stuck his mouth under the tap and turned on the cold water. He moaned while he drank. Any other time, drinking water would be his absolute last choice. Feeling his stomach distend, an uncomfortable feeling, and though he knew he should stop, but the water tasted so good and satisfied a need so deep, he kept drinking.

•　　　•　　　•

Bloated and satiated for the time being, Kyle walked through the cabin and found the washroom. There were three electric toothbrushes charging on stands. Droplets of water sprinkled the porcelain sink. People are staying here. They hadn't left too long ago. Kyle would have to hurry.

Leaving the washroom, he walked into a bedroom. A large unmade bed with dark brown bedposts was against one wall and a large wardrobe stood next to the window on the other wall. Kyle crossed the room and opened the wardrobe. Bright golf shirts and light blouses rested on hangers. He snagged a golf shirt and held it up. It was a men's style shirt. A little too small for Kyle, but it was better than the filthy shirt he was wearing now. It'd be snug, but it would fit. The real problem as Kyle saw it, was the color. Damn. Kyle glanced at the other shirts and thought out of all the shirts available, the one in his hand was the least ridiculous. A bright pink golf shirt covered with small red salmons; it is the best choice out of the lot. Holding it in one hand, he opened a drawer and picked out a pair of shorts. He squinted at the label. Too small. He wouldn't even be able to get them on. Dropping the shorts, he picked up Jockey underwear and a pair of socks. The socks had pictures of flamingos on them. Flamingos? Who is this guy?

In the washroom again, Kyle stripped off all his clothes and soaked a towel with warm water using water from the shower. He wiped all the sweat and grime from his skin as best he could. He cleaned the blood off his hands and the spatter on his face and in his hair. A ghetto shower, as his brother used to call it, even though they both grew up in the suburbs. Once clean, or cleaner than he had been, he put on the clean underwear, the clean socks and the tight golf shirt. He cringed putting his jeans back on. They felt grimy and oily with sweat. Grace's blood had left stains in his lap and blood spatter on his legs. His jeans were dark, so the blood covering him wasn't visible, but he knew it was there and it made him feel dirty.

Looking into the mirror, Kyle muttered. "Why couldn't this guy be bigger?"

His eyes fell on the toothbrushes. He ran his tongue over his teeth. Yeah. He had time.

•　　•　　•

With a minty-fresh mouth, Kyle left the washroom and passing the bedroom where he had pilfered his tight clothes, he stopped, mouth open noticing the time on the alarm clock by the bed. In bright green numbers, it read: 9:53 am. It wasn't even noon yet? Had the power gone off and the clock stopped or something? That can't be right, can it? This has felt like the longest day ever so far. He shook his head. Stop gawking and get moving, Kyle.

He returned to the kitchen, saw a loaf of bread on top of the fridge, took it down and placed it on the counter. He opened cupboards under the counter and plucked out a plastic bag. He stuck the loaf of bread in the bag and opened the fridge. Into the bag went a block of cheese, a package of black forest ham, mustard, mayonnaise, apples, one orange and oh boy, isn't he going to make the best, fattest sandwich in the world? You bet your ass! Oh, and look at that, two weird foreign beers. He snagged two bottles from the case. He closed the fridge, frowned, and opened it again. He grabbed two cans of Coca-Cola and stuffed those in the bag. He tied the bag closed, lifted it, frowned, grabbed another plastic bag from under the counter and double-bagged his goodies. Perfect. Time to go. He made to leave through the same door he'd entered and stopped. He saw a home phone on the wall right there in front of him. A rotary dial one and all. He hadn't seen one of those since he had been a kid.

"Hot damn!"

He picked up the phone and dialed his brother's number. He still didn't know what town he was in but that didn't occur to him. He saw a phone and knew his brother would help him out because that was what his brother did. That was what his brother always did. The phone rang and rang and went to voicemail. Kyle hung up and dialed again. After the third ring, a car door slammed shut outside. Kyle flinched and hung up the phone. He heard a man's voice outside followed by the laughter of others. They are very close. Kyle glanced at the back door and had another thought. The car. The people just arrived here in a car. Kyle pulled a knife from the block on the counter and carrying the bag of food with him, he ran into the bedroom on the balls of his feet.

-14-

The Chief returned to the scene in record time. He parked outside the crime scene tape, in the direct line of sight from Rubes to the pickup and stepped out as one of the crime scene officers fast-walked towards him. Rubes was standing outside of her cruiser, arms crossed, leaning against the door. She didn't glance at him. Strange.

"Chief?"

"Yeah."

"I'm Ralph. The phone keeps ringing. Texts are also beeping somewhat regular. I'm worried the phone's battery could die."

"Ok. Photo it, do whatever you guys normally do to document it and wait. Do you have a charger?"

"Yeah. We have multiple charging cables, for all the different phones, new and old."

"Good. Get them out and get it charging."

"Right. What should we do if it rings?"

"I'll answer it."

•   •   •

While Ralph and Brandy were documenting the phone before seizing it, the Chief checked on Rubes. He didn't like the way she wouldn't look at him. Made him worry.

The Chief said, "Hear anything back from the coroner?"

"Yeah. She called not long after I talked to you. Said she was on her way." Rubes checked the time on her watch and said, "She should be here any minute now."

"That's good."

Frowning, the Chief noticed that it wasn't him she wouldn't look at. She was avoiding looking anywhere near the pickup. Although Rubes was older than Grace by a few years, they had been in the same grade school together. And when Rubes was in Grade 12, Grace would have been starting Grade 9, so they knew each other, like people in small schools do. Rubes had discovered Grace, murdered, decapitated and he had kept her here, guarding a scene where Grace's body was still awaiting removal. The Chief thought, *I'm an idiot, a terrible boss, and yeah, a terrible human being.*

The Chief said, "Rubes. Go home. Get out of here. I got this. I can coordinate this from here. I don't need to be roving about."

"But…"

He lifted his hat off his head and scratched his crown. He interrupted her with, "I'm not asking Rubes. Go home."

She looked down at her boots and said, "I'm sorry Chief. I…"

"I'm the one who's sorry, Rubes. I should have known better than to keep you here. They talk about this in training all the time. PTSD and all that. There is nothing for you to be sorry for. Just go home. Talk to Rick, really talk to him. It helps. Trust me."

Nodding, she said, "Right. Sure. Tomorrow I'll…"

"I'll call you in the morning to see how you're doing and then I will talk to Rick to see how he thinks you're doing. If you both think you're up for it, I'd be glad to have you. Okay?"

"Yeah. Yeah. Okay."

Tires crunched over gravel behind them. They both turned.

The Chief said, "The coroner."

Brandy yelled to the Chief. She was standing by the front of the pickup. She held the phone up in the air. She said, "Hey Chief! It's ringing!"

Brandy and Ralph rushed over to the Chief. Brandy held the phone out in front of her in a gloved hand. Ralph kept pace beside her. He handed the Chief a glove and said, "Put this on!"

The Chief struggled to get the glove on and all the time the phone rang and rang and rang. Why was it so hard to get this damn glove on?

He pulled the plastic down over his palm and the thin plastic ripped at his wrist.

"Damnit!"

The phone stopped ringing.

The Chief said, "I'm going to have a heart attack here. Stupid glove."

From behind him, "Is this a bad time?"

The Chief turned, saw the Coroner, smiled, swiped a line of sweat away that had collected at his scalp and said, "No, not really-" and the phone started ringing again.

Using the gloved hand, the Chief took the phone from Brandy.

"Hello?"

"Kyle?"

"No. This is Chief Craig Evans."

"Ah, crap. What he'd do now?"

•   •   •

Steven Harcourt had been trying to keep Kyle out of trouble for what seemed like Kyle's whole life. After telling the Chief Kyle's name and age, Steven tried to find out why a police officer was answering Kyle's phone. The Chief asked the crime scene officers to have dispatch run queries on Kyle Harcourt and to have dispatch broadcast out to the patrol units the name of their suspect. The Chief also requested any photos found of Kyle sent out to the officer's computer terminals through the departmental email.

Steven said, "Is he under arrest? Do you need me to come up there? To be his surety or something?"

"Uh, no. To both."

"Well, where is he?"

"We don't know."

"What? What police service are you from? I mean, where are you?"

"I'm the Chief of Police for the City of Leonard."

"Leonard. I have no idea where that is or why Kyle's truck and phone would be there. Look, are you going to tell me what's going on or what?"

"Maybe you better come see me here. We can talk in person."

A pause and then Steven sighed and said, "That doesn't sound good. Wait, my other line is going. That could be him."

The Chief said, "Does it show the phone number on your screen?"

"Yeah, but, shouldn't I answer it?"

"In a second. Read me the number first."

"519-882-5677."

"Okay. Thanks, you can answer if you want."

"Too late. The person hung up."

The Chief gave Steven his personal cell phone number and told Steven it'd be best if he came to Leonard. They could talk then. The Chief thought it might be a good idea to have Steven around to help bring Kyle into custody safely. Generally, it was frowned upon to use family members or loved ones for negotiations. Sometimes the bad guy just wanted them there to witness their own suicide and or to try to kill them. Those tended to happen more often in domestic situations where some asshole husband wanted the last laugh at his partner's expense. This situation didn't fit that category so the Chief thought maybe it could help. It never hurt to have multiple options to explore. He asked Steven to stay on the phone while he called dispatch from his shoulder radio and asked them to query the phone number.

The Chief said to Steven, "If Kyle calls you and tells you where he is, I need you to call me, all right? Right away."

"Man. Just tell me what he did or why you want him so bad. I'm getting a sick feeling here."

"Well, we don't know that he did anything. An officer saw a man running from the pickup truck you say you helped Kyle buy. In the pickup truck was the body of a young woman. We haven't found Kyle."

"Oh no. Not again."

"Wait... what?"

The Chief's shoulder radio beeped in his ear. A loud insistent tone let him know that dispatch is trying to speak to him urgently.

To Steven, "Give me a second..." To dispatch, "Go ahead."

"That phone number Chief. It comes back to the Parker residence? The summer cabin people?"

The book kid. The Chief's face paled. His stomach free-fell to his ankles. "Send the closest units you've got. Hell, send all available units. Send them and tell them to be careful and one of you in there start phoning that cabin!"

-15-

If Kyle were to ask himself what he had planned to do in the cabin, he would have said hide-out, snag the keys and make a run for it, or rather, make a drive for it. Why did he take the knife? Just in case. That's all. Just in case. A knife could be a tool. Pry open a window, cut the tape on a box, a tool. It didn't have to be a weapon. After taking the knife for 'just in case' reasons he ran into the back of the house. At the very end of the hall was another door, one he hadn't opened yet. He pushed the door open, stepped inside the room and as he closed it behind him, the front door opened, and he heard voices at the end of the hall entering the house. A deep voice followed by a kid's voice? Or a woman's?

Kyle heard laughter and the jingling of metal Kyle associated with keys being tossed onto the counter. He pictured that in his mind. A hand tossing keys and the keys sparkling with light before landing on the counter. Turning his back to the door he tightened his grip on the knife handle and examined the room. A single bed and a Star Wars poster with the Jedi Rey staring intently at him while the glow of a lightsaber outlined her features above the frame. An unmade bed, books on a side table, and clothes in piles scattered about the room. Holding his breath, Kyle left the door and approached the window thinking maybe he could climb out the window, run in the front door, grab the keys and run back out. He wouldn't have to hurt anyone. But they would call the police, wouldn't they? And they would know who had stolen the car because who else would be out here stealing cars from cabins in the woods? Cops would flood the area and he'd be fucked. Could he tie these folks up? Could he intimidate two adults into complying with his demands? They would think about the kid, wouldn't they? The one who slept in this very room. They wouldn't be tempted into heroics with a kid around.

Kyle whispered, "Why is everything so hard?" He stifled a sob.

Peering out the window, the car beckoned to him. The bedroom door opened behind him and at the same time, the phone rang from the kitchen.

Kyle turned. A boy stood in the doorway with a book in his hand. He was wearing dark shorts and a red shirt with the word 'Muggle' on it. The boy's belly stretched the letters 'ugg' of the word on the shirt.

Kyle dropped the bag. The kid screamed, "Mom!" And Kyle stuck the knife in the kid's chest. The boy's eyes widened, surprised, and Kyle, just as surprised, thought, how'd that happen? He didn't even remember crossing the room, covering the distance from where he had been to the where the kid stood.

Footsteps approached from down the hall, but they were slow. Everything lost its hurry, and time lost its constant forward marching momentum. Kyle felt as though he was watching this scene from over his own shoulder, as though he had left his body and was only a witness to a terrible event and not the primary cause of it. He pulled the knife out of the kid's chest. The book dropped from the boy's hand and as his legs wobbled, Kyle stabbed the boy in the neck. That's where he aimed at, but he missed the neck and the blade sunk into the area where the neck meets the shoulder. Still, Kyle didn't feel like he was doing this horrible act. He was an audience member at a morbid movie. Not until the boy's father slammed into him from the side did time resume its normal pace. Kyle fell to the floor and his head hit a supporting leg of the bed and sparkles danced across his eyes. He thought, *the little man sure can hit hard*, and then Kyle got into the fight.

The man was screaming, a woman was screaming and their two different pitches described fear and anger perfectly. Kyle saw the body of the boy lying on the floor between the 'V' of his feet. The man jumped on Kyle's abdomen, taking the air from him. Kyle still had the knife in his right hand. With his left hand, he grabbed the man by the collar, but the man didn't seem to notice the danger or care. Screaming at Kyle, red-faced, streams of saliva crisscrossing his open mouth, he punched at Kyle, but he wasn't very good at it. His arms were flailing and Kyle, keeping his arms tucked in tight, deflected most of the blows. Kyle waited for his opening and when the man's flailing slowed, Kyle stabbed him in the side once, twice, three times, the warm blood running out and coating Kyle's hand. The man's screams quit. His mouth pursed and he sucked air in short gasps. His eyes bulged and his body twitched. The fight was leaving him with his blood. Kyle rolled him onto the floor. The man's mouth opened and closed. His hands clenched and unclenched on his chest. The woman knelt over the boy, a hand on each of his wounds. Blood squeezed out from between her fingers. She glanced at him and then at her husband bleeding on the floor.

Her eyes returned to Kyle. She said, "Please."

Kyle, sitting up and breathing hard, said, "I just wanted your car. That's all. Just your car. I didn't mean this."

"Don't let him die. Not my son. Please."

Wailing sirens carried to them through the open window. Kyle stood and stuck his face to the glass, his eyes roving from side to side. No sign of the police. Not yet anyway. On the ground by his feet was the bag of food he'd collected. The bottles had broken when he had dropped it and a puddle of beer pooled under the window. Damn. He's still hungry.

With the knife still in hand, he stepped past the woman and the boy and hurried to the kitchen. Glancing around, he saw the car keys on the counter, just like he had imagined they would be. On the counter under the microwave was the phone handle. It was off the hook. He remembered the phone ringing when the boy appeared in the doorway. Had someone been listening the entire time? He had an urge to hang up the phone. The approaching sirens convinced him to ignore the urge. He ran from the house with the car keys in his hand.

-16-

Constable Raymond Briere was a large, muscular and athletic man. He was the officer the Chief had thought of bringing with him when he had gone to visit Hank to tell him about Grace. He was relatively new on the job and excited about chasing down a crazy, decapitating maniac running loose through their town. Now, someone was dead, someone many people in town knew and he thought he should be sad about that. And maybe he was, in an abstract way. He did not know Grace. The truth was that he became a police officer to chase down the very type of person they were all after right now. A real-life menace to society and he couldn't help it if the whole situation excited him. It was only natural, right.

After being assigned to partner up with Jules Niebolt in the one car because there weren't enough cruisers for everyone, Raymond wore his professional I'm-taking-this-very-serious-face to mask his excitement. He found it a challenge considering he was trying to catch a murderer. An actual murderer! In their little town!

"You shouldn't look so happy."

Raymond was driving the cruiser and when Jules said that, his shoulders climbed up to his ears. He said, "Happy? No one's happy here."

"It's okay to be happy, but you shouldn't show it. It could give someone the wrong impression."

"I'm showing it?"

"You look like you just won the lottery. You ever see a picture of a lottery winner? In the papers when they're holding that big check? They look like they're so happy they could burst while at the same time so scared someone will walk up to them, take that check out of their hands and say, sorry man, we made a mistake, you didn't really think all these millions were for you, did ya?"

"Really?"

"Yeah. Really. That's your face. It's fine to be happy. This is the best part of the job, doing something useful instead of catching speeders or lecturing juvenile shoplifters. And I know we are patrolling an area most likely for this guy to be in when considering his last known DOT. That's direction of travel in case a rookie like you didn't know. And that makes you happy, but also worried because what if he doubled back and someone else catches him? That'd bum you out, wouldn't it?"

"No, no-"

"Yeah, it would. You wanna be the one to catch him. I get it. You're new and not jaded and don't yet realize the mountain of paperwork you would have to do if you did catch him. That's a good thing. But when we are out in the public, try not to look-"

Dispatch: *Unit 32, respond to Rural Road 43, Unit 12, the Parker residence. Copy?*

Raymond said, "That's us! Unit 32!"

Into the radio microphone, Jules said, "10-4. On our way."

Dispatch: *Be advised, Kyle Harcourt is believed to be there. Approach with caution.*

Just minutes prior to their conversation about inappropriate happiness, their dispatch had broadcast the suspect's name. A photo, when found, would be forwarded.

Raymond said, "That's him! That's our guy!"

Jules said, "Get a move on. A family lives there."

Raymond's brow drew down. He turned on the lights, the sirens and stepped on the gas pedal until it touched the floor.

-17-

Linda was a dispatcher for the Leonard Police Service. She has a gift for gossip and could turn the inanest piece of information into an entertaining tale of lewdness and infidelity. She routinely discussed with her coworkers who was sleeping with who, who was cheating on their spouse, and Linda happily sat in the center of this social circle of rumor spreaders. On the day Kyle Harcourt came to town, his actions were filling her day with one horror after another and her usually jovial disposition turned dark. She had known Grace. They weren't friends in high school or anything, but they had been friendly. The manner of her murder was a terrific shock. Decapitated? Grace? Then the phone call to the Parker residence they had all listened to. Linda hadn't called the home. It had been Marjorie who had made the call to the family that everyone in their dispatch den had run into at one time or another in town. A nice family. A nice, polite young boy, too.

Everyone heard the disturbance. Everyone heard the murder *happening*. A roomful of women with their hands over their mouths, eyes bulging and fear tickling their hearts inside their chests while over the speaker in their room they all heard the screaming, the fighting, the silence, and the crying. Hearing the family fighting for their lives made Linda sick to her stomach. She stood, dropped the headset, and with a hand over her mouth, said, "Excuse me, I have to go-" and she bolted from the room. In the washroom, the sounds of the struggling family played in her head on replay. And Grace's head floated across her vision. She hadn't seen the scene, but her active imagination didn't fail to conjure a disturbing image. Her stomach heaved, but only saliva spilled from her mouth and splashed into the toilet. This guy, this animal, he had to be stopped. Linda put the lid down, sat on it, and took out her phone. Making sure the lock on the stall door was engaged, she dialed.

"Tommy? It's Linda. Listen, you still working for Hank?"

Pause.

"Yeah? Good. Tell him the guy who killed his daughter is at Rural Road 43, unit 12. But you gotta tell him to hurry. He won't be around there for long. And don't go messing with any of the cops. They're good guys, alright? I'm just saying, if this guy gets past them, it might be good for you to be in the area, know what I mean?"

-18-

Kyle ran to the car door, tugged on the handle, locked, he swore, looked at the key fob in his hand, pressed a button and *click*, the door unlocked. He hopped in, noticed all the blood on his shirt and hands and muttered, "I just got clean…" and examined the fob again. There were keys attached to it but none that looked like a car key. He furrowed his brow and exhaled breath through the line of his lips. How the hell do you start this thing? With your mind? And he saw by the steering wheel a button that said Push To Start.

"Oh."

He pushed the button and displaying on the screen in the center console was an animation with words that said Depress Brake Then Push To Start.

He did that while saying, "How many goddamn instructions are there to start a stupid car?"

The car started and after turning around on the narrow driveway, he sped away from the cabin. The car rocked from side to side as though the tires were attracted to every erosion hole in the gravel road jerking Kyle around in the seat. He followed the road leading into a tunnel of trees with branches and leaves overhead making darkness out of the day. Kyle didn't know where he was or where he was going. All that he knew was that he didn't want to be anywhere near this place when the police showed up. The boy's shocked face when Kyle first stabbed him appeared on the inside of the windshield. His heart plunged. He muttered. "I didn't mean to. I didn't want to."

He slowed down for a sharp curving turn and a police car with lights flashing ran into the front driver side panel of his car. It pushed him into a tree bordering the road, but he didn't see the tree because the airbag punching him in the nose obstructed his view. He felt the abrupt jerk and stop of the car. Kyle had not put on his seatbelt and the collision had caused him to shoot forward and sideways into the expanding airbag. When his car hit the tree, the force of the collision yanked Kyle the opposite way. His ribs slammed into the hard plastic partition separating the driver's seat from the passenger seat and it stole the air from him.

He blinked, coughed, inhaled a deep breath and coughed some more. He winced with every cough. His ribs did not like the hacking for air. Tears squeezed from the sides of his eyes and Kyle wiped them away while blinking rapidly. Breathing in shallow, short breaths gave his ribs a break. A fine mist of white powder filled the interior of the car. A strong scent of plastic and talcum caused Kyle to wrinkle his nose. His upper lip was damp. He tasted blood on his tongue. Was his nose bleeding? He looked out the driver's side window. Where the hell was the police car? And why hadn't he heard it coming? Were they trying to be sneaky or something?

Kyle coughed. His palsying hand searched for and found the inside door handle. He cranked on it and the door popped open. He stepped out and his right knee didn't like supporting his weight and it buckled under him. Kyle yelped and fell onto his left knee. Keeping his right leg extended in front of him, he massaged the muscles around the knee. Peering around him, he had no idea where the police car was. A police car had hit him, right? That had happened, right? He hadn't driven into a tree on his own. Right?

Kyle gingerly made his way to his feet. He limped over to the front of the car he had stolen. The engine ticked. Liquid trickled to the ground. Oil scents mixed with the trees and other outdoor, woodsy smells. He blinked. Where had that maniac cop car gone?

His eyes swept the road. Tires tracks churned through the gravel and dirt. Two lines moved away from the front of his car and disappeared into dense brush. Favoring his knee and stretching it as he moved, Kyle walked to where the tire tracks left the road.

"Holy shit!"

The original owners of the home planted the trees bordering the gravel road to act as a natural guard rail and to keep visiting and leaving guests from driving off the road in the night and rolling down a sharp incline to their death. The road ran along a mini-escarpment maybe fifty feet at its longest and sixty feet at its highest, but the slant was steep and littered with large rocks and older trees. After the police cruiser struck Kyle's stolen car, it ricocheted off the road through a gap between trees that on any other angle it wouldn't have been able to squeeze through. Kyle saw the bright red brake lights fifteen feet down the sharp drop off. Massaging his knee, Kyle couldn't help but smile at the absurdity of the broken police car. When the driver side door opened, Kyle stopped smiling. A man's bloody face emerged from the door and peered back to see from where and how high they'd fallen, and he spotted Kyle.

The police officer yelled, "I'm going to get you! No matter how far you run, I'll find you!" Blood sprayed from his mouth.

Kyle backed away from the rough edge and following the road, he started running. He effected more of a hobble than a run because of his knee, but he moved quicker than walking and that's all he wanted to do: to get out of there as fast as he could.

-19-

The coroner was in a hurry. She arrived, examined the body in the truck, determined that yup, Grace was dead, and she ordered an autopsy and left the area without asking a single question about the investigation. Odd at any other time, but today, her disinterest was fine with the Chief. There was enough to deal with and answering the coroner's questions did not rate as his most pressing priority of tasks. Right now, the Chief sat in his SUV, holding the microphone in his hand, listening and waiting to find out that Raymond and Jules had caught the psycho bastard running through his town, murdering people, maybe even an entire family. The Chief's jaw ached from clenching.

The radio speaker came alive with Raymond's voice. "We need help here. Repeat: We need help. Jules is hurt. We are stuck in a tree and no one has been to the house yet to check on the family."

The Chief clicked on the portable and said, "What about Kyle?"

"He's gone. I saw him. He'll be on foot though. I can't get Jules to wake up. I think he's breathing. Uh, yeah, he's breathing. Send an ambulance."

"Right away. Uh, did you say you're stuck in a tree?"

•　　•　　•

The Chief sent two more cruisers (four officers) to check on the Parkers and to help Jules and Raymond. An ambulance crew was dispatched to also assist. The City of Leonard was part of Wellington County, Ontario, Canada. Wellington County was a large area of land with densely populated areas and sparsely populated tracts of woods and farmland. There are not enough ambulances to serve a county of that size and more often than not, people in an emergency waited a long time for help to arrive. When you're scared and worried, the waiting can feel much longer than it actually was. Considering that, it didn't take the first crew too long to arrive, but by the time they did, Mrs. Parker was a widow, and her only child was dead.

The Chief slammed his hand against the steering wheel when he heard the news. He really wished he hadn't sent Rubes home. He should be the one going out to the house to help and direct resources instead of being stuck here guarding a scene. He should be the one sitting down with Mrs. Parker while she tried to grapple with the destruction of her world. But he couldn't leave here. Not while the crime scene was still being processed. He had to secure the area while they did their work. The Chief did the only thing he could do while sitting there; he requested the volunteer Victim Services group to visit with Mrs. Parker and help her with locating and contacting her remaining living family members for support. Damnit! Kyle had to be stopped! Had the Chief caused this? Could he have done something to prevent all those deaths? Was there something he could do now to prevent more? Goddamn if he didn't feel some sort of guilty responsibility for what had happened to the Parkers. What he didn't know was the why of it. Was it because he failed them in some way? Or was it just a normal feeling that came along with the burden of responsibility. He was supposed to keep the people in his town safe. For three people, he has failed miserably.

He turned on his iPad and brought up Google Maps. His brow creased. He zoomed in and zoomed out with a pinch of his fingers. Anticipating where Kyle would go at this point will be an impossibility. The best thing to do, would be to protect the people nearest to his last known location and direction of travel. Draw a big circle around the area and tighten up. In the circle were two houses, the Benson's and, of course, the Grayson's.

"Hey Marjorie? Can you send a cruiser out to the Benson's place? Have them post up there and to keep an eye out, would ya?"

"You bet, Chief."

He tapped his nails against his front teeth. He wouldn't send anyone to the Grayson house. The Grayson's didn't like anyone on their land and that included the local police. Besides, from the stories he'd heard growing up, the Chief would be more worried for Kyle than he would be for the Grayson's if Kyle happened to make it there.

He didn't like just sitting around and waiting for Kyle to pop up somewhere. He needed to be more proactive here. What could he do right now to expedite the capture of Kyle?

He requested the K-9 officer re-attend to attempt another track of Kyle from the more recent car accident scene. He was told the K-9 officer who had helped earlier would not return. They would, however, try to send another one. The Chief called Inspector Greaves and asked for additional officers to help. He just didn't have the staffing to cover the large wooded area and he needed more resources roaming the area. Inspector Greaves said she would see what she could do.

His mobile workstation beeped. Another message. His computer had been beeping at him all morning ever since this craziness started. His eye was drawn to one email subject line. It was starred. It contained the results of all the queries on Kyle Harcourt. He clicked the link.

-20-

Rubes' stomach tingled and fluttered. Not like the precursor to a stomach flu, more like a queasy feeling, a pulling on the lower part of her stomach. She felt as though she was letting everyone down. She was letting the Chief down and all the other officers who came in on a day off or who hadn't even left work from their night shift to stay on-duty and help bring down this murderous runner by leaving. But how could she stay? The image of Grace's head wouldn't leave her brain. Grace floated there, behind her eyes, coloring everything she saw in red. The raw neck wound and naked torso snap-shotting and hijacking her vision. She wasn't any good to anyone like that. She knew that. And she knew the Chief knew that which was why he insisted she go home.

Driving away from Grace filled her with a tremendous sense of relief and once the scene was no longer visible in her rearview mirror, she burst into tears, the road blurring before her. She knew leaving, going home, was the right thing to do. All she needed was some time away from the scene to get her head straight and come back refreshed and ready to work. She needed a brief respite from the gruesome images and have time to process them. She needed to enjoy a calm and lovely day with her family to help her believe that the world isn't all horror all the time. That those visits of evil were never long because evil can't sustain itself. She just needed a little jolt of goodness. The kind a visit with her family would provide. So why did she still feel so bad? Why wouldn't this feeling of guilt leave her the hell alone? It wasn't like anyone else had seen what she had seen. Not even the Chief had seen Grace. No need for her to feel bad at all. Because even though intellectually she knew she shouldn't feel bad, she still did. The rational part of her brain needed to have a long discussion with the emotional side because at this moment they weren't seeing eye to eye.

Driving back to the station with her brain burning in her skull she was only partially listening to the chatter on the radio. When she had heard Raymond's voice on the radio asking for help, her mind returned to the present. She was nearby Raymond's location. She could help him and Jules. She picked up the microphone to tell dispatch she could go help when two things happened: Raymond said Kyle had gotten away and as she processed that information; she saw the same man who had run from her earlier this morning crossing the road in the rearview mirror behind her. He was wearing a different shirt, a bright pink one, but she knew it was him. If she had looked up a second later, she would have missed him.

She stomped on the brake pedal with the microphone in her hand wanting to broadcast who she had seen and where. There were a lot of voices competing for the air. Other police officers said they were on their way to help Raymond and the Chief was directing other officers to different assignments. She wanted to get on the air to tell them she had seen Kyle and which direction he was heading but every time she clicked the button, the sound indicating the radio air was taken would chime. And Kyle was getting away from her… again.

"Shit."

Exhaling, Rubes turned off the car and removed the keys. She turned her portable radio on, patted the gun on her right hip and the taser on the left side. Satisfied, she set off after Kyle at a run and the moment the radio air was free, she planned to tell everyone where she was and what she was doing.

Rubes lightly jogged along the roadway looking for the spot that Kyle had left the roadway and disappeared into the brush. She paused on the gravel roadside, looking for him within the trees. She thought she was in the approximate spot she had seen him cross the road, but she saw no bright pink in the dense trees. This guy can sure disappear. Houdini has nothing on this clown. A rivulet of sweat ran down her jawline. Walking along the gravel shoulder now and squinting into the trees, she looked for anything to catch her eye and there, a flash of bright pink. That had to be him. The only bright pink animal running through the forest today that she knew of is Kyle. She inhaled and shook her hands out by her side. Time to go. Time to get this bastard.

Rubes left the side of the road and her feet landed on an old trail. She clicked the portable button on her shoulder. The signal chimed busy again. Damn. Dangerous to go after him on her own without telling anyone. If she could keep him in sight long enough for her to get a chance to transmit her and Kyle's position, that'd be her best course of action. The safest plan. Minding her step and moving toward where she'd last seen the bright pink color, Rubes kept her forearms up in front of her face to stop the branches from raking her face.

Ahead, she heard rustling and snaps. She was getting closer. Kyle must be tired from running all morning. From running and killing people, she amended. Should she slow down? She clicked the radio button. Nope. Too much air traffic. Can't people just shut up for a second?

Yellow sunlight reflected from shiny green leaves. Earthy smells from the ground became more pronounced the deeper into the woods she traveled because the humidity trapped the scents and the heat. Rubes felt the sweat soaking her body, especially under her body armor. She picked up her pace when the trail widened enough for her to put her arms down and she didn't have to avoid the ground roots grabbing at her boots or tripping her. A constant stream of radio voices issued from her shoulder. She would have to update the rest of the officers soon. Maybe she should call the Chief on his phone? She didn't want to stop in the woods to do that though. Kyle could get further away while she stopped and made a phone call. Besides, he could be close enough to hear her make that call. Maybe he could hear her rad-

Rubes blinked. She was on her back looking up at the blue sky through a mesh of branches. How did she get here? On the ground? She couldn't hear anything, and her vision was blurry. Blood filled her mouth and she squinted at the shadow that appeared above her. A blurry shadow in a pink shirt.

The shadow screamed at her. "Why can't you leave me alone! Fucking following me everywhere!"

Her vision sharpened but only on one side of her face. The left side was dark. No, it was worse than that; it was what darkness aspired to be. There was nothing there. Kyle paced in front of her. Glancing in the direction she had come from, he moved his head from side-to-side angling for a better view through the screen of trees.

He knelt down before her. Face sweaty. Eyes wide. Small cuts and scratches marred his cheeks and brow. A swollen nose with dried blood mustached his upper lip.

Kyle said, "Anyone with you? Huh? You got a partner or something? Who you got coming, eh?"

Rubes focused on him and his words. Adrenaline spiked her blood and gave life to her limbs. She saw him holding a large rock in his scraped-up hand. He must have hit her with that. She hadn't even seen it coming. One second running and in the next? On her back gazing up at the sky. The worst kind of sucker punch. She raised a shaking hand to her head, and she touched the left side of her face under her cheekbone. She touched something on her cheek. A wet orb. What was that?

Kyle grabbed her hand and dropped it in her lap. He said, "Don't touch it. Makes me all shaky just looking at it. Man, I'm sorry about that. Hit you a bit too hard, I guess. Chasing me got me scared, you know? Still, didn't think I could pop out an eye like that. Crazy."

An eye? Her eye? She moaned and her body began shaking. She felt for the portable at her hip. Pressing whatever button she found under her fingers she hoped she activated the emergency one. The I NEED HELP RIGHT NOW button. There was such a button on all the police portables and a similar one in every cruiser. Once activated, a red screen would appear on every mobile workstation in every police cruiser showing where the signal was coming from. And as an officer, you would do whatever it took to get there as fast as possible. The portables were assigned to every officer at the start of every shift and linked to their police ID and patrol zone. The old portables had worked like cell phones, triangulating signals from the three nearest towers to find the most likely spot where the transmission had originated from. These new portables were equipped with GPS markers and were much better. They were accurate to within ten to fifty feet depending upon the signal strength. When Rubes pushed the I NEED HELP RIGHT NOW button every officer on the road could hear her and Kyle. Every officer was sent her location on their cruiser's mobile workstation monitor. And every available officer was on their way.

Rubes didn't know that. She hoped she had pushed the right button, but she didn't know. And this murderer had just knocked her eye out with a rock and was sitting here, making casual comments about her eye lying on her cheek. She had touched it. A shiver ran through her. Her right hand dipped to her gun. She removed it from the holster in one smooth movement and raised it when Kyle grabbed her hand with the gun and said, "What are you doing? Look at you, weak as a kitten. Here, let me take that."

He twisted the gun out of her hand and said, "Thanks. This might come in handy."

He stood and pointed the gun at her and she tried to say 'Don't' only it came out as "Gah," and a sharp pain ran from her jaw into her brain. Did he break her jaw too?

He smiled and said, "Nah, I'm not going to shoot you. Too loud. And besides, I don't think you'll be chasing me anytime soon. That eye, though. Man! I've never seen anything like that before. Gives me the heebie-jeebies!"

A siren disrupted the silence. Kyle frowned and glanced toward the road and then looked at Rubes. His eyes widened as he saw her fingers still pushing at buttons on her portable.

"You calling your friends? Is that what you did?"

He paced again with the gun barrel pointing down.

"Why can't you just let me go? I'd get out of this shit town and be gone! Fucking chasing me and chasing me, never letting up, never giving me a break! You did this, calling them on me!"

He pointed the gun at her head. She cried out and raised her hands. He lowered the barrel and said, "I'm not wasting bullets on you! I might need them later!"

He stepped close to her, so he was standing directly over top of her head. The bright pink shirt glowing from a ray of light piercing the overhanging branches made her squint with her remaining eye. He raised a foot; she screamed, and he stomped on her head. He raised his foot again. She gurgled. He stomped again and again and when he stopped, the officers rushing to Rubes in their cruisers heard Kyle say over the open radio channel in an out-of-breath, wet voice, "Why can't they just leave me alone?"

-21-

Tommy? Yeah. Listen. He's west of that address I gave you. Yeah. West of Old Town line. Get him." A cry escaped her, and she pulled it back and pushed it down. Linda said, "He's killing everyone out there."

-22-

Kyle had recently finished serving time for manslaughter. Before he could read further in Kyle's past, the emergency beacon sounded, and Rubes' and Kyle's voice dominated the police channel, transmitting through her portable to every officer on the road. Hearing her scream then Kyle's voice, a violent sound, a thump, a gurgle, then more thumps made the hairs stand up all over his body. On his mobile workstation, he could see all the police units and where they were on the map converging on the blinking little light in the woods west of Old Town Line. The Chief watched as the first unit announced they had found Rubes' car parked on the road. He let out a breath he hadn't realized he had been holding and waited. They found the cruiser and that was a good thing, but, goddamnit, where was Rubes? The Chief took his hat off and scratched at his crown.

Jennifer and Harold were the first officers to find Rubes. Years from now, suffering from PTSD, Harold would always see the image of Rubes' eye resting on the cheek of her misshapen head leaking yellow fluid from her ears. He'd later move to Guelph, an urban city, because any wooded trail brought Rubes' dead, murdered body back to him in vivid clarity.

Jennifer said, "She's here. We got her. She's, uh, goddamnit, she's gone."

•   •   •

The Chief saw Brandy of the crime scene unit approaching him from his peripheral. He was shaking in his cruiser clutching the portable microphone, knowing he should say something or direct someone, or do something a person in charge was supposed to do. His brain buzzed white noise.

Rubes was dead. She was supposed to be at home spending time with her family. She was not supposed to be dead in the woods. How did this happen? Think. What did he need to do? He blinked, trying to focus. He'd write a list, but his hands were shaking. He had to tell her husband, Rick. He had to secure that crime scene in the woods. Rubes' body, his friend, was a crime scene! So much. So much happening, so much to do. He scratched the crown of his head. He felt something trickling down through his hair from that spot. He stopped scratching and glanced at his fingernails. Blood. Everything was falling apart! He coughed and the acid taste of bile visited the back of his throat.

Feeling Brandy standing behind his shoulder outside of his car, he didn't want to talk to her. He didn't want to talk to anyone. He didn't even want to look at her. Not right now. Maybe not for a while. What he wanted to do was to go home and talk to his wife. To be near her, smell her skin and her hair, and hold her hand and have her tell him that Rubes' death wasn't his fault. Wasn't a result of something he failed to do. Didn't matter what he wanted right now, though did it? He is the boss. People are depending on him. And he had to catch this bastard. He closed his eyes and focused on his breathing. He picked up his hat from the seat beside him. He stretched his neck from side to side. He rolled down the window.

He said, "Yeah?"

"I uh, look, I'm sorry. We now have two more crime scenes to process. If you want, I can call my supervisor and get another crime scene unit out to help and try to get more constables out here to guard the scenes. After what he did, you'll probably want your own people to go after this guy. I know I would."

"Yeah. Uh, no. I mean, I would definitely like more officers out here. I'll take all the help I can get, that's for sure. But I think I would like more of your guys to help patrol and have my guys guard the scenes and protect nearby homes. They might not make the best choices right now. I wouldn't make the best choice right now. I was talking with Inspector Greaves earlier. She might be the best one to call. She's been helping with this already."

"Ok. Sure."

"So, yeah, if you could arrange that, I'd really appreciate it. I'll give you my cell phone number. Call me when you know if you can get the resources and what time you expect them here and I'll start planning on how to use them."

"That shouldn't be a problem, getting the resources. With a cop-killer running loose, you'll have a bunch of resources here soon."

"Thanks. Really. I appreciate it."

"Let me know if there is anything else I can do."

"I will."

Brandy walked away and pulled out a cell phone. The Chief's cell phone rang. He glanced at the phone screen. His wife.

"Hey."

"Oh, Chief, I'm so sorry…"

Hearing Natalie's voice, his reserve shattered, and the Chief started crying. He rolled up his cruiser window to talk to her privately.

-23-

Hank said, "She said he's west of that address. The one she gave us earlier."

Hank was holding a purchased police portable radio speaker near his ear. A police officer had misplaced the portable, for a heavy price. It was worth the cost, though. It was good for his business to know where the cops are patrolling and what they are up to at all times. Glancing at Tommy he said, "Looks like this guy killed a cop."

Tommy lit a cigarette. "That area will be crawling with more of them soon."

"Yeah."

"What do you want to do?"

"Kill him before the cops do."

Exhaling a cloud, Tommy said, "You think the cops will do him?"

Hank snorted. "Of course, they'll kill him. That's what they do. Oh, they'll say he was going to shoot them first or something, but they'll hide the fact they shot the guy in the back while he was running away or something."

Tommy scrunched his nose and adjusted the sunglasses on his face.

"Maybe some of them would, I'll give you that, but that Chief guy? I don't think he's the type."

Hank stared at Tommy, considering him like seeing him for the first time.

"You know, Tommy? You're smarter than you look."

"Thanks. Wait-"

"Get the boys on the phone. I want a bunch of them far west and slowly get them moving east. Like one of those skirmish lines. It'll keep us clear of any cops. They will be very busy for the next hour or two and we just might get in there and scoop this guy up before they get organized enough to do it themselves. Tell the boys I want this guy alive, though. I want this guy back in my shop tied to a chair. I have a blowtorch and a pair of pliers I want to introduce him to."

"Yeah. Ok."

Tommy flicked his cigarette butt away and lifted his sunglasses from his eyes to read the screen. Holding an iPad in his hand and manipulating a Google Maps screen, Hank shivered on this hot summer day.

This Kyle guy might be unknowingly running toward the Grayson place. On his screen, Hank was staring at the little house in the middle of a field, encircled by a screen of densely crowded old trees. He chewed the inside of his lip. They had to keep Kyle away from there.

-24-

After speaking with his wife, the Chief set about managing his resources. Rubes' body needed to be guarded. Actually, that whole scene needed to be guarded, and he didn't want anyone who had worked with her to stand there guarding her dead body for any amount of time if possible. Jennifer and Harold were stuck there now awaiting relief and who knew what standing over the body of their dead friend was doing to them. They had worked with Rubes'. Drank beer with her. Went to family functions. In a small police force like Leonard's, your shift-mates are a second family.

The Chief was told to expect nine OPP officers to arrive staggered throughout the day. He'll assign the first arriving officers to relieve Jennifer and Harold. He needed to get those two away from Rubes' body fast and send them home to their families. The Chief sent Rubes home for the same reason; to recover with loved ones. Only she never made it home.

Rubes didn't want to go home, at first. Would these two do the same? They might put up a stink about having to leave. They'd want to be around when and if Kyle is caught. If Jennifer and Harold protested hard enough, he just might keep them on. Maybe send them up to guard the Parker scene. He shouldn't. He really, really shouldn't. Being out here after seeing what they had seen wouldn't be good for them, but until they caught this Kyle guy, he needed every officer he could get his hands on.

What the Chief needed is more time to think. So far, he had been mostly reacting to Kyle. And it was not proving to be an effective strategy. Emergency after emergency was preventing the Chief from getting any sort of plan together. His head was spinning from everything he needed to do. Right now, visiting Rubes' family was the priority on his to-do list. He had to be the one to tell them before they found out from anyone else.

The Chief looked at the dashboard clock in his SUV and frowned. It wasn't even 11:00 am yet. Too much has happened in so little time and it made his head spin. Slow everything down. Tell Rubes' family first and go from there. The time of day meant Rubes' husband, Rick, would be at work right now. Who would be watching their little one? Rubes' mom or Rick's mom?

Using his cell phone, he called dispatch, "Marjorie? Could you find me a phone number for Rick's mom? Oh, and do you know her name? I'm drawing a blank here. I know I met her once, at their little one's birthday party, but I can't remember her name for the life of me."

"Yeah. Sure. Her name is Anne. I'll get her number for you."

"Can you text it to me? I'm thinking it'd be best to bring her with me when I go tell Rick."

"Yeah. I think you might be right."

●　　　●　　　●

Anne said, "This will kill him."

She was sitting on a couch in Rubes' and Rick's house. She kept her shiny eyes on her grandson, Rube's and Rick's son, Eddie, who was toddler-ing around, walking like the Chief imagined a starfish on land would walk, and pulling everything he could reach off the lower tables and shelves in the room. He called her and found out she was watching Eddie at Rubes' and Rick's house. He didn't tell her why he was coming to see her, but she knew what he would tell her before he even opened his mouth when she answered the front door. Her eyes shone and her mouth disappeared into a line as she invited him in. Some days, the Chief hated his job.

"You think you could come with me to tell Rick?"

"Of course I can." Her eyes locked onto Eddie. He gnawed, or gummed, at a plastic purple ball. Her lip trembled. She stood and picked up Eddie. She hugged him to her chest, and with tears spilling from her eyes and a steady voice, she said, "Of course I can."

●　　　●　　　●

The Chief followed Anne to her house. It was a short trip, and they deposited Eddie with Anne's husband, Jim, and then he followed her to Rick's work. When

Rick appeared in the lobby after the Chief requested him, he looked at him, smiled, looked at his mom, frowned and took two steps back and the Chief thought, he's going to run away from them both. He wants no part of this.

Anne said, "Richard!"

And he froze.

She said, "C'mon. Let's go."

He tucked his chin into his chest. His shoulders sagged. His body started shaking. He walked into his mom's arms. Watching Rick, the Chief thought that Anne was right. Rubes' death is going to kill Rick. Not literally, but his soul, his spark is dead along with Rubes. The Chief wiped at his eyes.

• • •

After a brief explanation of what the Chief knew, Rick wasn't up to asking any more questions for now. There'd be plenty of questions later on and he hoped by then to have answers. The Chief asked them (while looking mostly at Anne) if they would break the news to Rubes' parents and Anne said they would. The Chief walked them out to Anne's car. Rick was leaning on his mom and she was patting his head and whispering to him. She pressed a button, her car beeped and before they got to the car, Rick straightened and turned back to the Chief. Walking toward the Chief with clenched fists and a tear dampened face, the Chief removed his hat and scratched at the damn itchy spot.

Rick said, "You're going to get him, right?"

"You bet. Everyone is out there looking. Even OPP officers. We'll catch him."

"No. Not catch. Get. I don't want you to catch him. He's not some kid who stole a fucking chocolate bar! He's a murderer! Catch him? What the hell are you talking about? He cut off a girl's head, man! He's a sick animal and you know what you do with sick animals, Chief?"

Anne, hearing Rick getting louder and louder, appeared at his side and placed her hand on his elbow. He yanked his arm away from her touch and said, "You don't reason with them. You don't give them a hug and talk about how mean their parents were to them and if only they'd been given a chance their life could have been so different! You kill them! That's what you do! Listen to you! Catch him? Rubes' loved you, man! Talked about you all the time! Said you were a great cop! A great boss! A great friend, even! Where the hell were you, huh? When this animal killed her? Where were you? And where is your head at now? Catch him? What the hell? You kill him, that's what you do! You kill him for Rubes! You kill him for that poor girl whose head he cut off!"

Rick's face was inches from the Chief's. Anne pulled on Rick's arm again and this time, he allowed himself to be led away to her car.

The Chief said to no one who was listening, "I'm going to do my job."

•   •   •

Back in his SUV, the Chief cranked the air conditioning until the fan hummed. It was a scorcher. The pale hot disc hovered directly above in a light blue, almost white sky. Glancing at the map again, he saw where all his officers were positioned. He made sure the OPP officers were the ones doing the most patrolling while his officers secured scenes hoping one of them would find and arrest Kyle. His officers might be a little trigger-happy after what had happened to Rubes. They were probably angry at him for keeping them away from the hunt. The Chief could understand that, to a certain degree anyway. In his mind, they're cops and not executioners. And he wouldn't feel right knowing he had omitted preventing an opportunity for his officers to bloody their hands. The Chief remembering the book-boy shook his head. He thought of Rick's sick animal analogy. The Chief's stomach complained. When was the last time he had eaten? Six am? He should do something about that. Was he hungry or anxious? Might as well eat something and find out.

He drove out of the lot and headed to the McDonald's. He had done all that he could for now. Maybe, while eating his sandwich, he could finish his background homework on Kyle Harcourt.

-25-

Tommy said, "He might have gotten past us."

Hank scratched at the two-day growth on his chin. Two-days marked the beginning of the itchy stage. He planned to shave this morning until the unthinkable happened and after that, shaving lost all importance. A debt was owed. And Kyle was going to pay that debt with interest.

"How many people we got along this stretch of road?"

"Eleven."

"And they can see each other, right? Like I said?"

"Yeah Hank, sure."

"No. Not sure. Can they see each other or not?"

"As far as I know. I didn't check myself, but that's what I told them to do. I told them to spread out, but when they duck into the bush, they should be able to know where each other are and if they stood up or waved a hand, they should be able to see each other."

"Okay. Good."

Standing on a hill overlooking School Line Road, Hank scanned the trees hoping the object of his hate would appear. Hank had parked his car off the road, hiding it behind some bushes because the police knew the bikes and cars he owned, and he didn't want them to see his car.

He held binoculars in his hand. A pistol handle protruded from the back of his pants, in the middle of his lower back in easy reach. With the binoculars, Hank was hoping, praying to a God he didn't believe existed, that he would be the one to see Kyle. Tommy lit another cigarette beside him.

Hank said, "How many of those you got?"

"I got a carton in the car. You want one?"

"You know that cigarettes kill fifty percent of their customers? If you were going to jump out of an airplane and the instructor told you that fifty percent of the time the chute didn't open, would you jump?"

"Nope."

Tommy exhaled a cloud of smoke. Hank brought the binoculars up to his eyes and swept the bush area on the other side of the road.

Tommy said, "So do you want one?"

"Fuck off."

"Hey, why do you care if they can see each other? Wouldn't it be better to space them out further to see and cover more of the road?"

"No. Because then Kyle could cross the road and slip in between them, and no one would even notice."

"But he could cross the road further up where none of our guys are, right?"

"That could happen, yeah, but I don't think so. You grow up around here?"

Tommy sucked in some smoke and shook his head.

"I did and I know this area. Kyle was last seen heading this way, right? As reported by your friend?"

"Yeah."

"He's heading kind of west. The cops are coming from the east, and the north and the south... mostly. They are pushing him, whether he knows it or not, into this general area. The bush in there is not very forgiving. And when you're tired and don't know the area, you're going to take the path of least resistance. If what your friend said is accurate, he'll drop into the bottom of a natural bowl. If he goes north or south, he has a gnarly hill to climb through dense bush. If he goes east, he'll run into the cops. This little stretch here, the one we're covering, is the best spot for Kyle to come out at."

"If that's all true, why aren't all the cops out here, then? You think they would have figured that out."

"I think a couple of them have. How many patrol cars have you seen go past since we got here?"

"I don't know. Two?"

"Yeah. And we've only been here for fifteen minutes. More of them will figure it out and soon. That's why I wanted the guys off the road and into the bush. I don't want the cops seeing them. Another thing though, the cops are really busy right now. Kyle has left a few bodies behind him, we have a small police force, and so that gives us more time."

Tommy lit another cigarette with the end of the one he was smoking, ignoring Hank's raised eyebrows.

Tommy said, "Still brings me back to my original point. He might have gotten past us already. He might have crossed this road before we got set up."

"Maybe. But the distance he had to cover to do that would make him a world-class sprinter. This fucking loser is no world-class sprinter."

Hank raised his binoculars and swept the same area with a slow steady hand. He saw a bright pink something moving through a gap in the trees. The bright pink was heading toward the road. Hank smiled for the first time that day.

-26-

The Chief read all the information about Kyle Harcourt on the mobile workstation in his SUV. He burped, grimaced and popped an anti-acid tablet into his mouth and crunched it. He had eaten the Big Mac too fast. He wasn't even sure if he had chewed the thing. Just crammed it in and swallowed. Now it was sitting like a hardball in his stomach and his belly was disagreeing with the special sauce or something. It didn't help upsizing the fries and soda. The fries smelled terrific and the only reason he wasn't cramming those into his mouth too was because of consuming the Big Mac in record time. At least he'd ordered the diet soda, being calorie conscious and all. Sipping on the Diet Coke, his eyes read the convictions file of Kyle Harcourt.

There were a few assaults on his record dating back to when he was a teenager and it looked like he had stolen a couple of cars and committed a few break and enters, too. The Chief knew plenty of criminals who stuck to those basic crimes if they didn't happen to be drug addicts. The addicts would invariably have theft on their records and of course, drug convictions, but there weren't any of those in Kyle's past. The concerning charge on his record, the one drawing his eyes, was the one for manslaughter. He'd killed someone, and after serving his time, Kyle had been released from jail a little less than a month ago. No post-sentence probation order, so, no conditions either. Huh. Didn't take him long to kill again once he got out, did it? The manslaughter charge, that had been laid by the Haddonfield Police Service.

The Chief googled the Haddonfield Police Service. Another small service, just like Leonard's. He found the phone number and called the service. After talking to their dispatch and then being transferred three times to different people who couldn't help him, they put him in contact with someone who could help; Detective Bacon.

"Bacon? Like Kevin Bacon?"

"Yeah, yeah. But no relation. Listen, what can I do for you?"

"I was told you were the one who investigated and charged Kyle Harcourt?"

"Ah, man. What'd he do now?"

"You know, that's the second time someone has said that to me today."

•　　•　　•

The Chief explained what Kyle had been up to in his town and when he finished, only silence from the other end of the line.

The Chief said, "Hello?"

"Holy shit! I mean, what the hell? I can't see Kyle doing that and I can see Kyle doing all that at the same time, you know what I mean? But man! What do you need from me? How can I help? Wait, shouldn't he still be in jail?"

"It looks like they released him almost a month ago."

"Really? I wonder why he ended up in your town? Knowing Kyle, I'd think the first thing he'd do would be to hightail it to his brother's place."

"I think he was on his way there when he got... sidetracked."

"Sidetracked. There's an understatement."

"Can you tell me what your case was about? So, I can get more of an idea about who I'm dealing with here?"

"Yeah. Sure. I'd say you're kind of dealing with an idiot. Not stupid, but more like he can't control himself. He'd do something dumb, real dumb, and then scratch his head afterward wondering how the dumb thing he did had happened. You know? That kind of idiot."

The Chief said, "Yeah, I know what you mean."

"I'm sure you do. Stay on the job long enough... yeah. Not only does he have poor self-control, he can also be really mean if the mood takes him. And as you can see, that's a bad combination. You know, I thought for sure we had him for second-degree murder. But the Crown Attorney wasn't very experienced and a little nervous about the whole thing and going to trial and all that. So, when the defense offered manslaughter, he jumped at it."

"What happened?"

•　　•　　•

Detective Bacon explained the life and times, the condensed version, of Kyle Harcourt to the Chief. He spoke in an entrancing way and the Chief thought he'd do well as a host on one of those true crime podcasts. According to Detective Bacon, Kyle Harcourt was that guy in town who couldn't think ten seconds into the future. And because of this lack of foresight, his decisions, more often than not, were terrible. In Kyle's case, his behavior couldn't be blamed on bad parenting because his parents were genuinely good, normal, tax-paying, neighborly type of people. They did their nine-to-five jobs, kept their lawn neat in the summer and their driveway clear in the winter. Bacon guessed they probably weren't equipped to deal with a kid like Kyle. They were so low-key and laid back and Kyle was one very high energy kid who put the Energizer Bunny to shame because he was always going and going and going. They didn't know what to do with the kid and since it is generally frowned upon to correct your kid physically, Kyle had the run of them really quick. The only person in his family he would listen to was his brother because if he didn't, his brother would kick his ass. And most of the time, this worked well enough to keep Kyle in line. The only problem was, Stephen couldn't monitor Kyle all day, every day.

Kyle was only twenty-one years old the first time he killed someone. At the time, Kyle and Steven's parents had retired and sold their home to Steven at a family discount rate with the expectation that Steven would take responsibility for Kyle. Mr. and Mrs. Harcourt spent most of their time as far from Kyle as they could preferring to keep their relationship with him a long distance one requiring only the occasional obligatory parental phone call once a month. According to Steve, before his parents left, Mr. Harcourt was popping blood pressure pills like it was his job. The house was a great deal, but still, Steven sometimes wondered if the house was payment enough for having to deal with his disaster of a brother.

The Fat Pheasant bar in Haddonfield was frequented by an older woman crowd. It was a good place for young men to go to, or young women, it didn't really matter, for potentially no-strings-attached sex with a more experienced woman. On the night Kyle killed someone, he was inside this bar, flirting away with an older woman. Kyle is a good-looking young man and when he wants to be, he is very charming. Kyle was chatting and dancing with this woman and buying her drinks for most of the evening. It was clear to the witnesses that they were hitting it off very well. She would punctuate sentences by touching his forearm and pulling her hand back after she made her point. Soon enough, she didn't bother removing her hand. She left it there and rubbed her fingers along the muscles of his forearm. Yeah, Kyle must have been in a fine mood flirting with the pretty woman. Until the woman's ex-boyfriend showed up and saw what was happening and he took exception to their flirting. And Kyle took exception to him interrupting what was promising to be a good night.

The man pushed Kyle and Kyle popped him in the nose and the fight was on. The melee was met with the standard bouncer response dictating that they toss both idiots outside. Now, the ex-boyfriend, Dave Jackson, he'd had enough of Kyle inside. He was outmatched by Kyle and he knew it and once outside, he started walking to his car away from Kyle thinking, hoping, the fight was over. They were ejected from the bar, separated, and that was that. It should be over. All he wanted was to get into his car and get the hell out of there. Only Kyle wouldn't let him. Kyle followed him into the lot, pushing him in the back and calling him a 'pussy' a 'fucking coward' a 'turd puncher' and whatever else his uncreative mind could conjure up as to what he thought to be the most insulting or emasculating.

A small crowd had followed them out of the bar hoping to glimpse more of the fight and maybe record it on their phones and upload it to YouTube like everyone else was doing. It didn't occur to people to actually help other people. More important to record it first. The only good thing about capturing such social degradation was that most of what the police had, evidence-wise, explained Detective Bacon, was from these witnesses and from the not-too-great video captured on cell phones.

From one video, Kyle was seen closing on Dave's heels and as he got closer to his car, Kyle tripped him to the concrete. Dave stayed on the ground, facing Kyle with his hands up, telling Kyle he didn't want to fight anymore. He was done and he just wanted to go home. Kyle told Dave that he wasn't done with him yet. Kyle kicked at him and continued taunting him, trying to draw him back into a fight. When that didn't work, he grabbed Dave by the collar, slapped him across the face and pulled on him until he was standing. Dave still had his hands up, palms forward in the universal sign of surrender. Point being, it was clear to everyone there Dave didn't want to fight. Dave wanted to get out of there and go home and said as much over and over.

But like a bully on a schoolyard, Kyle wouldn't let him go. Kyle open-handed slapped Dave in the face a few more times. Dave blubbered. Kyle slapped him again and Dave started full-on sobbing with his shoulders hugging his ears and his hands shaking in the air by his head. Here he was, a thirty-four-year-old man crying in a dusty old parking lot because he made the stupid decision to try and reconcile with his ex-girlfriend at a bar and got high-school-kid jealous when he saw her with another man. Dave started backing up and pulling away and Kyle slapped him again. Dave broke Kyle's grip on him and reached for the door handle on his car. Before his hand could touch the handle, Kyle swept Dave's feet and pushed him in the back between the shoulder blades at the same time. Dave's head struck the door of his car right under the handle (Detective Bacon said he could hear the 'klonk' sound of Dave's head striking the metal door on the video and he'd cringed when he first heard it).

Dave's eyes rolled white and his body slid to the ground as though boneless. There was an oval indentation in the metal of his car where his head had struck. Dave drunkenly pushed himself up to his hands and knees. His elbows shook and his head hung loose and swayed giving the impression that something was wrong with his neck. Dave groaned and drool poured from his mouth to splash on the ground between his hands. The contact with the car had broken Dave's neck, but he didn't know it. He didn't know much of anything. His skull was fractured from the contact with the car. Bone had depressed parts of his brain. He probably didn't even know who he was. In that most vulnerable position, Kyle said, "Fucking-fuck!" and kicked Dave in the head. A witness said it was like someone with a giant scythe had swung through Dave's legs because he dropped to the ground and onto his face without making a sound. He might have been dead then. No one could say. Kyle was still calling him a 'pussy' and a 'candy-ass' and he raised his foot to stomp on Dave's head, as though Dave hadn't had enough yet, as though he hadn't learned whatever lesson Kyle was attempting to teach him, but before he could drop his heel on Dave's head, another witness, Trevor, bear-hugged Kyle and dragged him away from poor Dave. Kyle used the back of his head to break Trevor's nose. Trevor dropped him and Kyle went back toward Dave but then two more guys, friends of Trevor, stepped in and held onto Kyle until the police arrived. Another witness stopped using the camera on their phone long enough to call an ambulance. Dave exhaled his last breath before the ambulance could get there.

At the end of the story, the Chief said, "That sounds like second-degree murder right there. All those circumstances you're talking about, that's definitely second-degree."

"Yeah. That's what we charged him with. But like I said, the Crown was new, and Kyle had a history of getting into something stupid and not being able to control himself, I guess. She was worried about proving Kyle's intent to kill this guy because of his past idiocy. Intent is not really a thing with the charge of manslaughter. Once the Crown agreed to the reduced charge, the only thing left to argue about was the jail sentence. And you know how that goes. Kyle's young and hadn't ever been in trouble of this kind, and blah-blah-blah and so there you go."

"Well, damn. Second-degree would have kept him in jail longer."

"Yeah. That would have. Listen, if you could somehow get Steve in touch with him, that might help you out. He listens to Steve. He used to anyway."

"If I could figure out how to do that, I'd be able to figure out where Kyle is. All I know is that he's running around in the woods killing people like a goddamn Jason Voorhees."

"Who?"

●   ●   ●

The Chief called Steve. He knew Kyle the best and might have insight into what Kyle might do next.

"He cut off her head? Kyle? I can't believe it!"

After the Chief first called him, Steve started searching the web trying to find out why the cops wanted to find his brother so bad. Steve found out Kyle is a suspect in the murder of a woman he had decapitated. Details were scarce, but the media couldn't help but mention, over and over again, that the victim was minus a head. The Chief had been avoiding the news people on purpose and they hadn't been updated about the Parker's or Rubes' death yet. They'd find out soon enough though, from someone, and the media circus would come flying into town. The Chief wanted Kyle caught before the media wave drowned their small town. He'd have fewer questions to answer that way. Was he being naive about that? Probably. But a man had to hope, right?

"Look, I want to bring Kyle in, safe, and I'm calling you to figure out how to do that. You know him best. I want to know what you think he would do and if he's cornered, how could we get him to give himself up to us."

"This Kyle you're chasing is not the Kyle I know. It is, and it isn't. Kyle does stupid shit. He can't help it. You know that part of your brain that warns you when you're about to do something dumb?"

"Yeah. I do."

"Kyle doesn't have that part of his brain. He just does shit. He couldn't even tell you why half the time. And depending on how mad or scared he is, he might not even remember why. But cutting off a woman's head? Like... what? I don't know. This is, uh, I don't know. This is not any Kyle I know."

"He's running around in the woods right now and I want to bring him in before he runs into anyone else. If he's scared, like you say he might be, well, there's no telling what he might do. Is there anything you could tell me that might help?"

"I don't know, just block off the area you think he's in. He'll run into you guys, eventually."

"I'd like to think so, but it isn't that easy. The woods are big. Real big. I'd need a thousand more officers to do that effectively."

"I don't know what to tell you then. He'll be tired. He'll be scared. And with the way he's going right now, and I hate to say this, he'll be dangerous to anyone he runs into."

-27-

Kyle's sweaty hands juggled the gun. He'd hold the gun in his right hand and the gun would become slick so then he'd hold it in his left until he feared to drop the thing from that greasy hand and have to switch the gun back into his right hand again. Damn. It was so hot out. He's sweating through his clothes. His thick jeans clung to his thighs. He thought he couldn't be wetter than if he jumped into a pool with all his clothes on. Oh man, wouldn't that be nice? A nice cold pool, one without a heater and the deeper you sank under the surface the colder it got. He pictured himself at the bottom, floating and holding his breath, and looking up at the sun wavering through the filter of the water. Kyle closed his eyes and exhaled. He stumbled over a root and the gun slipped from his hand. It slid down a short dirt incline and disappeared into a bush.

"Really?"

He knelt down and stuck his hand into the bush searching with his fingers. He imagined a snake coiled in there watching his hand with its all-black eyes and its spear shaped head undulating from side to side. Kyle yanked his hand out and gingerly parted the branches with both hands. Peering into the darkness of the bush, he wished he knew more about nature. Are there even snakes out here in this area? The dangerous kind? He didn't know. He knew he didn't enjoy putting his hand into a dark place. Especially one hiding potentially aggressive animals.

Where was the damn gun? There. He saw the shape of the barrel and keeping the branches parted with one hand; he reached in with the other and picked the gun up by the handle. He sighed. Sweat rolled into one eye and he winced. Man was he tired. Every part of his body hurt. The right knee, the one he injured when he got hit by the cop car was stiffening up a bit and he stunk like moldy clothes mixed with something worse. A damp smell. A dirty armpit smell.

Walking on his knees to the nearest tree, he turned and sat with his back to the base. His stomach clenched like a fist. When had he eaten last? Seemed like forever ago and then longer. He could go for a fat, roast beef sandwich with onions and mustard on it right now. And a pitcher of beer to top it all off. He used the tree to scratch his back. The sweat was making him sticky and itchy. Probably the worst combination ever. The kid's face when he stabbed him in the neck. Why couldn't he get rid of that image?

"I didn't mean to…"

Get moving. Keep moving. Movement keeps the images away.

He stood. His knee cracked. He groaned and massaged it. Looking ahead, he saw a break in the trees. A road. There was a road up ahead. If he followed it while staying in the bush and ducking down whenever he heard a car approaching, he might be able to get out of this cursed town. The road could lead him to a house to find another car. With the gun, maybe he could frighten the people and take their car. He wouldn't have to kill them. No. No killing anymore. He'd done enough of that for two lifetimes. Just scare them, is all. His mouth tightened as he thought, *unless they gave me any shit about it.*

He slid the gun into the back of his pants. He tightened the belt on his jeans. He didn't want the pistol to slide down a pant leg. With his heavy feet scuffing the ground, he ducked under branches and parted others as he made his way to the road.

-28-

Hank said, "He's coming."

Hank and his own team used an app on their phones that turned them into two-way radios. You created a group through this app, opened it on your phone, depressed the button and just like that, instant communication with the whole team. It was a helpful and free tool for drug dealers and criminals to communicate quickly with the press of a button. Kind of like the cops using their portable radios hooked to their shoulders. He had the other members from their brother clubhouse install it on their phones too so they could all hear each other.

"Where? I can't see him."

Hank turned to Tommy and raised his eyebrows.

Tommy shrugged and said, "I don't know whose voice that is. Probably from the other clubhouse."

Hank used the binoculars to spot a unique marker for everyone to reference. Only a tree is a tree is a tree. Nothing unique about them. He couldn't very well say, he's coming out by that tree, could he?

"He'll be coming out onto the road soon. You can't miss him. He's wearing a bright pink shirt."

And there he was.

Brad, a member of Hank's crew, said, "Got him."

Hank said, "He's stopped right at the tree line. He's looking to see if it is all clear. Keep your heads down, boys. Wait til he gets to the other side. Can some of you guys maybe move closer to Brad? Keep out of sight while you do it."

A voice said, "Who's Brad?"

Another said, "Where is Brad?"

To Tommy, Hank said, "These fucks better not lose him."

Brad said, "He's coming out between that Dogwood and that Bitternut Hickory. See him?"

Tommy lit another cigarette and lowered his eyebrows at Hank and said, "What are those? Trees?"

Hank shrugged.

A voice, "The what and the who-zit?"

Brad said, "They're trees!"

The same voice said, "Hate to break it to you, man, but we're in a forest. There are trees everywhere!"

Kyle stepped onto the gravel sideroad. The bright pink shirt a beacon to all.

Brad said, "See him now?"

"Yeah."

"Got him."

Hank whispered to himself, "C'mon little piggy…"

They had no idea Kyle was carrying a gun.

●   ●   ●

Kyle sniffed and wiped his hands on the legs of his pants. Shaking his head, he didn't know which was wetter, his hands or his pants. Wiping them on his pants to get rid of the sweat was like trying to dry your hands on a towel that had fallen into a pool.

He turned his head from side to side. No one coming down the road. That's good but then again, was it? It'd be nice to see a car. He could step out into the road and when they stopped, he'd stick a gun in the driver's face, take the car and get out of this quicksand of a town. He was tired of walking in the damn woods. People did this for fun? Hiking and shit? And they called him crazy.

On the other side of the road, there was a small decline and then more bush. He could cross, stay out of sight of passing cars by walking at the bottom of the decline and follow the road. If he got lucky, which, considering how this day was going, very unlikely, he might come across a driveway with a car in it. Or he could wait until he heard a car coming and go with Plan A. The rural car-jacking plan. And if the car was a police car, he could lie down in the bush and wait for them to pass. Not bad as far as plans go. Simple and easy to remember.

He held his breath, listening. Forest sounds. No mechanical car sounds. He looked left. He looked right. No cars coming down the road either. Time to go. His stomach clenched. He patted it and said, "Yeah, yeah. I know."

He ran across the road, slipped on the gravel on the other side, caught himself and crab-walked sideways down the short, steep decline. He exhaled and smiled. He made it!

The bush came alive with sounds. Branches cracking, leaves rustling and through the emerald of the trees, two shadows running toward him. Kyle's eyebrows slid up and he turned to run away deeper into the woods. Off to his right, more sounds converged on him. The moving shadows were surrounding him. He pulled the gun from the back of his pants. He shot at the closest shadow. Hearing a grunt and seeing the shadow fall, he ran away from the rest of the sounds and shadows. Men yelled behind him. He didn't understand the words. Blind panic forced his vision to focus narrowly in front of him. Everything else around him faded. A small circular window of light drew him forward through branches, over rocks, over roots and sent birds and animals scurrying before him.

●   ●   ●

Holding the binoculars up to his eyes when the shot went off. Hank flinched and stiffened across the shoulders. Tommy was in the moment of lighting a cigarette, the lighter's flame almost touching the paper and tobacco end when the loud report of the gun made him jump. The cigarette popped out from between his lips.

Hank said, "How many of our guys got guns down there?"

"Three of them. Three shotguns."

"Birdshot or slugs?"

"I don't know."

Hank saw the pink shirt in small gaps between the branches running away. Following behind were two darker shapes. On the phone-radio someone yelled, "Terry is down! Terry has been shot!"

Hank muttered, "Shit."

Boom! A shotgun firing made a deep, distinct sound. The boys were firing at Kyle. Even though one of their guys had been hit, Hank hoped his guys wouldn't kill Kyle. He wanted to do that himself.

Pause.

Boom!

Hank saw clouds of dark smoke dispersing between the trees. The pink shirt appeared, disappeared, appeared again and was gone. The little bastard was fast.

Hank said, "How is Terry? Anyone?"

Brad, the tree expert, said, "Took one in the bicep. Looks like a through and through. He'll be fine." In the background, Hank heard who he presumed was Terry say, "Fine, huh? You a doctor and a master of trees? I just got fucking shot asshole! I'm not fine!"

Hank said, "Our boy is running toward the Grayson's. Me and Tommy will try to get ahead of him. The rest of you boys listening, if you can, meet us out there. We'll try to set up another skirmish line."

Boom!

Pap! Pap! Pap! Pap!

Silence. Not even the forest animals disturbed the quiet.

A voice on the radio, "Greg's down!" The shaky voice said, "He's fucking dead, man. He's dead!"

Hank ground his teeth.

After a beat, Tommy said, "Let the Grayson's have him, Hank. He'll be dealt with."

Hank said, "Maybe. Maybe not. All we know about them are fifty-year-old rumors. And I'm not giving him away to anyone. He's mine to deal with. Pliers, a blowtorch, and a shallow grave." Hank turned to Tommy and said, "You coming?"

"Yeah. You know I am."

-29-

The Chief was now playing catch-up. The day's events happened way too fast. He was afraid he was missing essential investigative steps to take and at the trial, he'd be ripped apart on the stand for all of those missteps. They had three crime scenes and every crime scene needed to be processed properly. What steps wasn't he taking that he should be? Was there something obvious he was missing? He also had to protect the citizens and have them feel like their police force was keeping them safe. The very best way to accomplish that was to arrest Kyle because their faith was certainly being tested today. Okay. Crime scenes first and then onto the problem of capture.

He opened the Google Map on his tablet. He had his people guarding Grace's scene and the Parker residence. Two OPP officers were standing by Rubes' scene. Thinking of Rubes, the Chief blinked back tears and said, "Focus."

Back to resources. Two of his guys for each of the scenes other than Rubes'. That is four of his officers being used for guard detail. He had two injured from the car crash, so they were out of it for now. Out of the two, Raymond didn't like that. He was itching to get back on the road to chase Kyle down. The Chief worried what Raymond might do if he happened to be the one to catch him. He worried about what any of his guys would do if they happened to be the ones to stumble upon Kyle. The Chief had to consider the safety of Kyle. The very thought of protecting such a person was starting to leave a sour and dirty taste in his mouth. Like sucking on a lemon dipped in shit.

He had to send Jennifer and Harold home, too. After finding Rubes in the state she had been in, he knew they would be no good to anyone. The Chief made a note to check up on them later. With the two in the hospital and the two he sent home; he was down four of his own officers. He had another two officers guarding the Benson farm in case Kyle ended up there. After tallying all of his resources up, he had ten of his own officers not looking for Kyle.

That was good and bad. He didn't think it would be good for the case to have any of his people finding Kyle (not after Kyle murdering Rubes), but that also meant he was losing out on those resources. Yeah, he had to keep the long-term picture in mind for when Kyle was under arrest and going through trial but first; he had to arrest Kyle. And fast. He's showing himself to be more than capable of killing anyone who gets in his way. The Chief contacted dispatch. "Hey, Marjorie? How many OPP officers we have coming in?"

"We have two already with Rubes, two doing patrol, a confirmed six more on the way and about ten more we are waiting to hear back from."

"Really? Ten more? That's more than our whole force if they all show up. That's good news."

"Yeah. It is. But it will take some time before they can all get here. They're coming from all over."

"Still, that's a better response than I was expecting."

Manipulating the Google map on the tablet in his hand, the Chief told Marjorie how he wanted the arriving officers deployed. When he got off the phone, he was a little more optimistic. If they all showed up, he'd have eighteen more officers in town looking for Kyle. And potentially more on the way.

Glancing at the map again, the Chief figured Kyle was either going to get lost in the woods and die from exposure (which wouldn't be a terrible outcome), run into the Benson farm where his officers were at or, he'd run into the Grayson place. On the map, the Grayson place, a white house in a field surrounded by trees, made the hair on the Chief's arms stand to attention. His cell phone trilled beside him. It was dispatch calling him.

"Hey."

"Hey Chief. The OPP officers, the ones guarding Rubes?"

"Yeah."

"They uh, noticed that Rubes' gun? It's missing."

The Chief's forehead beaded with sweat. He said, "Oh, no."

-30-

Kyle ran until his lungs felt hollowed out and his leg muscles protested every step with spikes of pain starting in his heels and ending in his lower back. His lower back had never hurt because of running before. Not that he'd ever run for this long.

To reduce his pain, he slowed his pace from running to walking and he still couldn't seem to get enough air into his lungs. Twitching at every noise, he studied the path behind him, suspicious of burly-bearded men or focused-faced police officers coming after him. Hungry, thirsty and dying for a cigarette, Kyle wanted this nightmare of a day to end. Who the hell were those guys? They definitely weren't the police. They looked like bikers. But what would bikers want with him? It was all so goddamn confusing. And they were waiting for him there, too. Like they knew he would be there or going that way. How the hell could they know that? He didn't even know where he was going at the time.

Kyle stopped and placed his hand on a tree, propping himself up. His lungs heaved. In his other hand, he held the gun. White motes dotted his vision. His guts twisted and his mouth filled with saliva. Kyle said, "Oh, shit-" and his stomach tried to leave his body through his mouth. Dry heaving against the tree, his knees shaking and with bile coating the back of his tongue, tears squeezed out from behind his closed eyelids. He didn't know if he should laugh or cry. What was his body trying to puke out? He hadn't had anything to eat for some time. There was nothing in his stomach to puke out. Yet here he was, weak-kneed and leaning against a tree while his body tried to eject the nothing in his stomach.

The convulsions subsided and he dropped to his knees and put his back to the tree. A bug flew into his mouth. He gasped, choked and spit it out. He muttered. "What the fuck?" In between breaths.

Kyle's heart jerked in his chest. Peering toward where he had last seen the men chasing him, he saw no shadows and heard no sounds of continued pursuit.

The earth of the forest mixing with his own stink crinkled his nose. Why had he stopped at that goddamn bar? Why couldn't he listen to his brother or anyone else for that matter? Why must he feel offended by anyone trying to give him direction or help him? Did he have a problem with the word 'no'? Or 'don't'?

Yeah, he knew he did. Not on a conscious level. That would entail self-reflection and Kyle did not do self-reflection. He really believed he was unlucky most of the time and any poor situation he found himself in was one not of his own making. To Kyle, events and people conspired against him.

Kyle ejected the magazine out of the handgun. The top bullet blinked in the sunlight. Should still be one in the pipe, right? And how do you count how many are left? He turned the magazine to see the back. There were vertical dots and beside each dot was a number. Empty spaces meant what? There isn't a bullet there in that dot? So, including the bullet still in the gun, he had eight? Nine? These bullet ends didn't line up with the numbers very well. Didn't matter. The gun isn't empty. That's all that mattered.

Crack!

Kyle flinched. A falling tree limb? After a few missed tries, his shaking hand slid the magazine back into the gun. Ready to rock. It was strangely silent after he loaded the magazine, like the forest was holding its breath. Time to get moving.

●   ●   ●

After a few steps, the ambient noises returned. Birds chirped. Animals scurried. And Kyle thought it very possible he might be dying. His stomach was pinching him, and his dry tongue stuck to the roof of his mouth. His muscles ached and throbbed. Places complained on his body he had no idea existed until now. Little bolts of pain made him blink and had him adjust how he walked. His hurt knee flared up in the most unexpected moments. Kyle favored that knee, but it didn't seem to appreciate his efforts. He needed food, water, and rest.

Being lost in a forest with the cops and some strange dudes chasing him made his heart jig and jag. Fear pulsed throughout his body and into his limbs. Would it be so bad if he stopped moving for a bit? Sit down under a tree and cover himself with branches and debris and if he could, get some sleep? Would that be so bad? It'd feel great but, still, probably not the best idea right now. Who knew if those men were still after him? Better to keep moving. Keep putting one foot in front of the other.

"What else you got in your lunch today?"

Kyle froze. He slowly dropped to one knee while peering around and through tree branches. He saw the white side of a cop car and the light rack on the roof, not flashing or blinking.

Kyle stifled a cry. Why couldn't they leave him alone? Everywhere he went someone was either running after him or waiting ahead for him. Tears blurred the scene. And then Kyle smelled, what was that? Eggs? His hunger roiled inside. His mouth watered. He stood, holding his breath, his eyes bulging.

Two cops stood outside of the car on the side furthest away from him. Kyle could see the shoulders and hat of one and only the hat of the other. They were looking away from him. Kyle saw a barn in the distance. That's what the two cops were looking at: the barn. But are they here waiting for him? Did they know he was coming this way or are they there just in case? Didn't matter, really. They were cops. They were hunting him. He should just turn around and quietly go the other way and he knew that. And he would have if except for that smell. Food! How could he ignore that? And there, on the dash of the car sat a canvas lunch bag almost like it is begging him to take it. The top of the bag was open, and all the delicious smells are being pushed out of the car by the air conditioner fan. Why they had the air conditioner on, and the windows open Kyle didn't know or care. The food, though. He did care about the food in that bag. A lot.

-31-

"What else you got in your lunch today?"

Officer Syed Singh watched his partner for the day, Officer Bobby Vella, bite into a lettuce wrap with some sort of meat inside after returning from their police car.

"If I tell you, are you gonna make fun of me?"

"Probably."

"Why would I bother telling you then?"

"What do you got in that wrap, there? Chicken?"

Bobby said, "Maybe. Maybe not. I'm not telling you." Bobby took another bite.

Syed shrugged, "Yeah. I can see it. It's chicken."

"Why do you care what I eat?"

"Cause I'm bored. Standing here is boring. And you eat weird shit and I want to make fun of you. It makes the time pass."

"Making fun of me makes the time pass?"

Syed said, "Of course. You say that like it's a shocking idea or something."

"Yeah, well, I'm not going to talk about how I eat."

"All right, then. No need to be so sensitive about it. It's just food."

"Exactly. It is just food. So, shut up about it."

Bobby bit into his wrap. Juice dripped out of the end and left a whitish-orange trail down the front of his bullet proof vest.

Bobby said, "Goddamnit!" And using his hand he wiped at it. It didn't help any. It only spread it in a wider arc.

Syed said, "What's in that sauce? Looks spicy."

"Will you give it up?"

"Is that wrap all you brought?"

"No."

"So? What else you got?"

Bobby finished the wrap. He didn't answer Syed.

The police radio squawked behind them. A strong breeze swayed the tops of the trees in the distance as though brushed by an invisible hand.

Syed said, "Wouldn't it be fucking awesome right now for Kyle to roll right up on us?"

"Yeah. That'd be better than winning the lottery, in my book."

"Fucking right."

"We'd have to shoot him, right?"

"No question about it."

"I mean, he's killed four people, he's killed Ru—, a cop, and he has a gun. I say we have no choice, when you think about it."

"You're right. And when you're right, you're right, man."

Bobby straightened and twisted his shoulders, stretching them out with a grunt. Leaning back against the car, he tapped his sidearm with the palm of his right hand.

Syed said, "Do you think it was quick?"

"What?"

"Rubes. Do you think it was quick?"

"Man. I hope so. She was good shit, you know?"

Syed said, "Yeah."

They passed the next minute in silence avoiding eye contact or even glancing in each other's direction. Both of their eyes shone behind their sunglasses.

Bobby said, "This wrap isn't going to do it."

"Now you're talking. You know Ted will deliver a pizza right to our cruiser here? I'll split one with you."

"No. I got some more healthy crap in the car."

"Ohhh, Mr. Healthy."

"Shut it."

Bobby walked around the back of the cruiser, getting a little tired of taking shit for his food choices. He opened the driver's door and reached in for where he had put his lunch bag. His hand swept the air and then the dash. Nothing. He leaned his head in and the bag wasn't where it was supposed to be. Frowning, he looked around the inside of the car. He checked the floor and the footwell on the passenger side. Not there.

He closed the car door and stood. He had just gotten the lettuce wrap sandwich out of the bag not more than five minutes ago. He had left the top of the bag open because he knew he'd be returning to it soon. Syed had been with him the whole time so he couldn't have taken his bag and hidden it as a prank. It should have been right there, right on the dash. So, where the hell was it?

He peered into the window again, in case he missed it, even though he knew he hadn't and yup, still not there.

Bobby quick-turned and gazed into the forest. Had someone come and taken it? And had that someone been the same person they should have been keeping an eye out for?

"Syed? I think we have a problem here."

●　　　●　　　●

Syed said, "We got to call it in, man. I don't see that we have any choice."

Bobby lifted the hat off his head with one hand and rubbed his hair with the other. He pulled his hat back on and said, "Do we? We don't know it was him. I didn't see him. Did you?"

"No, but who else took your damn lunch? It sure as hell wasn't Bigfoot, was it?"

"Look, our only job was to stand here and make sure this murderer didn't get to the Benson's, right? I mean, that is why we are here, or am I wrong?"

"No, that's right."

"Now, I'm not saying it was Kyle who came and took my lunch while we were supposed to be keeping an eye out because I didn't see him. So, since we didn't see him, and we can't be sure it was him, do we really need to tell anyone about this?"

Syed's gaze flickered to the trees. Sweat drew a line down his jaw. He exhaled.

Syed said, "The guy killed Rubes, man. He killed Rubes, and he killed a kid. If he was here, even if we only think he was, we need to tell someone. That way they have an area to look in, right? Doesn't the OPP have those drones? They'd at least have a place to start with their, I don't know, droning."

"We don't know it was him!"

"Yeah. We kind of do."

"Fuck." Bobby stretched his neck from side to side. He exhaled and said, "Okay. Okay. After we call it in, you know what I want?"

"What?"

"Ted's goddamn pizza."

"Damn right you do."

-32-

Kyle had fought an internal war with himself over the food in the cop car. Should he go for it or not? Risk versus reward here. Was whatever was in that bag worth going to jail for? He'd been to jail, and it was no joke. He'd been running in the woods, starving and sweating and killing people (not intentionally in his mind) to avoid going back to jail. Going for that food in the cop car... man, that was taking quite a risk.

And then Kyle's hand was reaching in through the open window. He didn't remember crossing the ground from the tree-line to the cop car. And now here he is, fingertips touching the canvass bag as the scent of eggs filled his nostrils. Kyle's hunger didn't wait for his brain to rationalize going for the food. His hunger decided for him.

"No. I got some more healthy crap in the car."

The cops are so close. His fingers clasped the bag and he slid it off the dash, taking care not to spill the contents. There was something heavy in it. Heavy is good. A string of drool spilled from Kyle's mouth. Kyle pulled the bag through the window and backed away, keeping low and his eyes trained on the officers' backs. Their voices faded. The tree limbs pulled the retreating Kyle into their embrace. Kyle disappeared into their depths, smiling with drool coating his lips and chin.

-33-

The Chief sipped on cold coffee, grimaced and put the cup in the holder beside him. He had spoken with Syed. It appears Kyle had stolen Bobby's lunch. They didn't see Kyle do it, but Syed was sure it had to be him. Who else would steal a lunch bag from a cop car? Someone on the run and starving, that's who. The Chief rubbed his thinning spot. He brought the map up on the tablet in his police car and viewed where he had deployed his officers. The Chief would have to reassess the positioning of his resources. Syed said if Kyle had come from the woods on the driver's side and then left the same way he had entered, then he'd be heading more or less toward the Grayson's. If not, and he passed the place, he'd end up wandering through more miles of wilderness. The Chief, if he had a choice, would prefer the latter. Then again, maybe not. Running into the Grayson's could solve a lot of other problems for the Chief. Like an expensive trial. But that was no way to think. Kyle should be brought in by the police to waste the next twenty-five years of his life in a tiny cell.

The Grayson place. If the rumors are true…

The Chief wondered if Inspector Greaves would be kind enough to see if the OPP could fly a drone over the area. He knew the drones had infrared cameras. They might pick up a human shape through all the trees. The trees were dense and tightly packed which could make detection difficult. In the winter, the trees wouldn't present the same problem. The branches would be bare of leaves and with the cold ground as a backdrop, a person's body heat would make them stand out like a glow stick on the grey screen.

The Chief exhaled. It wasn't winter. It was summer. No point in thinking about what he couldn't control or change like the seasons of the year. What could he do now? How could he improve their chances of bringing Kyle in without losing anymore lives in the meantime? Thinking about Rubes, the Chief squeezed his eyes shut, willing the tears away. He had no time for tears. Fucking Kyle.

-34-

Hank stood over Greg, rubbing the rough hair on his chin. Tommy lit a cigarette behind him.

Hank said, "Can't you go five minutes without having a smoke, man? You're fucking killing me here!"

Tommy, knowing Hank was in a mood, dropped the cigarette and ground it out under his boot.

Tommy said, "What are we going to do with him?"

Terry, the man who had been shot before Kyle had killed Greg was pressing a shirt against his shoulder. Blood dripped from his hanging fingers. Standing over Greg, Terry said, "We'll take care of him. He's one of ours."

Hank nodded, knowing Terry meant Greg had been from their clubhouse and they would look after him. Hank had meant to get to the Grayson's place fast and had been ready to run down from the hill he had been watching the action from and drive on over and get ahead of Kyle right away. Tommy had cautioned him against that. They had asked for help from the other club, and they had answered. One of them had been injured and another had been killed helping Hank. It wouldn't look good to run off and leave a dead man and an injured man behind. Not without at least checking in on them and offering to help. Tommy said Kyle was on foot and it would take time for him to get there before them, if he even made it to the Grayson's. They had enough time to check on the people who had helped them. Hank bit his lip and closed his eyes. Tommy was right. Even bikers, the one percenters, had politics. He had to play the game which was why he was standing here talking to Terry instead of hightailing it to the Grayson's.

Hank said, "Do you need anything from us, Terry?"

"Nah. We called some of our boys. They'll be here soon enough to help."

Terry winced and glanced down at Greg. Hank's eyes followed. Greg didn't even seem dead. He looked like he was sleeping. Except for the bloody holes in his torso. With his eyes on Greg, Terry said, "Heavy price, helping you."

"Yeah." Hank knew he would have to eventually pay for that help. And it would hurt. But that was something to worry about another day.

Hank turned from Terry and Brad, the tree expert. Tommy followed after Hank, their footsteps crunching over the dry ground.

Hank said, "How many men we got that can come with us to the Grayson's?"

"We're good, still. Six of us. None of our guys got hurt."

"Lot of area to cover with just six guys. Their property is big. He could slip right by us."

"We're not going onto the Grayson property, are we?"

Hank stopped and turned to Tommy. He said, "Why? You scared?"

Tommy lit a cigarette. He was careful to blow the smoke away from Hank. He said, "Well, yeah. Aren't you?"

Hank studied Tommy, turned and continued walking to his car. After a second, Tommy trailed after.

-35-

After stealing the cop's lunch, Kyle scuttled through the woods as though the bogeyman himself chased after him. Hugging the lunch bag to his side with one arm, he kept looking behind him expecting to hear a yell and the rustling of brush being pushed aside as the cops saw him and gave chase. When that didn't happen, he slowed down, stumbled over stones, tripped over roots and, exhausted, still he pushed himself onward.

Kyle was finding it hard to ignore the food under his arm for much longer. It smelled so good. It smelled like the carnival; popcorn and cotton candy; heaven for the nose. It smelled like a steakhouse, like a barbecue, and like paradise in a little canvas bag. His guts punched him from the inside, saying *hey man, I don't know what the hell you're waiting for, but it's time to eat!* And he wanted to give in to the smell and to the gastronomical demands, but if he did that before getting far enough away, he might as well walk into a jail cell and close the door himself. And to Kyle, no food was worth going back to jail even though the thought of the food made his mouth fill with saliva and his stomach continue to gripe at him.

Satisfied he had travelled far enough, he searched for a spot to hide out and eat. Kyle's skin, slick and slime covered only added to the discomforts piled upon discomfort. He needed to take a break. He needed to eat. Just a little further, he thought.

Kyle climbed a small hill and when he got to the bottom on the other side, he stopped and tilting his head, he listened. No sounds of pursuit. No yelling and no heavy footfalls. Kyle stumbled to the nearest tree and flopped down in front of it.

"Ouch!"

He'd sat on the gun in his back pocket. The hard metal pinched his skin between the gun and the ground. He removed the gun from his back pocket and placed it beside him on the dirt. He opened the canvass sack, saw the Coke Zero, and snatching it from the bag, he pulled the tab and cracked it open releasing the hiss of carbon. Kyle chugged the drink, pressing the can so hard against his mouth it clanked against his teeth. His throat moved. The sweet liquid spilled into his stomach.

He put the can down with less than half left. He opened a plastic rectangular container. Three white hard-boiled eggs glistened. He plugged one into his mouth and chewed. He moaned and kept chewing. He swallowed the egg and giggled. Who knew a can of Coke and a hard-boiled egg could make him so happy? He reached for the next one, bit it in half and picked up a plastic drink container. A clear plastic container with a twist-on lid, he could see the drink inside. It was beige with a light tint of green. Squinting at it and chewing, he twisted the lid off. He sniffed the liquid. Caramel? And what was that other smell? Cinnamon?

Kyle lifted it the container to his mouth and sipped it tentatively. Damn. It tastes good. He drank the rest of it as fast as it would go down. After the whatever-drink, Kyle finished the eggs and the last of the Coke. Rubbing his bloated stomach, he massaged a burp out. Leaning back against the tree and straightening his legs out in front of him, he rubbed his thighs and massaged his aching knee. A sunbeam penetrating the tree leaves above lit upon his chest. Warm. A pleasant blanket of fog settled over his mind. Kyle blinked. It was a long blink. The next time he closed his eyes, they stayed that way.

-36-

The Chief glanced at the digital clock on the dashboard. 2:34 pm. Is that all? Is this still the same day? How can all that has happened fit into such a small window of time? His stomach growled. Hadn't he just eaten? The Chief rubbed his eyes. They burned in their sockets. His nostrils stung, like after a good cry. Had he cried yet? When Natalie called, that was the last and only time so far today, but he'd been close a couple of other times too. Man, this day…

His ringing phone buzzed in his hand. He twitched and looked at it as though it had appeared by magic.

"Hello? Uh, Chief here."

"Hey Chief. Long day, huh?"

"Inspector Greaves. Yeah. You could say that."

"Look, the reason I'm calling is, uh, how many resources do you have? How many people you got out there patrolling and guarding scenes, houses, perimeters and stuff like that?"

"Uh, I don't know. Give me a minute here. I can look at the computer here and-"

"Don't worry about that right now. The reason I'm asking is that we don't know how long this will go on for do we? And you need to look after your people. You can't have them out there forever. I know you have a lot on your plate, and this is the last thing you should have to worry about, but I want you know that I made another call for more OPP officers to come out and assist, especially after what happened to your officer, Ruby, right?"

"Rubes. We called her Rubes."

"Yeah. After that, I had officers calling me to volunteer and come out to help. I mean, they don't even want the overtime. We'll pay them, of course, only all I'm trying to say is that, when we get more staffing out here, you can start sending your people home. To rest, spend time with their family, whatever they need. And whatever you need. I got authorization from the top. We got your back."

The Chief pressed the phone to his chest. His eyes spilled, and he sucked back a cry. Too much has happened today. And now this. A simple offer to help reducing him to tears. But that wasn't the whole reason. No. The generosity, the kindness that could only have existed because of a tragedy pulled down the walls of his self-control.

From his chest, a muffled, "Chief?"

He wiped his nose and eyes with his other hand, quick-checked his eyes in the rearview mirror (they were a bright red), and after swallowing a few times, he said, "Yeah. That's great. That's uh, great."

"Yeah. I thought so too. So, for now, the officer's pouring in will be delegated to patrolling the perimeter of your town lines. It wouldn't do to let Kyle get out of your town."

"No. It wouldn't."

"And then, when you're ready, we can start replacing your guys with our guys."

"I have to say I appreciate everything you have done and everything you're continuing to do. Only I don't think any of my officers will want to go home. Not until Kyle is caught."

"I can understand that. But you're the Chief. And you got to look at this from that standpoint. The political standpoint."

"Inspector-"

"I hear things. Your guys are talking. Talking about what some of them want to do to Kyle if they see him. If he ends up dead, there will be questions. Ones you won't be able to answer."

"Where'd you hear that?"

"Does it matter? I'm hearing it. That's what matters. So that means your guys are talking. Are you saying you haven't heard any of this?"

"No." As soon as the Chief said that, he knew that wasn't true. He'd heard some grumbling even before Rubes was killed. Ruby herself said it wouldn't be that bad to let Hank find Kyle after what he'd done to Grace. Maybe because his officers knew what he thought of vigilante justice, that he thought it wasn't any justice at all, maybe they had kept quiet around him knowing he disapproved.

"The talk is real. And if they kill Kyle, someone, some reporter will hear how your officers were talking about it. That wouldn't be good. I suggest you send them home whether they like it or not. Let them have a few hours of overtime, so they feel they're not leaving as soon as their shift ends, but, really, you should send them home. They need the break."

"I uh, I'll think about it." What the Inspector said rocked him a bit. His officers are talking, but not to him. Even though he knew the reason, or thought he did, it still hurt. Or maybe he was being too sensitive on an already sensitive day.

"And you too, Chief."

"Me too what?"

"You should take time for yourself. I can look after things for a while, if you like."

The Chief frowned. Is that what she was doing? Trying to take the investigation from him? Was all this niceness simple political maneuvering for the biggest arrest in a long time? Or was he being a paranoid cop? Viewing any generosity with a skeptical eye, wondering what the angle was and how the generosity would benefit the person offering. Yeah. Cop thinking. And who gives a shit if she took over the investigation? She has more resources. What matters the most is catching the bastard, right? Rubes' face flashed in his mind. Kyle needed to be stopped. But the Inspector was right. His guys needed a break. And the Chief also knew he needed a break too. Might not be a bad idea to head home and spend some time with his wife. But not yet.

"Thank you. I may take you up on that offer. Probably early evening though. Eat dinner with my wife at home."

"Whatever you need. Let me know."

"Will do."

-37-

Hank said, "What do you think?"

Tommy glanced at the iPad screen and squinted. The sun's glare made the screen hard to see.

"Dave, can you and that big head of yours block that sun? I can't see the screen here."

Dave scowled. The other men laughed. Dave did have a large head. Or did he have narrow shoulders? Either way, the effect was the same and Jesse had once teased him for having 'shoulders like a trout'. Dave had been mixing speed with cocaine that night and he didn't find the joke all that funny. Dave had broken Jesse's nose, knocked out a tooth and fractured Jesse's ribs. Although everyone laughed at Tommy's joke about Dave's big head, Jesse didn't. Jesse's nose no longer being in the center of his face took the humor out of any jokes concerning Dave's head and its unusual size.

Dave moved his head between the sun and the iPad. Tommy said, "Not much better, is it? Can you adjust the brightness?"

Hank picked up the iPad and turned it around, squinting at the edges. He said, "How do you do that?"

"Give me the damn thing, old man."

Tommy swiped up on the screen and toggled the brightness to the end of the line. Putting the iPad back on the hood of the car, he said, "That's the best we can do."

Using his fingers, Tommy pinched the screen to zoom in on the satellite image. A white house stood in the middle of a field. There was no road or driveway leading to it. The emerald field appeared well cared for. The field stretched for approximately one hundred feet in a circle around the home and was bordered by a ring of dense trees. Vern, leaning over the shoulder of Hank said, "You ever see such a thing? I mean, how do they bring groceries in? Are you sure people even live there?"

Hank said, "They have been seen in town getting groceries."

"But are they living there? How do they bring the food to the house? Walk through a forest and then through a field to get to the front door? Carrying bags of food? Doesn't make sense."

Hank shrugged and said, "Who gives a shit? If no one is living there, good for us and bad for Kyle. If someone is living there, bad for them, and bad for Kyle. Doesn't change a thing. Not to me. Anyway, I plan on getting to him before he even gets to the house. We need to position each other so we can see him approaching."

Jack said, "What if he doesn't even come this way? He could get turned around in the woods easy. Hell, I grew up in these woods, and I could get lost." He paused, "Maybe not. But this boy could."

Hank waved him off and said, "What can I do about that? Either he comes this way, or he doesn't. All I know is that this is the last direction we saw him heading in so here we are."

Jack swatting at a mosquito near his ear said, "How long we going to sit here for?"

"As long as it takes. You got a problem with that?"

"No, Hank. No problem here."

"We'll be here until we hear the police have caught him or we learn they spotted him somewhere else. Right, Hank?" Tommy interjected. He didn't like the red flush rising on Hank's face. Putting a finger on Jack's chest, Hank said, "As long as it takes."

Tommy said, "Okay. We'll position everyone first and then I'll go get food, drinks and bug spray for everyone. Sound good?"

Hank nodded.

• • •

Tommy bought dark vinyl coats with hoods, flashlights, Subway sandwiches and soda, and set about delivering them to the men positioned in the woods. The bugs were thick and unnervingly large in some places. Dave and Vern heartily welcomed the coats and the bug spray. Tommy made sure everyone had a gun of their own because Kyle sure as shit had one and he wasn't exactly shy about using it.

As Tommy approached Vern, the thick cloud of bugs hovering over him zipped to Tommy to taste the new guy. Tommy dumped his gifts and hustled over to Dave, who wasn't faring much better than Vern. Actually, it'd be fair to say he was faring worse. Raised, red bumps decorated Dave's forehead and cheeks. Dave's hands were constantly waving away the bugs from around his head and his frown was so pronounced it disfigured the shape of his jaw. Tommy raced away from Dave as soon as he dropped the items into Dave's hands fearing another bug attack if he lingered too long. Tommy enjoyed a smoke talking to Jesse and another one later when talking to Jack. Jesse and Jack are in a better area and weren't being bothered by the insects near as much as Dave and Vern, but they welcomed the coats and spray just as much. Even though they weren't being pestered by the insects too much yet, nighttime woods was a different animal than daytime woods.

Hank's sitting spot enabled him to see the front door of the home. Only the bright red door marred the brilliance of the white siding in the sun. Trailing smoke from a cigarette, Tommy stepped over a log with his bags of goodies.

Tommy sat on the log and peered at the red door to see what Hank was so interested in.

Hank said, "Doesn't look like the place is abandoned, does it?"

Tommy, exhaling a plume, said, "Nope. Look at that satellite on the roof. It's one of those good ones. Probably get channels from all around the world."

"How would you know what a good satellite looks like?"

"It's a Bell Satellite. You don't get much better than that. Unless it's Rogers."

"Why not just get unlimited internet like everyone else?"

"Maybe that's what that satellite is for. The Internet. Can you see any company running fiber optic cable out here? Doesn't matter. TV or Internet. That satellite looks newer. Not like those giant backyard dishes you used to see in the 90s."

"Yeah."

Tommy dragged on his cigarette. Pointing at the house with the red ember he said, "The place looks better than mine."

Hank snorted. "That's not saying much."

"Yeah. I know. It is weird though. Vern is right about that. How do they bring groceries in? Or anything for that matter? You could only get to the house by foot."

"I don't know."

"You ever see a house without a driveway before? I mean, even trailer parks have driveways. Hell, remember Dwight? That old coot whose wife kicked him out of the house, so he set up a pop-up tent just off Old School Line Road?"

"Yeah."

"Even that tent had a driveway. Gravel and all, but still a driveway."

Hank smiled. "Fucking Dwight. He sure seemed a lot happier in that tent than living with his wife, didn't he?"

Lighting another cigarette, Tommy nodded and said, "Yeah. He did."

Hank said, "Do all the boys have a gun?"

"Yeah. Kyle has one. Seems only fair."

"Kyle with a gun is a problem. And being here, where we are, on this land, this could be a problem too."

"Do you think what they say about the Grayson's is true?"

"They say a lot about these people. Do I think they're a family of cannibals feeding off anyone foolish enough to cross their land? No. Do I think they're a coven of witches and warlocks, summoning demons, monsters and worshipping Satan under the moon? No. I don't believe that either. I haven't believed in monsters since I was a kid. From what I've seen, and done, I'd say people are way worse than any movie monster. Still, what I know is that you don't get the reputation they have without good reason. Maybe that reason happened a long time ago and it's been following them ever since and they're stuck with it, you know? Remember Billy Redmond?"

"Yeah. Tootsie Roll. Sure."

"See? That's exactly what I mean. Billy was in what? Grade three, grade four maybe, when he took off his swim trunks and that tootsie roll looking turd in his shorts rolled across the change room floor changing his life in this town forever. One moment, one stupid accident, and he's forever known as Tootsie Roll. This could be like that. Something from long ago that still affects the family to this day. Small towns. They have long memories."

"Sure. Wait. So, you think everyone has the wrong idea about them?"

"No. All I'm saying is that some rumors don't fade with time. Some rumors become etched in stone and it don't matter if things have changed. To other people, they are what other people say they are. But that opens up other questions."

Tommy exhaled and said, "Like what?"

"Look at this house here. It is well kept. The grass is green and weed-free. People are living there."

"Yeah?"

"Well, where are they then? They are seen in town, but it's a rare event. And why don't their kids go to our school? How do they make other Grayson's? Inbreeding? And if the bad rumor, whichever one you want to believe, happened a long time ago, why aren't they doing anything about it? Why aren't they joining one of the churches or the Knights of Columbus or some shit? Why not cut down some trees and put in a driveway?"

"You're kind of all over the place here. Are they bad or not?"

"The reason you don't cut a road through the trees and put in a driveway is to keep people away. They don't want anyone driving up to their house. Why?"

"You have a fence around your property. With a camera and a gate."

"Yeah, but I'm a criminal. I steal shit and sell drugs. I have a reason for the security. And if these people are criminals, I would know about it. Can't have too many criminals in one small town without knowing about each other. Since they're not criminals, what reason could these people have to keep other people away?"

"Shit. I don't know."

"Me either. And that's what worries me. Not knowing that information worries me."

Hank turned back to the house. He said over his shoulder to Tommy, "Do me a favor and tell the boys to keep their eyes open."

"They know."

"Tell them again, Tommy."

"I'll call them."

"Good. But first, what food you got in that bag for me? Anything good?"

-38-

"Dad?"

"Hey, Lindsay." The connection made her father's voice sound far away, as though at any moment the call's communication tether would snap.

"It's hard to hear you." She heard ruffling like a microphone rubbing against cotton.

"How's that? Better?"

"Yeah. Uh, the reason I'm calling is, there are people on the property. It looks like they are watching our house."

"Huh. Police?"

"No. Not these guys. They look like... well, they look rough. Like they walked off the set of that TV show, *Sons of Anarchy*."

"Bikers?"

"Yeah."

"Where's Samuel?"

"That's why I'm calling. He's out."

"Damn."

"Yeah. And he's been gone for almost a week."

"That's not good."

"What should I do?"

"There's nothing you can do. Either he returns when they are there, or he doesn't." She heard a loud exhale.

He said, "This doesn't make any sense. What are they doing out there? If they are townies, they should know better, and if they're not, I can't even think of a reason why anyone would be around our place. Have you been listening to the police scanner?"

"No. I should have been. The moment I saw them creeping into the woods. See? That's why I called you."

"Nah. You would've thought of that before long. Check the scanner, watch the news or something. There must be a reason people are on our property. Has to be."

"Yeah. I know."

"Hold tight. Me and your mom will head home as soon as we can catch a flight. We moved most of what we had to move anyway. There's no rush to get the rest of it done."

"Ah, don't do that. This is the first time you guys have been away in ages."

"That's not true. We do one of these trips every couple of years. We can go away again. I'd only sit here and worry. And so, would your mother."

"I can take care of it, Dad. I'm sorry I called. Momentary lack of confidence. I can handle this."

"I know you can. Tell you what, call me tomorrow first thing in the morning. If the problem hasn't been resolved, me and your mom will catch the next flight home, ok? I really couldn't stay here the whole time worrying. If the situation was reversed, could you?"

"No."

"Right. So, call me tomorrow. All right?"

"Yeah."

"You sound worried. Listen, they can't get in. They'd need a goddamn tank. Do they have a tank out there?"

"I'm not worried about me. I'm worried about Samuel. On the cameras, these guys, they all have guns."

"All of them?"

"It looks like it. Yeah."

"That's really weird. Man. What are they doing there?" A pause. Her father's breathing from thousands of miles away. "You got the shotgun handy?"

"Always."

"I wouldn't worry about Samuel. If those guys are still around the house when he gets back, it won't go well for them. No matter how many guns they have. But still. Lock the doors. At least until Samuel gets back."

●   ●   ●

After the phone call, Lindsay returned to the security room. The wall of monitors reminded her of the eyes of a fly. She'd seen a close-up image of a fly once and the multitudinous eyes appeared as alien lenses. In the security room, with the screens shining on her, she felt as though she was the one being watched and not the watcher. She didn't like the security room which was why she didn't go in there often. Lindsay had set an alarm to notify her when the cameras picked up movement so she wouldn't have to spend any more time than necessary in that room. The sensors had been calibrated to only sense movement of a size worth noting. The thick forest surrounding their home teemed with wildlife, but Lindsay was only ever interested in the man-sized wildlife. Since she set up cameras in the woods, she also set up sensors at every access door of the house. Every time any door leading outside opened, a chime sounded. She had set the system up a long time ago. It had been tricky getting it all to work to her satisfaction but in the end, it was definitely worth it to her.

She remembered her father smiling at her when she showed him how it worked. Like most people past a certain age, he had no affinity for new technology. It seemed to her most people got comfortable with the equipment of their time. Her dad could program a VHS player and record songs from the radio onto an analog cassette tape like a boss, but that was it. Her security set-up proved useful because no one in the family had to hang out in the security room. Once a week they could check the recordings on the hard drive to see if anyone had been sneaking around. Then whoever's job it was to check the recordings that week would also erase the hard drive and set it to record for the following week. There was never a lot of footage to go through. The occasional bear might activate the sensors, but not much else. In Lindsay's opinion, prior to today, the entire system seemed pointless. The last time someone had come snooping around their home was well before she had been born. Her daddy had been a little boy himself at the time.

The alarm she set up to notify her of movement was a soft doorbell chime. No one rang their doorbell out here so the sound wouldn't confuse her. And she liked the tone of it. It was a pleasant ring. It was unusual to hear the alarm sound at all and when it went off today, she looked up at the ceiling as though it held the answer to the strange jingle breaking her concentration on the job in front of her. She had been working on replacing the old and inefficient solar panels on the roof with Tesla tiles, and when the chime sounded, she put down the instructions and stared at the ceiling. She had a fleeting, crazy thought. Was someone at the door? And then realization. Her eyes widened. Her nostrils flared. The alarm. Someone or something is on their property.

Lindsay hurried to the security room. Multiple screens projected images of six different men from different locations on their property. Not bears this time. She sat in a chair in front of the monitors. She bit her fingernails. What are they doing? She typed in a command on the computer and it brought up the recording from the time when the cameras first picked up the strangers. They had been standing on the fringes of the forest. The hood of a car, tires, and two motorcycles were visible at the bottom of the screen. A big man, strong through the chest and shoulders, pointed into the woods. The six men separated. Lindsay continued to watch. They all took up different positions on the property. Lindsay noted the camera numbers on a pad.

On the wall hangs a map of their property. Numbers were scattered over the map. The numbers mark where the cameras were placed and their corresponding ID's. The men had surrounded her home. What was going on here? Four of the men moved off camera. There is too many woods and too little cameras to cover the entire area, but since these men didn't set off another camera in a different quadrant, she could discern their general area. She saw one man approach the others. He had a large bag slung over a shoulder. The man handed items to two of the men she could see. He handed one man a long rifle, and although she couldn't be certain, it looked like he handed another man a pistol. Why are these men surrounding her house and arming themselves? Are they after the rumored Grayson gold like those men had been all those years ago? That rumor couldn't still be alive, could it? Unsure and worried about Samuel, she had called her dad. He had made her feel better and even though, like she said, she didn't need to call him; she was glad she had.

Back in the security room, she turned on the police scanner and a wall-mounted TV connected to the Internet. She queried local news. Within a few minutes, she understood. These men aren't here for her or her home. They were here for Kyle. She didn't know why, not really, but a hunted multiple murderer in their town and strange men showing up on her property was too much of a coincidence to dismiss. Both events are related.

She glanced at a wall panel. She pressed a button and the click of all the locks in the home engaging at once drowned out the police radio for a moment. On a monitor, she watched two men sitting outside her house, one of them smoking a cigarette. She shook her head. These men shouldn't be here.

-39-

While Hank and his men sat in ambush, some at war with bugs, others at war with boredom, and an anxious Lindsay gnawed at her already short fingernails waiting for Samuel, Kyle slept into the early evening.

-40-

The first person the Chief visited was Jules Niebolt in the hospital. He had a slight concussion from the car crash and a dislocated knee. Raymond had broken his nose on the airbag and the hospital staff was worried he may also have a concussion and they were monitoring both officers closely. Raymond wasn't happy about having to stick around in the hospital. Other than the double bruised eyes and the bright white bandage across the bridge of his nose, Raymond said he felt fine. Raymond knew what had happened to Rubes, knew Kyle was still running free and was pissed there was nothing he could do about either fact. If the hospital staff would just let him go, he could at least contribute to the latter.

"I should be out there, Chief. I know this town. I grew up here. I played in these very woods. I'd find him. Damn right. I'd find him and I'd make him pay." His lip trembled. He said, "After what he did to Rubes..."

"Maybe it's best you aren't out there. We need to be thinking clearly, to do our job."

Raymond's eyes measured the Chief. He said, "I am thinking clearly. Clear as a bell. The question is, are you Chief?" He said the word 'Chief' with a sneer.

Raymond crossed his arms and turning away from the Chief said, "Jules is still out of it. He'll say something and forget he said it and then say the same thing again. His wife is in the room with him. You should probably say hi."

"All right. Look, they are not going to clear you to go back to work."

Raymond's head turned back to the Chief. His eyes flared wide.

The Chief held up his hands and said, "That's not up to me. You know that. They just want to make sure you're not concussed. You should go home. Get some rest. I'll need you tomorrow for sure."

"I can't sleep. Not while that piece of kid-killing, cop-murdering garbage is running around free."

"Up to you what you do tonight. I can't use you, though. Not until tomorrow at the earliest."

•   •   •

Raymond had been right about Jules. He was definitely out of it.

"Hey Jules. How's the knee?"

"My knee? Fine. Fine, right?"

Jules looked at his wife, Celia, and said, "My knee's fine, right?"

She said, "You were in an accident. Your knee was dislocated, but it's been put back."

"Accident?"

The Chief said to Celia, "Let me know if you need anything, ok? Dinner, coffee, whatever. I'll have it sent right over."

Celia said, "Thank you."

•   •   •

The Chief next visited Syed Singh and Bobby Vella. They refused to leave their post at the Benson's. Bobby asked to get relief at his post for only an hour or more so he could go home to replace the lunch he was sure Kyle had stolen (he couldn't go through with ordering pizza because it seemed too unprofessional). The Chief arranged for two OPP officers to replace them so they could both go home, but they said they would return soon and hang out until at least midnight.

Syed said, "It's better to have more officers looking for this guy than not. If we're here, guarding this place, that leaves at least two more officers free to find him, right? I have to ask though, why are we still guarding this place? I mean he stole Bobby's lunch. Would he come back? Kind of stupid if he did. Not that I wouldn't welcome the chance to get my hands on him."

"As far as I know, Kyle is not a woods kind of guy. It's easy to get turned around out there. One tree looks just like the other, you know? He might end up back here just because he got lost."

With a smile that didn't reach his eyes, Bobby said, "That would be very okay with me."

•   •   •

Jennifer and Harold, the two officers who had found Rubes, were already at their respective homes and surrounded by loved ones. The Chief stopped by Harold's house first, only because it was closest. Harold was holding a bottle of whiskey in one hand when he answered the door. He said, "You find him?"

The Chief said, "Not yet."

"I hope it isn't you that finds him, Chief."

"I know, Harold."

"I hope it's someone who knows what to do to a thing like Kyle."

"If you don't feel up to work tomorrow, that's fine Harold. The OPP are really stepping up. Let me know in the morning, or when you can. Take care of yourself."

The Chief walked away. At his back, Harold said, "You didn't see her, Chief. You didn't see what he did to her."

When the Chief turned back, the door closed.

●　　　●　　　●

Jennifer answered the door. She said, "You get him?"

The Chief shook his head. Jennifer's partner, Candace, appeared beside her. Like Harold, they didn't invite him in.

"Hey Jennifer. I just wanted to stop in and check on you and see if you're okay or if you need anything."

"Thanks Chief." Her eyes welled, "I don't think I'm ok. Not right now. I uh, I keep seeing her."

She put her face into her hands. Her shoulders shook as she cried. Candace put her arms around her.

The Chief said, "Call me if you need anything. Anything at all. At any time."

Candace said, "Sure. Thanks."

●　　　●　　　●

The Chief had no one else to visit. He called Inspector Greaves and said, "I'm going home. I'll have the radio on, and my cell phone glued to my hand."

The Chief drove toward home but took his time arriving there. He drove down dusty roads and past wooden fences bordering farmland. He drove toward the sun lowering to the horizon.

He knew his job was to bring in the bad guy. To do it right and in the process, not become the bad guy. His role wasn't to be a judge. And it certainly wasn't to be an executioner. His first job though, his most important one he thought was to protect the innocent. He wasn't doing a good job of that, was he? If it came down to it though, he knew he couldn't kill Kyle if Kyle decided to give himself up. It wasn't something he'd ever be able to do. He knew that as sure as he knew his own name. But should he put so much effort into preventing others who could?

-41-

Sitting on a stump with a vinyl hoodie pulled down low over his eyes, Dave felt a bug crawling around on his nose. He peered at it, crossing his eyes, and yup, definitely a big sucker sitting there on the end of his nose as though it was taking a load off, tired from hovering aloft. He swiped the bug away and it flew away. He zipped up the hoodie as high as the zipper allowed and arranged it to cover the bottom part of his face so only his eyes showed.

"No way am I staying out here all night, that's for sure. I'll sit out here until dark and that is it." Dave frequently talked to himself. Even when other people were in the room. He liked to talk out loud because it helped organize his musings. Speaking his thoughts bullied out the other internal voices bouncing around and trying to compete for the spotlight in his head.

He pulled the gun out of his coat pocket and turned it around in his hand. Four bugs immediately dropped upon the exposed flesh of his hand looking for a meal. He stuck his hand with the gun back into his pocket.

"Goddamn bugs. I never knew there were so many bugs in one spot. They sure do love me, don't they? Not staying out here forever, man. This is too much."

Dave huddled inside his coat, almost wishing he smoked just to give him something to do. And maybe the smoke would keep the bugs away, like one of those lemon candles. Dave stiffened. His skin rippled as the hairs straightened on his body. He stood and removing the gun from his pocket, he turned in a circle. What was wrong here? Something has changed. What was it?

Out of the group, Vern was the closest man to him. Keeping the gun in one hand, he raised the walkie-talkie to his mouth and said, "Vern? You there?"

"Yeah."

"You see anything?"

"Like what?"

"I don't know. Anything."

"No."

Hank said, "That you asking, Dave?"

"Yeah."

Hank said, "What's wrong?"

"Nothing."

"Why are you asking if Vern has seen anything then?"

"I don't know. Just a feeling."

Silence.

Hank said, "All right then."

Dave put the walkie back in his pocket. The feeling of wrongness didn't go away. His reptilian, ancestor brain was picking up on something his senses weren't detecting. He scanned the trees, pointing the gun where his eyes were looking. Nothing but woods and silence.

"It's too goddamn quiet. That's the problem."

Dave grew up in the town of Leonard and spent part of his childhood exploring the woods with his friends pretending to be soldiers. As he got older, his parents often took him hunting and that particular skill is something he continued to develop yearly with his friend or sometimes, even though it was frowned upon for safety reasons, sometimes he went out alone. He knew the woods was an alive place. Animals were always moving; birds were always tweeting and whistling. There were always the ambient noises of life. Dave could hear his own breathing, the buzzing bugs flying close to his face, and that was it. And truth be told, the silence was starting to freak him out. He knew from all of his years spent hunting that the only reason the woods went silent was because there was another predator nearby.

When Dave first arrived, the area was quiet. He didn't think anything of it because he expected the quiet. If he waited long enough, he knew the forest animals would get used to him and they'd return to their usual business of being animals. So, for the woods to go silent again meant someone or something else was nearby. Something new. Something the animals were trying to figure out if it was hostile or not. Is that why he asked Vern if he had seen anything? Because he knew something was off?

There are bears in the area. Despite their cuddly depiction on TV, they are animals, and they are very, very dangerous. And they aren't like other apex predators. Large cats or wolves, when going for the kill, went for the soft spots, like the throat or the stomach. They did that to kill their prey quickly and to prevent any injury to themselves while the animal fought them to live. Prey can't hurt the predator if it dies quickly enough. A bear is an entirely different predator. Unless you had a large gun, you could not hurt a bear enough to stop it from killing you if it set its sights on you. That'd be like a toddler trying to hurt Arnold Schwarzenegger in his Mr. Olympia prime days. It was just not going to happen. And because it was the toughest animal in the woods, the baddest on the block, it wasn't worried about being hurt or injured. It doesn't have to kill you quick. It doesn't have to go for the soft spots. It could put a paw on you and pin you to the ground. Then it could take bites of you at its leisure. A bear was one animal that Dave would prefer not to tangle with.

Dave looked at the gun in his hand. A .38 caliber against a bear? Might as well shoot spitballs through a straw.

"I wish I had a rifle right now and I wish the goddamn woods would start talking again."

A breeze pushed through the trees. It rippled the nylon jacket on his back. Dave wrinkled his nose and coughed.

"Goddamn that stinks!"

He twisted to see what had produced the sudden stench with his gun leading the turn. He never saw what hit him.

-42-

The Chief pulled into his driveway and parked beside Natalie's green Camry. He turned the SUV off, shaking the keys in his hand before stuffing them into his pocket. He didn't feel right about leaving the manhunt for Kyle to the OPP. He didn't feel right about a lot of things that had happened today. The dead child. The dead officer, his friend, Rubes. Stopping at home to have dinner and relax would give him time to think, but was that a good thing? And was it just an excuse to get out of the game for a while, out from under the mountain of stress slowly and inexorably crushing him flat. Thinking tended to lead to introspection. What terrible revelations awaited him there? Could he have stopped any of the killings after poor Grace? What decision of his, or lack of decision, had caused more deaths? Would these stupid questions ever go away? He suspected no, they never would.

The Chief put the key back in the ignition. He had work to do.

"Chief? You coming in?"

Natalie stood with the screen door open. One foot on the front step and the other still inside the house. He closed his eyes.

She said, "C'mon. I have a hot dinner and a cold beer ready."

The Chief removed the keys and sighed. He stepped out of the cruiser and walked up the front steps. His reserve broke at the touch of her hand. He stood crying on the porch with her hand on his shoulder. She pulled him inside, closed the door and hugged him. The Chief wept against her cheek.

He said, "The boy and his father. And Rubes. I couldn't stop it. I couldn't stop any of it."

"I know."

•　　•　　•

He took the radio off his belt, unclipped it from his shoulder and put it on a chair beside the dinner table. The radio was quiet concerning Kyle sightings. Like he had suddenly disappeared. The Chief hoped Kyle hadn't made it outside of Leonard. He didn't want any other deaths to occur because they couldn't catch him in his town. The Chief's eyes stung, and his nose burned from the sudden cry-fest at the front door.

He said, "You're getting really good at this, you know?"

They were eating carbonara with pancetta.

"My technique is getting better. Getting the egg on the hot pasta without the eggs cooking on it and becoming grainy is the tricky part. I think I almost have a handle on it."

"I'd say you most certainly do."

"I have a cherry pie keeping warm in the oven."

"Bless you. Tell you what, I'll cook you whatever you want when this is all over."

"That's a deal."

●　　●　　●

After eating the pie and following it with a coffee, the Chief put the dishes in the dishwasher and wiped the table and counter clean. Natalie said she would do that, but the deal had always been the cook never cleans and even on a day like today, he was holding to that deal. He wanted the normalcy. It kept his self-doubt at low ebb.

He clipped the radio to his belt and shoulder, kissed Natalie on the cheek and said, "Thanks. I needed that."

"I know."

The Chief walked to the door, and she said, "Listen. You take it easy. Make sure you bring your old-man ass home to me."

He peered over his shoulder, trying to look at his own ass and said, "Old?"

"Yeah. Old."

He smiled and nodded at her.

"Lock the door behind me."

On the front step, he inhaled the evening air. Summer nights are the best. No sun baking your exposed skin, yet the air was warm. Any other night, he'd take the time to enjoy it. Summer was too short and not to appreciate it, seems like a crime all by itself. No more time for musing. Time to work.

The Chief didn't know where to start looking for Kyle that wasn't already being covered. Truth be told, because they hadn't found him yet, that realization depressed him.

-43-

Hank was prepared to stay out all night waiting for Kyle. In the coming darkness, he reevaluated his stance thinking maybe he was being a bit too stubborn about it all which was adversely affecting his rational thought. There was no guarantee Kyle would head for this house. The woods are huge. It was getting dark and it would be so easy for Kyle to get lost or turned around out here. Hank had to further consider the darkness. The summer trees are thick with leaves. Even if the moon was bright tonight and the sky clear, the light wouldn't penetrate through the organic roof. Kyle could possibly walk within ten feet of them and not be seen. The only reason to stay out here was for his own stubborn pride and his razor sharp need for revenge.

Hank said to Tommy, "What do you think? Should I call it?"

Tommy said, "We wouldn't see him in the dark. Even with that bright shirt on."

Hank smiled and said, "You think the bugs have carried off Dave and Vern yet?"

"They are not in a good spot, that's for sure. And with it getting darker, I don't see their situation improving much."

"Yeah. I suppose I'll put them out of their misery. Good of them for sticking with me for so long."

"Hey. We all loved Grace, Hank. This fucker needs to pay."

"Yeah."

Hank raised the radio and clicked the button. "Hey guys. I'm shutting it down for the night. I'll see you back at where we came in."

Vern: "Thank Christ."

Jesse: "You got it, Hank."

Jack: "Heard."

Tommy lit a cigarette while standing behind a tree. If someone was watching from the house, he didn't want them to see his ember.

Tommy said, "Did Dave say anything?"

"No. Only Vern, Jesse, and Jack. I'll call him. Make sure he heard me."

He lifted the radio. A light turned on in the house.

Tommy said, "Well, look at that. Someone is home."

"Could be on a timer. You ever see Home Alone?"

Tommy, staring at the house from behind the tree, didn't answer him.

Into the radio, Hank said, "Dave? You hear? Quitting time. Let's meet back at the car and bikes."

No answer.

To Tommy: "Who is the closest to Dave?"

"Vern."

"Hey Vern? Can you go check on Dave?"

No answer.

"What the hell is going on? Now Vern's not answering?"

Vern: "What's that?"

"Can you check on Dave? He's not answering."

"Yeah."

Hank said, "Let's pack up and get out of here."

"We coming back tomorrow?"

"If they haven't caught the prick, you bet I'll be back."

"We. We'll be back."

"Appreciate it."

Hank stood and stretched. The radio chirped in his hand.

Jesse said, "Hank. Something's here." Jesse's voice was whisper soft.

Hank stared at the radio. He whispered because Jesse whispered, "Kyle? Is it Kyle?"

"No. I don't know. I hear… steps. Heavy steps."

"We're coming."

Vern: "I'm coming too."

Hank said, "No. You check on Dave. Me and Tommy will go to Vern."

Hank said, "Put out that smoke, would ya?"

The red ember sparked as it hit the ground.

Hank said, "You remember where they are, right?"

"Yeah. But let's get there before full dark. Places in the woods look different at night. Even with flashlights."

· · ·

Hank and Tommy hurried through the forest. Tommy was breathing hard as he followed the bouncing backpack on Hank's back and the flashlight beam in Hank's hand. Hank turned on the light when they could no longer see the house.

Sweat flowed from Tommy's hairline. He licked it off his upper lip. Salty. Tommy concentrated on Hank's feet. Stepping where he stepped and moving how he moved.

Hank said, "Are we close?"

Out of breath, "Yeah. I think so."

"You think so?"

"Yup, we're here. See that? A Subway bag, right there."

Hank's beam pinned the bag in its light. They walked toward the bag. Tommy turned on his flashlight and for a reason he couldn't articulate, not even in his own head, he scanned the forest behind them.

Hank said, "A bag, a soda can, some cigarette butts, and no Jesse."

"Call him."

Into the radio Hank said, "Jesse? Where you at?"

No answer.

Hank said, "What in the holy hell is going on?"

Tommy said, "I don't know. I don't like it, though. I know that."

"Me either."

Vern on the radio said, "Dave's not here."

"Are you in the right spot?"

"Yeah."

"How do you know?"

"One of his boots. It's here. And it's hard to tell because it's so dark, but I think, I think there's blood on it."

To Tommy, Hank said, "Kyle, you think?"

"I don't know, man. It doesn't feel right, though." Hank stared at Tommy. None of this felt right. Nothing left of Dave but a bloody boot? No sign of Jesse except his garbage. And no sign of Kyle. A shiver ran through Hank.

He said, "You feel that?"

"Something. I feel something."

"I feel like we're being watched."

"Yeah."

From the radio Vern said, "Help me! It's got me, Hank-"

The radio cut off. In the distance was the unmistakable sound of a gunshot and following that; screaming.

-44-

Ahhh! Ouch-ouch!"

In his sleep, Kyle moved, and his neck cracked. The bones in his neck throbbed. He had slept on his left arm and with his weight removed from the arm, the blood rushing back into it stung like a thousand needles stabbing him all at once. He stopped moving. It hurt less when he didn't move. He had fallen asleep in an awkward position. When the waves of pain passed, he relaxed and expelled a breath.

The sky had darkened. The surrounding forest was shadowed. Creaks and cracks menaced. Falling asleep! What a stupid thing to do! Are they creeping up on him now? Was that what he was hearing? And who would it be? Rough men with guns or police officers with guns?

He stood, grimacing as he pushed himself up. His knee creaked. His muscles pulsed, protesting his movements. His own body odor overpowered the scent of the dirt and the leaves of the forest. Rubbing his knee and leaning back against the tree he had fallen asleep on; he studied the woods. He had to keep moving. He had to find somewhere else to be, somewhere safe and preferably inside before night's curtain fell. Pushing off from the tree and making sure he still had the gun, he continued forward. He didn't know any other way to go. He didn't know it, but Kyle was roughly two miles, as the crow flies, south east of Hank. Stumbling in pain and exhaustion, he closed the gap.

-45-

Hank said into the walkie, "Vern!"

No answer.

"Goddamnit Vern! Answer me!"

"Call Jack."

Hank said, "Jack? Where you at?"

No answer.

"Jack. Let's meet up and get out of here together. Where you at?"

Silence.

Hank said to Tommy, "What in the holy fuck is going on, man?"

Tommy said, "Let's get out of here."

Hank whirled on him and said, "And leave our friends? You fucking crazy or something?"

"They're not answering. And you heard Vern. Someone is getting us one by one. I say we fuck off and come back in the morning with more guys, more guns, more of everything. And then we rip this place apart."

"I'm not running. You? You can fuck off. But I'm not running. You don't know that they're dead. You can't know that."

"It's not running. It's dark, and it will only get darker. There is only you and me out here. I call it a tactical retreat."

"Nah. Fuck that. This has something to do with that house. Strange shit happens by that house. People disappear by that house. I say we go there, kick in the fucking door and get some answers. We might even find our friends."

"I'm with you. A hundred percent I'm with you. But not tonight. Tomorrow. With more men. With more guns. When we can see whoever the fuck is hunting us."

"Hunting us?"

"Yeah, man. Hunting. Someone is taking us when we're alone."

"Yeah. That's right. Taking us. So, they could still be alive."

"Sure."

"You don't sound like you believe that."

"Man. Look. If they're alive, then this person knocked them out, right? They're unconscious, right?"

"Yeah. Or really hurt."

"If they were really hurt, we'd still hear them. They'd be screaming or asking for help, so I'd say if they are alive, they've been knocked out."

"Ok."

"You and I both know how hard it is to knock someone out. It's not like the movies at all, and you know it. So, this person knocked out four of our guys? Four tough fuckers, like our guys? No. Not likely. They're dead."

"Dead, huh? I thought I was the cold one here. Listen to you."

"I'm not cold. I'm fucking scared man! I'm afraid to fart in case I shit myself I'm so scared. We need to get out of here. We are on this person's turf. This is their home. We're just trespassing tourists. And we're paying the price for that trespass."

Hank turned away from Tommy. He could see a faint light through the trees. Are those the lights of the house? Are his friends in there?

"I can't go. You go, Tommy. Get help. Bring it back tonight though. I'm going to watch the front of the house." Hank glanced at his watch. "I'll wait three hours for you. And then I'm going in."

"Jesus Hank. You're going to stay out here alone? Like Jesse, Vern, Jack, and Dave? That's fucking crazy, man. Let's compromise. Come with me. We'll get help together. We'll get more guns, more lights, hell, get Clay up here with his bulldozer and tear a road through the trees right to the front door of that house and then we'll light that place up!"

Hank's eyes returned to the house. He didn't say anything. He rubbed his chin and ran the same hand through his hair. Hank sighed and said, "All right. We'll go and come back. Bulldozer is a little stupid, but sure. A compromise."

"Yeah. Yeah. Okay. Let's go."

Tommy turned and getting his bearings using his phone's GPS, they headed off to the car. He lit a cigarette and then after one drag, flicked it into the dark.

Hank followed Tommy wondering if the reason he had agreed to leave was because it was the smart and strategic thing to do or if he was as scared as Tommy to be out here.

•   •   •

"How close are we?"

Tommy checked his phone. The glow lit his features, turning his face into a skull with shadows. It was very dark out here now.

"Not far. A couple hundred yards and we'll be out of the trees."

"Good."

Tommy's flashlight beam cut through the dark, casting as many shadows as it dispelled. Hank's beam lit up Tommy's back and every few feet, he turned the beam behind him. Walk-walk-walk, turn, walk-walk-walk, turn... the light revealed glowing eyes.

"Fuck!"

"What? What'd you see, Hank?"

Tommy crowded into Hank, his flashlight scanning their back trail.

"Eyes. I saw eyes."

"Like a squirrel?"

"A squirrel? You think I'd fucking scream over squirrel eyes? No, man. It's big. And tall."

"What is it?"

"I don't know! A bear?"

"There are fucking bears out here?"

"It's the woods, man! Of course, there are bears out here!"

"Not all woods have bears!"

"Shh! Listen!"

Silence. Their lights danced over trees, bushes, and leaves.

Hank said, "What am I listening for?"

"I don't know. It's like... silent. There's no noise."

"Ah man. I don't like this."

A stench of decay, dampness, and the metallic odor of blood wafted to them. Hank said, "Tommy. Let's get the fuck out of here."

"Yeah." Tommy checked his phone, raised his head and pointed his flashlight and said, "That way."

Something moved into the beam. It growled. Hank said, "What the fuck!"

Hank was lifted off his feet and flew up and over Tommy's head. Branches cracked (reminding Hank of the time he had broken his forearm falling off a motorcycle), and he hit the ground with a thud knocking the wind from him. White dots clouded his vision. Darkness followed.

●　　●　　●

Tommy ran. He gibbered. He stumbled over terrain. The flashlight jumped and darted in his hand. It flashed on a tree, a root, dirt, a branch, and stones on the path. Tommy didn't know if he was running the right way or not. He knew nothing except the terror-driven desire to escape these woods and to escape whatever had attacked Hank.

His breath grew ragged, and for the first time, Tommy thought maybe smoking as much as he did wasn't a great idea. Behind him rose the sound of heavy steps, deep breaths, and a rumbling growl.

"No, no," Tommy gasped.

A push from behind propelled him forward. His head struck a tree. His spine compressed, spots swirled in his vision, and before he lost consciousness, he thought he'd heard a low growl.

-46-

Kyle's stomach grumbled. He tripped on a root and fell to a knee. Tired. Any other time in his life that he thought he had been tired, he had been horribly mistaken. He hadn't known what tired meant until today.

He slapped at a bug on his neck. He felt the wetness of it against his palm. The woods were dark now, not that the daylight helped him much. He didn't know where he was going then, and he certainly doesn't know where he is going now. The moon was bright only in the breaks in between interwoven branches and leaves above. Shafts of silver light painted circles on the ground. He stood, eyeballing the next circle of moonlight.

Kyle rubbed his aching knee. He said, "One moon circle at a time."

He stumbled forward, hungry, tired, and reeking of sweat, blood, and an unwashed active body. His teeth were filmy in his mouth. His exhales were hot leaving his mouth. This has been, by far, the weirdest day of his life. He smiled. The boy's surprised face when Kyle had stabbed him removed the smile. Kyle said, "Don't think of that. You can't take it back, so don't think of that."

He stopped at the next circle of light. Holding up his hand, he watched the light turn his hand and forearm silver. Over the tops of his fingers, he saw another light through the trees. This light originated on Earth. This light was man made.

Kyle said, "What's that?"

A soft yellow light floating in the night, far away, but there. Was it real though? Kyle had been out here for a long time, running, and sleeping on the ground. He's exhausted and lightheaded. Wouldn't that effect how he saw the world? Was it possible his mind was conjuring images that aren't real? Not that it would matter. That light meant civilization, or at least the promise of near civilization. The alternative was to turn away from it and continue circling the woods until he collapsed to the ground without the energy to pull himself back up and he imagined the ground, the roots, nature itself growing over him and through his body, little green buds appearing on his arms, and tree roots pushing through his cheeks. Strange, but the image seemed peaceful. He shook his head.

He said, "No." He wasn't ready to quit. Not ready for that. Now, if he walked toward the light, and it was the headlights of a police cruiser, he'd be shit out of luck because he sure wasn't running anymore, but at least he wouldn't be dead (if they didn't shoot him on sight, of course). And he knew the police would feed him and give him a mattress to sleep on instead of on the dirt ground. That'd be good. Sleep and food. The dream combo.

If he made it to the light and it happened to be a figment of his imagination, he'd be no worse off than he was right at this moment. He'd still be clueless in the dark.

Kyle moved forward. Crickets rubbed their legs; trees exuded their piney scent and animals moved in the underbrush. The light grew brighter. What casted the light couldn't be discerned. Kyle dodged branches with his hands and divots, stones, and roots with his feet through his sense of touch. It was too dark right now to see anything but shapes and shadows.

"A house!"

Through the trees, Kyle saw the white sideboard, the light spilling from the windows and a glowing light above a red front door.

Houses had food. Houses had beds. Kyle trembled. His stomach twisted imagining the potential food available to him inside. Kyle walked faster, or thought he did, and his eyes dipped to the ground, to the branches in his way and back to the front door.

The red front door was closed. He shifted his eyes to the ground to navigate the terrain, then to a branch that had scratched his arm and then back to the house. The front door stood open. Kyle paused. He saw a shadow moving inside and the door closed. He hadn't seen who had closed it. Someone was home though. Kyle's hand patted the gun in the back of his pants. It didn't occur to him to not go to the house. In that house was food. In that house was a place to crash. In his mind, those things in there were his, and if the person inside didn't like it, well, too fucking bad. The kid's face flashed before him.

Kyle growled, "Not now." He removed the gun and held it in his hand. He swayed. Hungry. Tired. He'd solve those problems soon enough. Everything he needed was inside that house.

●   ●   ●

Kyle circled the home, focused on not being seen and avoiding standing up in front of windows. His concentration and his need for food caused him to miss certain details about the house he surveilled. He hadn't noticed there was no driveway. He hadn't noticed that this house did not have a garage.

Every light on the main floor shone. He peered into each window, moving slow. Kyle had heard somewhere, maybe in a movie, that fast movement drew the eye and he concentrated on moving with slow deliberation. He didn't see anyone inside the house. No one sitting in a chair, watching TV or moving about. When he made it all the way around, the front door was still closed. Someone had closed it, though. He hadn't seen anyone through the windows. Where are they?

Squatting and walking with the gun in his sweaty hand, Kyle approached the window next to the back door. He lifted his head until his left eye could see into the room. Saliva flooded his mouth. A stainless steel, double door fridge gleamed as though a spotlight was shining on it.

Kyle said, "Well, all right."

He reached for the doorknob and his fingers closed on it. He twisted it and it turned. Unlocked.

He opened the door. A chime sounded. He noticed it but didn't care. He stepped inside and closed the door behind him. He pivoted his gun back and forth, pointing it at each entryway into the kitchen. The entryways were tall and almost flush with the ceiling. One entryway lead into a hallway with rooms branching off it and the front door was at the end of the other hallway. Listening for running footsteps, something, anything to let him know someone knew they had a trespasser inside, he waited. Nothing.

The fridge beckoned.

-47-

Lindsay unlocked the doors of the house when she saw Samuel returning from the surrounding trees on the monitors in the surveillance room. He carried two men inside and put them on the floor in the front hallway. He left and returned with another two. One more trip brought in two more. Six men in the front hallway. Lindsay saw the men, rough and bleeding. Once inside, Lindsay and Samuel stood staring at the pile of men. She was holding the shotgun, but with Samuel standing there, she knew she didn't need it.

"Are they all alive?"

Samuel nodded. Samuel carried each man downstairs one at a time because of the narrow staircase.

Lindsay followed Samuel down as he carried the last unconscious man. After Samuel put down the last of his human baggage, Lindsay hugged him and said, "Are you ok?"

Samuel nodded.

"They didn't hurt you at all?"

Samuel shook his head.

A chime sounded from a speaker set into the wall. Lindsay and Samuel shifted their gazes to the ceiling.

Lindsay said, "Somebody else is here. It's getting to be a regular party around here."

-48-

Kyle leaned over at the waist, nose deep in the fridge with an ear-touching grin stretching his face as his eyes surveyed the food options under the bright, white light. He shifted the gun to his left hand. He removed salami, mustard, mayonnaise, and pickles and put them on the counter. He saw a cold beer inside the door of the fridge, moaned and said, "Sweet Jesus." He clasped the beer by the neck and closed the fridge door.

"What are you doing in here?"

"Ahh!" Kyle dropped the bottle of beer. It clunked against the floor. Kyle noticed it hadn't broken and filed the information away for later.

He turned and shifting the gun to his right hand, pointed it at the woman casually leaning against the frame of the entryway. Behind her, Kyle saw the front door. She was pointing a shotgun at him. She held it at her waist, confident, like she knew how to use it. A frown pinched her eyebrows together.

Kyle said, "The door was unlocked."

"A closed, unlocked door is not an invitation."

"I was hung-"

"You're Kyle, right?"

"How do you know my name?"

"You're all over the news. You're all over the farmers' CB radios and the police radios. You're somewhat of a famous killer around here."

He flinched when she said killer. Then his mouth tightened into a line and he straightened his shoulders. He raised his gun to eye level and said, "Yeah. I guess that's right. I am a killer. But right now, I'm hungry and I'm going to make a sandwich and I'm going to drink that beer."

"No."

"No? Look. I don't want to kill you. I don't. I didn't want to kill anyone. I've just been having one bad, fucked-up day that just doesn't seem to ever want to end. I just want to eat. I'm starving. I'm tired. Fuck it. Tell you what." He put his hands down and pointed the gun at the floor. He said, "Let me make a sandwich, take that beer to go and I'm out. Be less than a couple of minutes and I'm gone."

"Oh, I can't let you leave now."

A smell filled the kitchen. Damp, musty, reminding Kyle of Spencer, the dog he had as a kid when they let him inside from the rain. The distinctive and ever unpleasant wet animal smell. Heavy breathing behind him. He turned but before he could complete turning, he felt a sharp pain on the top of his head. He collapsed to the floor.

Kyle said, "Ahh," and tried to push himself up.

Lindsay said, "You're not the only killer around here."

-49-

At the time Kyle was being introduced to Samuel, the Chief was driving the back roads of farm country and then onto the farm roads used by the farmers to transport hay bales on slow moving vehicles. The roads more often than not lead the Chief to a locked gate barring continued driving. He'd make a three-point turn and travel down another unpromising road. So far, no sign of Kyle from anyone. Citizens and cops alike. Nothing. Zip. Nada. Zilch. The Chief tapped the steering wheel, peering out through the windshield with the SUV's high beams on. It'd be great to see the bastard dart across the road in front of his car. It'd be great to be the one to bring Kyle in.

What if he had gotten out of Leonard despite their best efforts? Had Kyle waved a car down, killed the driver and stuffed the poor soul in the trunk and is now driving to see his brother? The Chief ground his teeth, realized he was doing that, and relaxed his jaw. Grinding his teeth like that always gave him a headache. He had enough problems without adding that to the list.

Over the course of the evening the radio chatter died down. There was less light to see by and the officers, after a long day, were getting tired. His dayshift officers must be just as exhausted as he was. Even some of the OPP officers have been out here patrolling and guarding scenes for hours now. Everyone was getting rundown. And still no Kyle.

The Chief pulled over to the side of the road. He turned on his iPad and brought up Google Maps once again. Last he knew, Kyle had been going toward the Grayson house. Kind of. It was a small house in a large wilderness. It would be some kind of weird luck to stumble upon it. In the dark though, it'd be the only place with lights. That might draw someone in from the darkness provided they were close enough. Even considering that, finding the house in the darkness and the vastness of the woods didn't seem likely. Even though Kyle has been, so far, channeling the luck of a leprechaun or something, the odds of finding the house must have getting-struck-by-lightning kind of odds. But would it actually be lucky for Kyle to find the Grayson home? Maybe. Maybe not. There are some interesting stories about the Grayson's and none of them are of the cheery, sunshine and roses type of tales.

The Chief pinched the map screen with his fingers and zoomed in on the area around the Grayson home. Huh? There was a road nearby. It didn't get close to the house, but he could drive out there and maybe see what he could see. He wasn't doing much of anything else right now. But first, do the rounds, check on his employees and see if they need a break. They'd say no, but it'd be better if they all got some rest, so they'd be fresh for tomorrow. And who knows? One of them might take him up on his offer.

The Chief visited his officers. He brought coffee to some and guarded scenes long enough for them to get food or use the washroom for others. After his visiting, he drove out to the Grayson house. In the dark he missed the dirt road Hank and his men had used to park their vehicles. The road wasn't visible on the Google satellite image. The trees in the image were too dense. He drove past the road he didn't know existed tapping the steering wheel. He said to no one, "Where had Kyle gotten to?"

He hoped Hank hadn't caught up to him. He hoped one of his officers hadn't caught up to Kyle and dispensed street justice on him either. That wouldn't be good for anyone. Rubes' smiling face floated to the front of his mind's eye. Or would it? He shook it away.

The best result to this mess would be to catch Kyle alive. The second-best result would be for Kyle to get lost in the woods and die of exposure. That way, no one would be at fault.

He said, "Maybe that'd be for the best."

The night road swallowed his headlights.

-50-

Dad?"

"Hey darling. How goes it?"

"Samuel came back all right. He caught seven of them."

"Seven? All alive?"

"I think so. One of them might not be, and if he is alive, he won't be for much longer."

"You figure out what they were doing out there?"

"One of them is a killer the cops are looking for. Killed a few people and a cop out here in town."

"Really? Holy crap! What's going on out there?"

"I don't know. I think those guys around our house, I think they were waiting for this Kyle guy."

"That the killer?"

"Yeah."

"You see any cops poking around yet?"

"No."

"Huh. They will be. If those men were there waiting for Kyle, then the cops won't be too far behind, I don't think. Listen. Those guys waiting in the woods? They had to have driven out there. You'll have to get rid of their cars. Put 'em in the service tunnel garage. I'll chop them up when I get back."

"Okay."

"Did Samuel get hurt at all?"

"No. He's fine. Excited, but fine."

"Yeah. I bet he's excited. He hasn't had people in a long time. They might even keep him through the winter. He might not have to go out hunting for a while."

"Maybe. I mean, he seems really excited. I've never seen him like this before."

"Well, that's because no one has been foolish enough to come onto our land in a long, long time. And he hasn't played his game for a long time. The last time he did, huh, yeah, it would've been before you were born. I was a young boy, then."

"Whoa. That is a long time ago."

"Easy now. But you know what you're supposed to do, right?"

"Yeah."

"Are you ok? You sound, I don't know, off, I guess."

"Yeah. I think so. Everything I have to do is running through my head too fast. I have to slow it down. Once I get rid of the cars or whatever, I'll probably be able to relax. I'll have one less thing to worry about, at least. I don't need any more people out here snooping around. Especially the police."

"That's for sure. But those men? Are they all secure? Your mother and I will be home in four days, but like I said, we can come home earlier. Not a problem. You know what? Maybe we should anyway."

"No, no. Samuel's got them all in cages. And even if they weren't, they couldn't get up here to me. But anyway, they're not going anywhere. I have to say, though, I feel kind of bad for them."

"Yeah. I know. This can be hard, especially doing it all alone. But Samuel won't let them go. Not once they trespassed. That's the one rule we could never change with him. There is no talking him out of it. And Samuel's our family. Those men are not. Still, it is a good thing something like this doesn't happen too often. I doubt I could take it if it did."

"I know."

"Look. Don't worry about them. What will happen will happen. Just get rid of the cars and hang out upstairs, read a book or watch TV. Samuel will come get you when he is ready to start. Tell the men the rules and leave. Close the access door and just forget about them as best you can. You won't hear a thing."

"All right."

"Oh, and when you're explaining the penalty for trespassing, try not to look the men in the eye. That makes it harder. It's better if you look at your feet. And when you're done, leave them for Samuel and wipe them from your mind. Because after you're done your speech, you'll never see them again."

-51-

A muscle spasm woke Kyle. Metal bars pressed against the back of his thighs, buttocks and back. Bent over, his chin was tucked against his chest and between his bent knees. He twisted his head to get a view of his surroundings. In a cage suspended from the ceiling around him were four other men. Three were to the right of him, and one was to the left. Guns and knives sat in a pile on the hard-packed dirt floor out of their reach. The guns had been disassembled and rendered useless. In a smaller pile beside the weapons was jewelry; gold necklaces and silver rings. Walkie-talkies and cell phones, the batteries and parts scattered and shattered, made another pile. Lighters and sets of keys made the last group of items.

Caged lights swung from chains between them. They were in a cave of some sort, maybe underground. Lying in another cage of iron bars not suspended from the ceiling were two men. It was a large cage assembled on the ground, big enough, in Kyle's estimation, to hold all of the men here. Not comfortably, but more comfortable than sitting in these little cages, bent over and squished. How did someone even get them into these cages? Had to have been someone strong.

Kyle felt like Hansel sitting helpless in the cage as the witch stoked the oven. Even though there wasn't an oven or a witch in this room, something was going to be done to them. Something no one in here was going to like much at all.

Kyle turned his head to take in more of the room. His neck cracked and he winced, hissing in a breath. His back spasmed and stiffened up, cramping accompanied by painful scalpel cutting, lancing pains running down his spine. He had to get out of this cage before his body fell apart. This was way worse than being caught by the cops. The police didn't do this sort of shit. They fed you, put you in a cell with a mattress and checked on you from time to time. If you were cold and asked nice enough, they might even give you a blanket and pillow. This medieval-hanging-suspended-from-cages-shit wasn't in their playbook. Kyle knew that whatever was about to happen to them all was not going to be pleasant.

Where in the actual hell was he? The walls of the room surfaces made him think they had been hacked at and chipped at with rough tools. They were unsmooth, with pockmarks, and divots. The dirt ground smelled rich, and for some reason, an image of worms squirming on the sidewalk after a prolonged rain came to him. A hard shiver ran through his body. His teeth clacked together. To the left of him, a man said, "I know you."

Kyle turned to the man. The man pressed his face tight against the bars. Blood covered the right side of his head and coated the right shoulder of his shirt. Kyle opened his mouth to reply, and he had to swallow a few times to moisten his dry tongue.

He said, "Oh yeah? Well, I don't know you, buddy."

"You killed my daughter."

Kyle had killed two women over the past, what was it now? A day? Two days? Didn't matter. What matters was that he didn't know which one had been this man's daughter. Probably not the cop, but what did he know? He decided not to reply. The chain groaned as he shifted in the cage. He spun away from the man.

"Aren't you going to say anything?"

"Would it help if I did?"

Another man said, "Hank? I think Tommy is dead."

"You sure?"

Vern said, "No. I'm not sure. His head doesn't look right, though. And I can't see his chest rising, but no, I'm not sure."

"Hey Jack? You closest to Tommy?"

"Yeah."

"Well? Is he dead or what?"

"I don't know. I can't see out of my one eye. There's like a white spot, I uh, I don't feel too goo-" Jack puked. It splashed on the floor. The acid stench made Kyle's nose twitch.

Hank said, "Shit."

Chains creaked. Kyle watched Hank trying to turn his cage so he could see the two men lying in the larger cage on the floor. Hank said, "Tommy!" No answer. He said, "Dave!"

Neither man moved. One man's arm was red and swollen. The shape of it resembled a sock filled with Jell-O. Who could take out seven men like this?

Hank said, "Did anyone see who took us out?"

A door creaked and then slammed. All conscious eyes turned to the sound. All the awake men held their breath. Silence stretched.

Kyle said, "I don't like this."

Hank said, "Shut your fucking face, asshole."

-52-

Lindsay smelled him before she heard him. Sitting in the kitchen with a warm cup of coffee in her hand and a frown on her face, Samuel's distinct smell preceded the sound of his feet on the floor.

"Okay. Let me finish my coffee. I'll be right down."

His hand touched her shoulder. She gave it a squeeze and let go. He turned away. His footsteps receded.

Lindsay sipped her coffee, but it was no good now. It tasted like dirt. She grimaced. She stood and poured the rest of the coffee down the sink. She rinsed the cup and put it in the dishwasher. Her heart pounded. Sweat beaded her brow. Her dry throat made it hard to swallow.

Seven of them. Against Samuel. They didn't stand a chance.

•   •   •

Her dad told her to keep her eyes down and she reinforced his advice in her mind on the way down the stairs, humming it under her breath the same way she used to when studying a tricky concept for an exam. She wanted to keep his advice at the front of her mind and make it impossible to ignore. Looking at the men would make them real.

At the bottom of the steps, she opened the steel door and stepped through, muttering, "Eyes on my feet, isn't that neat? Eyes on my feet, can't be beat," down a long hall of carved stone and wooden reinforcement beams. She stopped at another steel door. Her hand hovered over the handle. Once she stepped through, she'd be committed. She'd have to deliver the rules and leave the men to their fate. She hated this situation. But she had no other choice. Samuel is her family. He needed her to do this.

Lindsay inhaled, gripped the handle and turned. She stepped through. Five sets of eyes burned into her.

"Hey! Get us out of here-"

"Help us lady-"

"What are we doing here?"

"I think one of our friends is hurt bad. Maybe even dead-"

Then one voice, hard inflection said, "She's not going to help us."

"I told you to shut your fucking face!"

"Oh yeah? Or what? What are you going to do, huh?"

Lindsay studied the toes of her shoes. She saw the separate piles of property. Her eyes stopped on the pile of keys. She stepped to the pile, picked up the different key rings, and stuffed them in her pocket. It will be a hell of a lot easier to move the vehicles with the keys.

A voice said, "What are you doing, huh? Those are our keys."

It took all of her will to not look at the man who asked. She stared at the toes of her shoes.

"I told you she isn't here to help. She's going to hide your cars or drive them far away. That's why she took the keys."

"What are you talking about, idiot?"

"We're locked in cages that were here long before we showed up. You know what that means? That means this situation isn't new to her. This has been done before. And having a room to put people into cages is never a good thing. My guess is no one is getting out of here. Not alive."

The men quieted. Chains creaked and clinked as the cages shifted with their weight. She had their attention, that's for sure. She shouldn't have looked at them. All of them in their cages, trapped, expecting her to help them and only one of them knowing she wouldn't. She knew what she had to say only with all those eyes on her; she didn't know if she could. Just start. It won't be over with unless you start. Then you can go back upstairs, concentrate on moving the cars, and getting those pleading eyes out of your head. She inhaled.

She said, "Some of you may know my family. You know there is a history of people disappearing around here. Uninvited people coming onto our land. Sometimes they come to do us harm. Sometimes they come to take something from us. And sometimes a person, or people, stumble onto our land by accident. I don't know what category you fall into-"

"I don't know who the fuck your family is, and I don't care."

Hank said, "You should fucking care. She's right. This place has history. And even though I never thought much of that history, I still respected it enough not to come around here. Until you murdered my girl."

Lindsay raised her eyes. She couldn't stop herself. She said, "You're Hank."

"Yes."

"I heard about your daughter."

"Did you know this rat-fuck cut her-" voiced thickened, "head off?"

"Yes. I heard it on the police scanners."

"Then you know why I'm here. I never meant to disrespect your family. And none of my friends would be here if it wasn't for me. None of this is their fault. What could I give you to make it worth letting us go?"

Lindsay dropped her eyes. She said, "I can't help you. You're Samuel's now."

The door behind Lindsay opened. Heavy walking steps approached and stopped behind her. A shadow fell on her shoulders.

Hank said, "What the fuck? What? Wha?"

A man beside Hank started crying.

• • •

When the woman from the kitchen walked into their room of cages, Kyle's stomach sank into his toes. The other men all competed with each other begging for her to let them out, let them go, like that was going to happen. She was not help. She was the last person Kyle saw before waking up in this cage. It wasn't like she would let him or anyone out now. No. Something was planned for them. And it wouldn't be a nice dinner and a movie. After he told everyone she wouldn't be helping them, he tuned her out. The burning in his cramping back and the spasms in his neck demanded his attention more. His head was throbbing from being hit earlier and little glass shards of grinding pain flared in his knee. Besides, it made little sense for him to care about what she had to say. Stuck in the cage the way they all were, she could do whatever she wanted to them and there wasn't a damn thing any of them could do about it. She could jam a hot poker up his ass and the most he could do would be to ask her to stop. A lot of help that would do.

Hank mentioning Kyle had cut off his daughter's head brought his attention back to the people in the room. Grace. She had been Hank's daughter. He didn't remember cutting her head off, but he didn't think that small detail wouldn't help him any with the woman or with Hank. It interested him because this horrible day had started with Grace and it would end here with her dad. Fuckin' Karma. Maybe there was something to that mystical junk. The only problem with Karma was that Kyle could not believe the universe gave a shit how nice he was to children, old people or whoever. And besides, some people are assholes twenty-four hours a day, seven days a week until the day they died, and Karma never caught up to them. People like that? They were the bad thing that happened to others. Kyle couldn't be one of those guys. He was hanging in a cage, awaiting something. No. Kyle was of the opinion that shit just happened. You are either who it happened to or you are the person who made it happen to others. Until now, Kyle had been the person who happened to others. Kyle thought Hank could probably be described as the same. Now they are both going to pay. Not because of Karma though but because, sometimes shit just happens.

Kyle heard Hank ask what he could give to the woman to get out of this mess, but it was elevator music to him. Kyle closed his eyes, trying to shut out the burning pain in his body from being stuffed into this tiny, swinging cage. Hank yelled. Kyle opened his eyes. One of the men started crying. Seeing what stood behind the woman, Kyle understood why.

●   ●   ●

Slouching, its head still brushed the high ceiling. Towering over the woman, Kyle estimated it at eight feet, maybe even nine feet tall. Amber reflective eyes in a fur-covered face studied them. A monstrous hand ending in claws rested on the woman's shoulder. She patted the hand the way you would the hand of someone familiar to you, someone you knew and cared about. A dark coat stretched across its shoulders exaggerating, rather than diminishing, the apparent strength of the creature. And that's what it was. A creature. Something from before time. An animal from an era when forests covered the earth and everything had claws, teeth, and hunted for flesh, blood, and viscera. A nightmare stepping out of the dream world and into the real. It was a werewolf, a Sasquatch, or the missing link in human evolution, the potential source of nightmare stories and folklore over the millennia. It wore a coat, and Kyle now saw, dark jeans, ripped and shredded at the knees. A monster effecting the civility of man but failing miserably. Its chest rose and fell, stretching the coat. A rumble echoed in its chest. The woman looked up at the thing and extended an open hand. The creature dipped its chin into her palm and the woman scratched the furry chin. The creature closed its eyes and the rumble in its chest rose an octave.

It opened its eyes and issued a clipped bark. The woman said, "Yes. I know. I'm getting to it."

She dropped her hand to her side. She lowered her chin to her chest.

"This is Grayson land. Samuel is a Grayson, and he protects us, and he protects our land. He has caught you trespassing. It is now his duty, his right, to mete out the penalty."

Jack must have noticed the jewelry on the floor because he said, more to himself than to anyone else, "Is that my chain on the floor?"

The woman said, "Samuel likes shiny things."

"But, it's mine."

Kyle said, "Jesus Christ on a crutch, man! No one gives a fuck about your chain."

Hank said, "Jack. Be quiet. We need to hear this."

She hugged her elbows into her stomach. She took a deep breath and exhaled.

She said, "I will soon open the cages. It will be up to you to get yourself out of here. Samuel will hunt you. There are many tunnels, and many exits down here. But there is only one tunnel that leads to an exit you can use. You make it out of here and off our land, you're free. We do not allow Samuel to hunt people off our property and so far, he has listened to us."

Hank said, "What the fuck are you talking about? That thing? Hunting us? For sitting in the woods outside your house?"

The woman held up a hand and said, "I'm not finished!"

"Yeah, you are! This is fucking crazy! You are one crazy bitch, you know that? Tell you what, you let me out of this cage, I'll fucking gut you! I'll wear your guts for garters and then-"

The creature growled and stepped in front of the woman.

Kyle said, "If you don't shut up, that thing will go after you first." Hank glared at Kyle. He said nothing else. Kyle wondered why he had warned him. Other than the creature, Hank was the most dangerous to him. Maybe because they were both human and that thing in the black coat and ripped jeans was not. It wore the clothes of a man, but a man it was not.

The woman said, "The cages will open at the same time." She held up a black device she had taken from her back pocket. "This will open them remotely when I've left this room. Samuel will be here, waiting. When they open, I'd move quickly if I were you."

She patted the thing on the back. Samuel chuffed his approval. The woman turned to leave.

Kyle feared her absence from this room. After she left, they would be alone with the creature. The doors on their cages would open, and it would choose who to pull apart first. Kyle's cramped muscles would need time for the blood to return to them before he'd be able to move, never mind trying to get away. Until that time, he'd be at the thing's mercy. She needed to stay, and he could tell she didn't feel comfortable doing this, leaving them to this fate. The way she wouldn't look at them and how she hugged her arms to her chest told Kyle that much. He didn't know what to say, but he had to keep her here. Even a second longer is better than nothing. Kyle said, "Hey! What are our chances here? Has anyone made it out before? Has anyone else survived?" Stupid question. Why did he ask that? He already knew he wouldn't like the answer.

She stopped. She didn't turn around to look at them. She said, "No. No one has ever made it out alive."

Stunned by the blunt delivery of her words but not their content, Kyle's words left him. She turned a corner and was gone. A door slammed. A lock clicked. Seconds later, with an audible snap, the cage doors swung open on creaking hinges.

-53-

Inspector Greaves called the Chief again closer to one in the morning.

"Hey Inspector. How's your night going?"

"I'm calling you to ask the same thing."

"Ah, you know. Tired." He stopped himself from saying 'I'm scared instead of finding Kyle we'll find more bodies in the morning,' and 'I'm sad I'll never see my friend Rubes smile again and that a young boy will never see another birthday.' He had to stop himself from saying those words even though they bubbled at the back of his throat. If he started talking like that though, he'd soon be a blubbering mess. Thinking about it paused his breath and prickled his eyes.

"Look. Let's do a switch up. I'll keep my guys out here patrolling for the rest of the night and you send your people home, let them get some rest and if Kyle hasn't been found before lunch or so, bring them back out. My crime scene guys have processed all the scenes except for Ruby's. They want to return to the scene in the morning with the daylight. So, for the most part, we'll just be patrolling and answering the odd Kyle sighting call. We can handle that."

The Chief liked that idea. He liked it a lot even though he felt guilty for liking it. And then he pictured crawling into bed with Natalie, smelling her smell and hearing her breath and he craved the contact. He could use that right about now.

"You know what, Inspector? I like that idea. I think I'm going to take you up on the offer. I don't know how to thank you for all your help. You've all been great."

"Nothing to thank me for. Really. We're all cops and Kyle needs to be caught."

"All the same, thanks. I'll round up my people, send them home and I'll have dispatch contact you directly for any calls?"

"No. I have a field supervisor out there for that. But I'll call your dispatch and arrange all that. You get you and your people home."

"Will do. Really though, thanks."

-54-

After the woman left and before the cages opened, the thing, what she called Samuel, paced back and forth in front of them, his eyes passing over each one, probably deciding what food he'd choose first. When the cages did open, it paused its pacing and stood watching them, hands opening and closing at its side.

If Kyle hadn't been so terrified and worried it would pick him first, he might have smiled at the scene. Five men who had been crammed inside the too small cages, for who knows how long were now free. Watching these men trying to work their cramped and battered bodies out of these cages was like waiting for molasses to pour from a carton. Grunting, groaning and grumping, what Kyle's brother would call the three 'Gs' of a whiner.

Drool spilling from Samuel's mouth trailed shiny liquid down his hairy chest. His shoulders rose and fell. Kyle could feel the hunger in those amber eyes. A keening noise rose unbidden through Kyle's own lips. Panic was rising. He knew it but was powerless against it. Have to get out! Get out!

Kyle pushed both feet through the cage opening. His sore knee cracked, and he pulled back the curse sitting on his tongue. He forced himself to cease the keening noise. He didn't want to attract the thing's attention so the less noise he made the better. He slid his hips forward, and using his hands, he pushed against the cage. One of his feet touched the ground. His back spasmed. A sharp pain ran from the base of his spine to the back of his skull. He froze, afraid to move, waiting for the waves of pain to fade.

Kyle heard something hard hit the dirt. He rolled his eyes toward the sound. A man was out. Dust from his impact slowly settled. He rolled on his side to an elbow. Samuel grabbed the man by the foot and lifted him into the air.

"Hank! Help me, Hank!"

"Jack! I'm coming, man!"

Hank was having a hell of a time trying to get out of the cage. Not surprising considering the size of him. He managed to get one foot out, but Kyle could see the other leg bent back behind him. He was in a tight spot. Hank wasn't getting out soon.

"Hank!"

The thing held Jack by the foot, so the bottom of his boot touched the rough ceiling. Samuel leaned his head forward, and from his posture, it looked to Kyle like he was smelling the man the way a person does a plate of steaming food before digging in.

Samuel dropped Jack to the dirt. Jack's hands were hanging above his head, closer to the floor and when he fell, some of the strength of the impact was deflected. The way Jack's mouth opened in an 'O' with no sound issuing, Kyle could tell the wind had been knocked from him.

Samuel put a heavy foot on the man's chest. Jack's hands grabbed at it, trying to press the foot off him. Samuel reached down with a clawed hand. He fingered the man's stomach. Drool plopped onto Samuel's hairy foot. The claws pressed into Jack, digging. Blood filled the hole.

"Jack!"

The other men were in various positions of escape from their cages. They all started yelling. They all started screaming at what they were witnessing and unable to prevent. Kyle, monitoring Samuel, gritted his teeth and slid from his cage. He could give a fuck about Jack and if he had to admit it, happy the creature had focused on Jack instead of him. What he knew for sure was that being eaten alive was at the top of his 'how not to die' list.

Samuel pulled out a red balloon of gore from Jack's opened stomach. Intestines slid through his fingers and he grasped at the slippery entrails with both hands. Samuel leaned down. He opened his mouth and slid the bloody spaghetti-like pile into his maw. He crunched down. Blood poured from the sides of his mouth. Jack's eyes bulged. His bloated face couldn't issue a scream. Samuel's heavy foot had him pinned to the ground.

"Jack!"

"What the fuck!"

Men fell to the dirt floor, yelling, struggling to stand, and moving toward Samuel and their doomed friend.

Kyle crawled away, staying low to the ground, doing everything he could to leave unnoticed. Crawling around a corner with the screams echoing behind him; he stood. He couldn't stand straight. His lower back had stiffened in the cage. Placing his hand on the wall and bending over, he shuffled away from Samuel and the screaming men.

-55-

Hank did not understand what the word helpless had meant in relation to himself. When other people used it, he'd crease his forehead, and wonder about such an idea. No one was ever helpless. If you happened to be in a helpless position, it was because you put yourself there and if you planned properly and took the necessary precautions, you'd never be in a helpless position. To Hank, helpless was just another word for carelessness or, more bluntly, idiocy. But now he had a firm understanding of the word. Trying to squeeze out of this cage while his friend was being eaten alive in front of him by a monster, (cause that's what it was, a monster,) he now understood what helpless truly meant.

There was no way he could have prepared for this. The only careless action he had undertaken was to wait for Kyle on the Grayson land. He knew there were rumors about the Grayson's. People disappearing and even hidden riches (which sounded to Hank as likely as finding buried pirate treasure in your backyard). Only the difference between a rumor and fact tended to be, in his experience, vast. Most times, facts didn't even resemble the rumor. All he had planned to do was wait for Kyle and hope he'd show up. He hadn't planned on doing anything else. So, was it even a careless action? He couldn't have planned around this thing. Because that thing shouldn't exist. It'd be like planning a job around vampires. Stupid thoughts to circulate in a moment such as this but they were there. It was like there were two Hanks. The Hank about to piss himself in a cage, terrified, almost gibbering, wanting to save his friend, but also wanting to abandon that same friend and save himself and the other Hank seeming to hover above it all, calmly contemplating the true meaning of helplessness and the veracity of local rumors.

Hank noticed Jesse slipping out of his cage and getting to his feet with his trembling knees almost knocking together.

"Jesse! Help me get out of here, man!"

An open sewer smell filled their cavern. From hunting, Hank knew the smell happened when the intestines were perforated by a careless gutting knife.

Hank glanced at Jack. His hands flailed weakly at the large foot on his chest. Spatters of blood dotted his face. Hank turned away from the scene. Kyle's cage was empty. There was no sign of him. He sneered.

Hank said, "Fucking Kyle."

Jesse fell against Hank's cage and recaptured his balance by clinging to the bars. Vern escaped his cage and was staring at Samuel eating his friend, wide-eyed and mouth agape.

Hank's right leg was cranked back and put a painful strain on his knee.

Jesse said, "Hank, you gotta lean back and get your foot out in front of you!"

"I know, man! Don't you think I know that? The toe of my boot is caught in the bars. I need you to push it out!"

"Okay. Yeah. I see that."

Over Jesse's shoulder, Samuel was hollowing out Jack. There was no saving him now. And what would that thing do when it finished with Jack? It would turn its amber, remorseless eyes on them. They would be next.

Hank said, "Hurry, man!"

"Yeah, yeah! I know!"

Jesse pushed on Hank's foot from the bottom of the cage. His foot popped free and leaning his torso back, he rotated his foot to the front. It hurt. A lot. The strained, static position had stretched his muscles and tendons from the hip to his ankle. Now free, they complained at the rough treatment. With clenched teeth and sweat pouring from every pore, Hank slid out of the cage and onto the ground.

Vern sat on the ground, in the same position as before and watching the carnage while still as a statue.

"Vern!"

No response. Only the sounds of chewing and empty cages swinging on creaking chains.

"Vern! You fuck!"

Vern's head spun to Hank. He blinked, closed his mouth, and opened it again.

"Hank! It's eating Jack!"

"Yeah! I know! Now let's go before it starts in on us!"

Mesmerized, the brutality acted as a magnet on Vern's eyes. Samuel reached down, took a hold of Jack's forearm, and with a tear and a pop, pulled his arm off at the shoulder.

Hank said, "Jesus!"

Vern threw up on his own lap.

Jesse covered his mouth with the back of his hand.

Jack's eyes rolled back, and the rest of his body not being pinned by the monster started bucking and twitching.

Samuel slid the sleeve of Jack's shirt off the arm and staring at the men, he opened his powerful jaws and ripped a strip of meat off the arm as though it were a drumstick.

Hank said, "We gotta go, gotta go now, can't stay, have to go!"

He was leaning on Jesse for support while his leg recovered. He stepped away and his right leg collapsed under him. He fell to the ground.

"Jesse! Help!"

With Jesse's help, Hank stood. He yelled, "Vern! Let's go, man!"

Vern scrambled to his feet, and with some effort, caught up to Jesse and Hank.

Passing the open cage with the unconscious Dave and Tommy inside, Jesse said, "What about them?"

Hank, gritting his teeth, said, "They're on their own."

-56-

Kyle shuffled away from the screams and the yells. The more corners he turned and the further he ran drastically decreased the noise. Soon enough, all he could hear is his own labored breathing and his feet scuffing the ground.

Kyle said, "Shit!"

He stopped and looked back. On the ground he saw his footprints. If that thing wanted him, it just had to follow these size ten patterned breadcrumbs he was leaving behind. Hank could do the same if he was still alive. What could Kyle do about it right now? Nothing. Not a damn thing. He decided to keep going and maybe something would occur to him.

The ceiling lights in the tunnel were spaced farther apart than they had been in the cage room and because of that, there were more shadows and more dark spots. The lights above were still too high for him to reach with his hand and he didn't have anything to break the lights and hide his tracks using the dark. The tunnels must have been carved out to accommodate Samuel's large frame. Thinking of the lights and Samuel, what Kyle really wanted was a weapon. The best idea was to keep moving forward and hopefully, he'd find something useful. How long had that mantra been going round and round in his head for now? Keep moving forward? He felt as though he had been running forever, but it must have been, what? Not even a full day yet? Or was it morning now? Samuel had knocked him out, so he had no idea how long he'd been unconscious in that cage. Didn't matter. Getting out of here and not getting eaten? That's what mattered. That was priority numero uno.

His knee ached, his back ached, his neck ached, and he was still starving, and every step was a struggle. Man. Nothing ever worked out for him, did it? Thinking about his footprints, he realized breaking the lights would be just as bad. If Hank and his crew wanted to know where Kyle had run to all they had to do was enter the darkness and follow the sounds of broken glass underfoot.

Yeah, but would they want to? With that thing running around down here? It knew the tunnels. This was its home. Those reflective amber eyes, like a wolf's, could it see in the dark? And what if Kyle reached a dead-end and had to backtrack? He'd have to go through those dark parts himself. His stomach clenched at the thought. Not since he had been a kid did he believe the dark held monsters with claws and teeth.

Find a weapon first. Then revisit that breaking glass-hide-the-tracks strategy. Who knows? He might even make it out of here on his first try. Might not even have to backtrack at all. Maybe being positive like all those hippy doctors at the jail suggested was the way to be. He wanted to laugh, but a cry escaped him instead.

-57-

Tommy's head burned. His skull, the actual bone casing protecting his brain shifted as though not a complete, singular unit anymore. He hissed an inhale through teeth clamped tight as a sprung bear-trap. Every part of him ached, throbbed, or complained in some way. His armpit hairs hurt. Was that a thing? Was that something that could hurt? He blinked. The bright light lasered his brain. He shut his eyes, holding his breath, waiting for the pain to let him go. Sweat dotted his body. His fingers clenched the dirt at his sides.

What had happened? Above him, he saw a rough ceiling and a bulb on a chain. Where was he?

Something big had chased him, gaining, breathing heavy, footsteps drumming the ground, and then his head met a tree. Where was Hank?

Tommy blinked. The light became more tolerable with every blink. He worked his eyes open. He didn't move his head. Not yet. It didn't feel ready. The bones were too loose and he worried his brain might slide out between the cracks. He didn't really think that could happen. It was more like he felt it might happen and he visualized it happening, which was more than enough to keep him still. He saw metal bars everywhere his eyes roamed. What is this?

A passing shadow flowed over his eyes. It scared him, he twitched and that hurt. Heavy steps vibrated the ground. Tommy turned his head. His neck bones grated, and he closed his eyes, waiting for the new pain to stop. When it did, he opened his eyes. A monster stared at him.

"Ahhh! Jesus!"

The creature squatted and placed its palms flat on the ground in between its legs. It moved closer to Tommy.

Tommy pushed against the ground with his hands to scoot away and knew his brain was telling his heels to dig in and do the same, but his feet ignored his commands. And as the creature closed the gap in silence with the heavy coat it wore scratching the ground the only sound, Tommy understood the reason his feet were not obeying his commands. It wasn't just his feet either. Below his waist, his navel to be exact, an absence of feeling made itself known. He couldn't feel anything. A void, an absence, a big fat nothing below his waist. Paralyzed. His lower body wasn't listening to him because it couldn't.

"No. No, please. Stay away."

The thing leaned over Tommy. Its amber eyes studied him. It sniffed Tommy. A large tongue darted out from between sharp teeth.

"No. No." Tommy turned his head and closed his eyes.

The thing's breath wafted over Tommy. Blood. The smell of a platter of meat bleeding beside a BBQ before it was cooked. Tommy shivered.

"Go away. Please go away. I don't see you. You're not here. I won't tell. I promise I won't tell anyone."

Clawed hands slid under Tommy's back, cutting him open. The creature's other hand slid under the back of his knees. It lifted Tommy from the ground. He screamed. The pain was enormous. It was the Titanic. It was Mount Everest. Vertebrae ground, skull bones gaped and closed, electrifying his body with pain. He stopped screaming only to vomit. The chunks stuck in his mouth, his throat, choking him, and on top of the panic of not being able to breath, there was the pain!

The creature twisted Tommy and put him over its shoulder like Santa with a sack. The puke spilled from his mouth. White motes danced in his eyes. The ground bounced. He caught sight of Dave unconscious (or dead, he couldn't tell) on the ground in the cage they were leaving. Next, bouncing past something else on the ground. Something bloody and… meaty. Tommy had the impression of a man only he couldn't think, couldn't concentrate. Movement was pain. Each bouncing step brought fresh agony.

The creature turned corner after corner, walked down tunnel after tunnel, all looking the same to Tommy with the rough stone walls, spaced beams of older timber, and lightbulbs on chains, the passing scenery a nonsensical blurring of images to Tommy's jouncing frame. A pause, squeaking hinges and they entered a different room. A room with shiny metal walls and a hard linoleum floor. A cold room. Tommy's breath made visible in his exhales. Hunks of meat hung on hooks. Moose. Deer. A bear's head on a metal shelf. Tommy didn't see any more details and he didn't try to. The blood pounded through his tender skull until his eyes filled with pressure, such pressure he imagined his eyes popping from his skull like a cork from a champagne bottle. The image kept him from using his fragile neck to lift his tender head.

The creature stopped and the world spun as it flung Tommy to the floor. The bones in his skull shifted. His neck grated. His ribs pressed against his internal organs. He screamed and screamed and screamed. He didn't hear the creature close the door, locking him in the darkness of the freezer. He was screaming too loud.

●   ●   ●

The door opened. Tommy squinted. The creature's tall frame blocked the light. Every beat of his heart brought blood to his injuries and fresh agony. He was shaking in the cold room and was trying not to. The micro-movements were too painful. He became insensate with the pain. He said, "Help me, hey? I need help, a hospital, right? My legs. I can't feel them."

The creature walked into the room carrying something, or someone else.

"Dave? That you?"

The creature stopped before a hook and slid the man off its shoulder. It held the man in front of it off the ground by the armpits with no visible effort. It tilted its head. It leaned in and sniffed the man. The dim light from the open door did not illuminate enough of him for Tommy to see the man's face. The clothes and the body shape made Tommy think the man being held by the thing was Dave but he couldn't be sure. The creature chuffed. It raised the man and lowered him onto the hook.

The man stiffened. His legs snapped straight and shook. His fingers splayed. The thing let go of the man. The hook turned and Tommy saw Dave's eyes, wide as dinner plates and a cavernous mouth opening and closing like a fish out of water and drowning on the shore. And just like a fish, Dave wasn't making a sound.

Tommy twisted onto his stomach. His legs didn't turn over with him and pain shot up his spine.

"Ahhh!"

Tommy returned to his former position, his chest rising and falling, tears streaming from his eyes.

"Dave!"

Dave's eyes found Tommy. His mouth opened and closed.

The thing turned from them, left the room and closed the door leaving them both in darkness. Tommy's breathing and the twisting hook the only sound.

-58-

Hank, Vern, and Jesse fast-walked away from Samuel down long tunnels with more long tunnels branching off those long tunnels. How big was this place? It must have taken them forever to build it.

Jesse said, "Where are we going?"

"Does it look like I fucking know?"

They had no phones, no weapon, and no walkie-talkies. They had their legs and their fists. Against that thing? Hank wanted to laugh. His eyes welled and his lower lip trembled instead.

Vern said, "It don't feel right. Leaving Tommy and Dave like that."

Hank said, "I know."

They walked forward with Hank ignoring the branching off tunnels. He didn't know if that was the right decision. They could have walked right past the one tunnel that would take them out of here and he wouldn't have known it. He had nothing but his wits and right now, that seemed about as useful as a paper umbrella in a rainstorm. A weapon would be more useful. Or running into Kyle. That would be beyond good. Kyle couldn't be the one to escape from here. Not after all this. That'd be all sorts of wrong.

Vern said, "How many tunnels are down here, do you think?"

Hank said, "I have no idea."

"Would have taken a lot of work. A lot of years to clear this place out. Do you think just the Grayson's did this? Over the years?"

"I don't know."

"What'd they do with all the dirt they took out of here?"

"Your guess is as good as mine."

"You think they were moonshiners? Back in prohibition days?"

Jesse said, "Canada never had prohibition. That was a U.S thing."

Vern said, "How you know that?"

Jesse said, "History class. Tell you what though, the Canadians made a hell of a lot of money selling booze to the mob. But it was all legal. It was only illegal, on the States side, to smuggle it across."

Vern said, "A mine then? Did this use to be a mine of some sort?"

Jesse said, "I don't think so. There are no rails to move anything. No shafts leading down or up. I could be wrong, but it looks like a den. A big one, but, yeah. Then again, what the hell do I know."

Their boots scuffed the hard packed dirt. Their breathing was controlled but labored from managing the pain of their injuries. Hank thought they were quite the sorry bunch. Not the tough drug dealing bikers they were known to be. They were licked and they knew it. Running from a fight and leaving their friends behind was something Hank thought he'd never do.

Hank had been terrified. A feeling he didn't know he was susceptible to. That thing, the Grayson family pet, Samuel showed him how wrong he had been. Samuel had made him feel not only terror, but powerlessness, a truly alien concept to Hank.

Samuel was like a lightning strike, a tsunami, a hurricane. A force of nature that reminded you how laughable your idea of control really was. There was no controlling lightning. It either struck you or it didn't and that had nothing to do with you. Nature was indifferent to you. And if it swatted you, it wasn't personal. Nature didn't know you existed. It didn't care about you, your family, your dreams or your aspirations. It stomped on your chest and ripped out your intestines. It tore off your arm and stripped flesh and muscle from your bone with razor teeth. And there wasn't a thing you could do to stop it. The only thing you could do, what actually was in your control, was the decision to run, or not to run. So, he ran and left his friends behind. He ran on jellied legs and panic electric under his skin with only a stumble away from his rational brain devolving into a gibbering shell that once thought it had been human and the absolute lord of the natural world. Compared to Samuel, they were weak. They are civilized, hairless monkeys and once Samuel started to hunt them (if he already wasn't), they had no chance. All they are doing down here in this cave system, Samuel's home, was delaying the inevitable.

Hank rubbed his eyes and sniffled. What was wrong with him? He wasn't a quitter.

Jesse glanced at Hank, and then caught the eye of Vern. Hank sensed their exchange and he coughed and straightened. He turned his head away from his friends to avoid their scrutiny. Down another hallway, tunnel, whatever they were, stood a door. An actual goddamn door!

Hank said, "We're not beaten yet, boys."

-59-

Lindsay's arms trembled. She watched her distorted reflection in the water of the toilet bowl waiting for her stomach to stop performing backflips. Not real backflips. She knew her stomach couldn't do that since it didn't have a back, but it sure felt like that. All of those men looking at her for help, for her to release them from the hanging cages and not realizing (at first) that she was their jailer and also their executioner by extension.

If there had only been one of them, then maybe she wouldn't be sweating and trembling with her face hanging over a toilet bowl waiting for her stomach to give up the goods.

"Ack!" A dry heave only. Saliva flooded her mouth and she spat it into the water. Her saliva had an acidic taste to it. She grimaced.

"Come on, Lindsay. You can't stay here like this all night; you have to hide the cars. Stop thinking about them. They're already dead."

●   ●   ●

Lindsay stepped outside the house and the summer night air chilled her sweaty skin. She went up to her room and put on a sweater. She stepped outside again and locked the door behind her. She didn't want any more surprise people popping by.

She had a good idea of where the men would have parked their cars. There weren't too many places around here to do so. Normally she would have taken the tunnel they use to bring in groceries, new furniture, or anything else they needed for the house, but those men were down there with Samuel.

"Don't think of them."

She tried. She focused her attention on the beam of her flashlight turning the black parts of the night into day. A black claw becomes a branch. A dark blob becomes a grey, rounded stone. A beam of sunlight in her hand. There wasn't enough out here to distract her from those men with their pleading eyes staring at her from swinging metal cages. And she left them for Samuel.

"Stop thinking of them, damnit!"

Her eyes flooded, the dark path became a blurry dark path. She stopped and wiped away tears. Her nostrils burned and she felt one dripping.

"Should have brought a Kleenex."

Seeing Kyle in her kitchen and knowing what would happen to him, she didn't feel bad then. She figured he broke into her home, he was going to steal from them, and he was on a cross-town murdering spree. She thought whatever happened to him, he had earned it. Those other men though? Did they deserve Samuel happening to them?

She knew what he could do, sure she did. He brought home fresh meat all the time. Deer, elk, and even the occasional bear. To know he ran those animals down and ended them with a powerful swipe of his claws, she was aware of Samuel's power and potential for violence.

She'd also witnessed Samuel's potential for kindness. She had grown up with him. Samuel used to pick her up when she was little and carry her around in his arms, running with her through the woods at tremendous speeds, exposing her to a freedom, a rush, she had never experienced before. In those arms she felt invincible. She knew Samuel would let nothing harm her or her family. Samuel loved them and they loved Samuel. They were tied to each other through their love. He was as much a family member as anyone born into it.

She loved hearing the stories about how Samuel had become a part of their family. Amazing to think how long ago it had been. How old Samuel must be. Her father would always start the tale with a wink and a croaky old-timer playful voice with, "It was the winter of 1863…"

And the magical tale would follow. Winter in Canada was always a bitterly cold experience. Back then there were no roads or snowplows. The wind molded drifts taller than any man. Their ancestors ploughed through this snow and through the wilderness pulling a covered wagon carrying their life and everything they owned inside. Food was scarce and the wolves were bold. It wasn't unheard of for a pack of them to stalk and attack an entire family and escape with some poor child in slavering jaws dripping with blood.

And Claire Grayson, on a bitingly cold winter day so long ago, heard a child crying.

• • •

"Stop the horses!"

"What now, Claire?"

"Didn't you hear that?"

"I ain't hearing nothing but you jawing at me."

"Mr. Grayson, you stop these horses now, and listen!"

Jedidiah Grayson pulled back on the reins, "Whoa, now."

They stopped. The wooden wheels and the carriage boards silenced. The leather gear holding the horses in their traces ceased straining. A grey winter day peppered with fat white flakes drifted to the ground on cold air. A silent, white world.

"Jed! Why we stopping?"

"Claire heard something!"

And then they all heard it. The screaming wail of a child.

"There!"

"I heard it."

Jed stood in the driver's box and reached inside the wagon bow behind the seat and picked up his Sharps carbine rifle. He dropped down into the snow. He looked into the breech of the rifle to see a bullet gleaming at him. He tucked the flap of his coat behind his Colt Walker.

"Wait here, Claire. I showed you how to work the shotgun, right?"

"Yes."

"Get it ready."

From behind him, the men from the other wagons approached with weapons in hand. Clyde, a week past his twelfth birthday, walked beside his father with a rifle in his arms. Jed's eyes paused on Clyde, but it wasn't his business to tell another man how to raise his children.

Clyde's father, Frank, said, "Where you think it's coming from?"

The child wailed again.

Jed pointed with his chin and said, "I'd say from over there, but you know how sounds are out here. No way to tell for sure, except to look for ourselves."

Frank said, "How do you wanna do this?"

No one spoke of not doing anything. This vast wilderness possessed no feelings or thoughts for the life of others. Nature was indifferent. The pioneers knew this and would help each other out because it was the right thing to do and also hoping the gesture would be returned if they should ever need help in the future.

Jed said, "Run a skirmish line, I guess. Fifty paces apart. Make sure you can always see each other, and we walk that way, towards the crying."

Frank said, "Right." The other men nodded.

Taking the lead, Jed said, "All right, then," and he moved toward the distressing cry of a child.

●   ●   ●

Jed came upon the pack of wolves first. So, intent on what they had chased up the tree, they didn't sense his approach. It didn't hurt either that Jed made sure to stay upwind as he searched for the child.

Five wolves encircled the base of an old tree. Snarling, legs splayed, they were ready to pounce. Bright marks marred the tree bark from their claws. The child cried, and Jed could only see a portion of the kid, but he had an impression of something hairy. A brief thought of the child being a native, dressed in animal furs, crossed his mind, but then that didn't matter, did it? A child was a child. Even a native one, he supposed.

He brought the rifle up to his shoulder and fired. A wolf jumped, yelped and its blood painted the bottom of the tree. It made no further sound. Four wolves turned to face Jed, snarling, growling and they moved to encircle him. He hoped the men with him were making their way to him by now. He knew they heard the rifle boom. If they heard a child in this wilderness, they certainly heard the damn rifle.

He had no time to reload the rifle. The wolves would be on him before he'd even get a bullet out of his belt. Jed dropped his rifle in the snow and unholstered his pistol. A wolf crouched, tensed muscles, ready to pounce. It bared teeth. Jed shot the wolf in the face and its skull disintegrated in red mist.

Teeth bit into the back of his calf.

"Ahhh!"

A wolf pulled Jed off his feet. The wolf whipped its head from side to side with Jed's leg in its mouth. Jed slid along the ground; a bola of pain concentrated in his lower leg. Another wolf gripped his free hand in its teeth and crunched through bone. Jed bit his own tongue and yelped. He winced, and holding onto the pistol, tried to find the third wolf. He knew it was out there waiting for an opening. Jed knew it would rush in for the stomach or the throat; the soft spots. Flung from side to side, torn and pulled on by teeth in his flesh, Jed tried to spy the last wolf. If anything, the unseen wolf was the most dangerous to him.

Jed swung his pistol and when it connected with the head of the wolf crushing his hand with its teeth, he heard it whine. He pressed the barrel against what he hoped was the skull and fired the pistol. Warm blood splashed his face. The tight grip on his hand disappeared. Still being dragged through the snow by the wolf tearing at his calf, he heard the last wolf before he saw it. It barked, growled out of his sight and Jed twisted his torso, desperate to see it. There, between the trees, he saw shiny eyes above a curled snout. When Jed met its eyes, it burst from the trees. It rushed at him through the snow, mouth open, teeth like white scythes, a grey, sleek powerful animal, intent on making a meal of him. He swung the pistol toward the wolf knowing he'd be too late this time. His reaction had been too slow. Jed's last thought was of Claire, seeing her in the wagon and holding the shotgun waiting for him. The wolf rushing him didn't see the hairy creature charging it from the side. The creature slammed into the wolf. The wolf yelped, rolled and hit a tree so hard it shook snow from the branches above. Now was Jed's chance.

He shot the wolf ripping at his calf in the chest and again in the stomach. He brought the pistol around to the wolf at the tree. It was on its feet now, baring teeth and Jed shot at it, but missed and clipped the tree behind it. It lunged at Jed. Holding his aim steady, his bloody tongue sticking out of the corner of his mouth, he fired. It took the wolf in the head. Its dead body dropped and plowed a furrow in the snow. Jed pulled the trigger again, but the hammer fell on an empty chamber. It didn't matter. The wolf was dead.

He leaned his head back and closed his eyes. Little arms wrapped around his chest. Jed, smiling, dropped the pistol and patted the child on the back. Quite the hairy coat the kid was wearing. He was so warm. Like a rock warming by a campfire.

Frank said, "Is he alive?"

Jed's eyes popped open. Standing over him was Frank and Clyde. The child stirred in Jed's arms.

Clyde brought his rifle to his shoulder and said, "It's a demon pa! A demon has got Mr. Grayson!"

Jed said, "You better drop that rifle, boy! This ain't no demon. This here child saved my life!"

Frank levelled his rifle at the child clinging, shivering, and now mewling against Jed's side. He said, "That's no child, Jed. I don't know what that is, but that ain't no child."

Jed struggled into a sitting position and leaned forward to catch a glimpse of what had his companions so concerned. Jed's eyebrows climbed his forehead and he gasped. Then it opened its eyes. Amber eyes, reading him and Jed reading them in return. It was an animal, that's for sure. A scared animal that saved his life. They had saved each other's life and if there was a more unique and powerful bond on this earth, Jed didn't know of one. Looking into the creature's eyes Jed knew he wouldn't allow anyone to shoot or even hurt the frightened creature. It was possible he might regret that decision in the future. Wild animals can turn on those caring for them and Jed knew that. And if he allowed this creature to grow into an adult there was no telling how powerful and fearsome it would be. But that was the point. There was no way to know the future. He knew the present though. This animal had saved his life. He wouldn't repay that in blood.

"Don't matter none. Nobody is going to be shooting it today. Now put those rifles away."

•　　•　　•

Claire looked after Jed's wounds when he returned to the carriage. His entire calf had turned a bright purple, but at least the teeth of the wolf hadn't penetrated the thick layers of his clothing. His hand hadn't been so lucky. It had swollen to twice its normal size. Teeth marks oozed blood. Claire fashioned a sling and Jed's arm hung immobilized and useless under his coat.

The creature fascinated Claire. Initially, her lip curled in disgust at the sight of it and as Jed told her the tale and how the little creature had put itself in harm's way to save Jed, her feature's softened and she smiled. The creature, sitting on Jed's lap in the covered wagon, moved his lips in an attempt to imitate her smile.

Claire beamed, and said, "What a darling thing!"

Her tentative hand reached for the creature's head, and it jumped from Jed's lap to land on hers.

She said, "Oompf!"

Then the creature wrapped its arms about her waist, rocked back and forth, and purred against her bosom.

She patted it on the back and said, "Samuel. That's his name."

"How do you even know it's a boy?"

Even in the dim covered wagon, he saw her blush. She said, "I saw it's… bit."

"Claire!"

She giggled with a hand over her mouth.

•   •   •

The other people in their party were not so accepting of Samuel.

Robert said, "We can't keep it! I won't have some spawn of the devil travelling with us! It's bad luck, is what it is!"

Sitting around a fire after beef stew (light on the beef as they were running low on meat) and black coffee, the men approached Jed, concerned because the little creature was still with them. Not only that, they heard Claire had named the thing! A good Christian name, too! Travelling overland the way they were doing entailed enough risks without adding any further. And a creature, a monster, was bad luck. The consensus of the gathered men had been to leave it behind or kill it. As long as it wasn't travelling with them.

Frank said, "What if its mudder comes looking for it? The little beast is dangerous enough! You only need to look at its claws and teeth to see that! Imagine an upset mudder! I don't want to be around for when that little critter's mudder comes a'looking!"

The women congregated in one wagon listening to the men debate the fate of the little creature outside. Claire sat in her carriage with Samuel. The men had forbidden their wives and children to visit Claire and see the creature even though they were all powerfully curious. The men worried the creature's scent would get on them and that wouldn't do if an angry mother followed on their heels.

Jed sipped on coffee. He smelled cigarette smoke from the circle of men. He spotted the source and said, "Henry? You mind rolling me one of those?"

Jed's hand and leg hurt something fierce. He had been tempted to dip into the whiskey he had, but knew it'd have a better use in trade. Besides, he wanted a clear head when dealing with the group of men here. Upset men can be dangerous.

"Sure, Jed."

Frank said, "Are you listening to me? To us? I says its bad luck and it needs to get gone!"

Muttered assent from others reached Jed.

"I'm listening. And I will respond. In the end though, it won't matter a lick of difference what I say. There ain't no way I'm sending Samuel away. Now let me ask you something. Saving Samuel netted us five pretty durn nice wolf pelts, wouldn't you say?" Holding up his bandaged hand, he said, "At no cost to you. To any of you."

"Now Jed-"

"That ain't anyone of yours fault. That's just the way it is. Now, maybe if we knew Samuel wasn't a human child, we wouldn't have risked our lives for him. But we didn't know. And I risked my life against five wolves to save him. You ever hear of that? Someone besting five wolves?"

Frank said, "No. No, I ain't."

"Me either. And I wouldn't have if it wasn't for Samuel. It's true I saved his life and yes, he saved mine so that, in your eyes, I guess that makes us even. But for me, it's just not that simple." Jed drank the rest of the coffee in his tin. He said, "Henry? You about ready with that smoke?"

"Yes."

Henry stepped around the fire. The flames turned his features into flickering orange and black shadows. He passed the rolled cigarette to Jed and using his thumbnail, he lit a wooden match.

Jed inhaled. The end glowed like a red eye in the night. He exhaled a plume.

Jed said, "I don't expect you to understand. All I'm saying is, we're not, Claire and me, we're not leaving Samuel behind. We can't. I don't know how to say it any plainer than that. So, you can leave us behind. That is up to you. I'd naturally prefer you didn't, but I'm not going to lie to you and tell you we'll leave Samuel behind somewhere on the trail in the future."

Frank said, "How come you so keen on that... thing?"

"I don't rightly know. We found Samuel for a reason. And I aim to find out what that reason is."

Frank said, "Well, we'll talk about it, us men, and decide what we're going to do. Now, you're certain? No matter what, you ain't leaving him?"

"That is a fact."

Jed stood, nodded at the men, and returned to the wagon.

●   ●   ●

Before turning in for night, Frank, speaking on behalf of the men, told Jed they would all stick together... for now. However, if any bad fortune happened to them on the trail that didn't make any sense, some devilment, then they would leave Jed, Claire, and Samuel behind.

Jed said, "That's fine."

Jed and Claire whispered late into the night. Every man took a turn at sentry duty in the darkness. Keeping the fire going and checking on the horses were added duties to keeping the group safe in the night. It wasn't unheard of for Indians to sneak into a camp and take all the horses without making a sound. Out in this country if a person didn't have a horse, they'd soon be dead. Sentry duty was taken very seriously and, in the past, people had been shot for falling asleep. Jed's injuries kept him from sentry duty, and he didn't like it. Jed always pulled his own weight. At least for now it gave Jed and Claire the opportunity to discuss their future.

Jed said, "I don't know if staying with them is good or bad. You think when we get to where we're going, they won't talk about Samuel?"

Claire said, "They'll talk. They won't be able to help themselves. He is such an unusual creature."

Samuel was curled into a question mark on the plank floor of the wagon. He held one of Jed's shiny coat buttons in his hand cradled under his chin. Jed had put a wool blanket on him, but within minutes, Samuel pushed it off. Jed smiled. He guessed being covered in fur kept Samuel warm enough.

Jed said, "Maybe we should leave them."

"You're in no shape to be leaving anyone. You need to heal up. Get your strength back before we consider leaving the group."

Jed sighed, "Yeah. You're right."

She patted his thigh. She said, "I know I am."

• • •

Jed and Claire had a decision to make as they creeped ever closer to the Hudson's Bay Company trading post and toward civilization. Jed, Claire, and Samuel would have to part ways with the group before they reached the outpost. They still had a long way to go through this rough and unforgiving country after the outpost and going out on their own did not bode well for their chances. They had moved through the untamed land with the group for close to a year now, since running into Samuel. Jed had fully healed. He noticed an ache in his hand whenever a storm was on its way but other than that, he could pull his own weight again and that suited him fine.

They endured a hard winter, a brutally hot summer and back into a cold, unforgiving winter. Jed wondered if this damn country had a spring or an autumn. There didn't seem to be an in-between. The weather seemed to go from one extreme to another. If it hadn't been for Samuel, they would have very likely run out of food when winter had struck the second time. A point Jed made sure to make to the group whenever the opportunity presented itself. The animals were scarce in the cold and the deep snow and they were running through their rations of hard tack faster than they anticipated. They considered rationing what they had left and that worried them. Food kept you warm. Food kept you strong. To ration it meant a lesser portion of those essentials to keep you healthy. It had been good for the group that Samuel couldn't stand the hard tack.

Samuel didn't like anything the group of travelers fed themselves. Jed offered Samuel the hard tack only once. Samuel took it in his clawed hands, sniffed it, sneezed, and dropped it on the ground. Jed said, "I'll eat it if you don't want it. You don't have to drop it."

After that, Samuel started hunting for himself, and for Jed and Claire, proudly dropping the carcass of deer, rabbit and whatever else he had caught when away from the group. The fresh meat soon drew the attention of everyone in the wagon train and, with the influx of fresh meat, the group's mood brightened.

Samuel disappeared into the woods often as he grew. Sometimes he'd be gone when they woke, and they wouldn't see him until they stopped for the night. Jed and Claire worried about him while waiting for him to return throughout the day. He might have been attacked by another pack of wolves or a bear even and they were always relieved when he walked back into the camp carrying a dead animal with him.

He'd drop the carcass by the fire, tear off a hind leg with a rip and a pop and sit on the back of Jed and Claire's wagon to consume the flesh raw. Jed and Claire would then butcher and clean the rest of the meat for them and the group. Samuel grew fast in their company. He soon towered over Jed. His body thick with muscle all over. His strength was prodigious. He wondered if Samuel could take on those wolves that had attacked him all on his own now. It would be quite the battle, that's for sure.

In the beginning, when Samuel first started bringing in the products of his hunts, Jed's swollen, and broken hand prevented him from carving into the fresh meat. He needed help and he knew the best person to ask was the one who had protested Samuel's presence the most in the first place. On the first day that Samuel dumped a still warm dead deer at Jed's feet, and after Samuel took his portion of the food with him and sat at the back of the wagon to eat it, Jed realized his opportunity. This was the second such dead animal dropped before them and Jed thought now would be the perfect time to weaken the overall resistance to Samuel. And he knew the first person in their group to start with.

Jed said, "Frank! Fresh meat here! What say we cook this up?"

Frank's grinning face parted the flaps of his wagon.

"Fresh meat?" He climbed down from the wagon, removed the knife from the sheath on his waist and said, "Where did this lovely come from?"

"The unlucky one. Samuel. He caught it."

Frank's steps paused, his smile wavered, and then his eyes fastened on the deer and smacking his lips, he said, "This is a big un!"

They ate very well after that. Samuel got them fresh meat and more hide in that first winter than two years of trapping would have earned them. Although Samuel became a much-valued member of their community, Jed and Claire knew it still wouldn't be enough to keep him safe. People would talk about him when given the chance. Once they reached a community, Samuel would be in jeopardy.

It wouldn't matter that Samuel was simultaneously feeding them and creating wealth for them with his fresh kills. It didn't matter Samuel was gentle with the children and became fiercely protective of their community and alerted them when starving wolves prowled too close. He was a creature no one in their group had ever seen or heard of before and because he was different, he would never be truly accepted by them. People tended to destroy the different. You only need to see what had been done to the natives of this land to see that.

The group did enjoy speculating around the fire at night after dinner about what he could be and why people hadn't seen more of Samuel's kind in this country or anywhere else. There were outlandish suggestions, (Robert insisted Samuel had to be a daytime werewolf) and no satisfactory answers. Samuel was a mystery. An anomaly. And that meant someone in their group would talk. Jed thought it as inevitable as the sun rising in the morning. He and Claire occasionally talked about the problem late into the night. They would have to leave the group at some point; what they continually discussed was when would they tell them. They wouldn't be able to tell them where they were going. They'd have to lie about that. Once people learned of Samuel, they would come for him to see for themselves.

Two days before Jed and Claire planned to tell the group they were leaving, Samuel entered their camp on a cold sunny morning with a deer over one shoulder and a piece of gold the size of his fist in his other hand.

Robert noticed the yellow rock first and knew what it was right away. Every man going into the interior knew what raw gold looked like. Every man dreamed of finding a vein of gold lining the hills or glints of the rock shining in the bed of a river, twinkling in the sun.

Pointing with one hand while the other framed the side of his face, Robert said, "Samuel! Where'd you get that?"

Samuel chuffed, furrowed his brow and studied the deer. He held the deer out with a straight arm and no apparent strain.

"Not the deer! That gold!"

The word "gold" drew people from all over the lunchtime camp. Clyde dropped the bucket of oats he'd been carrying to feed the horses. Frank spilled the firewood bundled in his arms into the snow. The women and smaller children poked their heads out of the covered wagons. Dave, who had been relieving himself behind a thick fir tree, yanked up his pants and hurried toward Samuel through the snow.

The men all approached Samuel and stood around him, bent over and looking at the golden rock in his hand.

Jedidiah said, "May I see that Samuel?"

Samuel handed it to Jedidiah.

All the men hovered over the rock in Jed's hand.

"Is it real?"

"Yeah, is it?"

"What say you, Jed?"

Jed squeezed the gold in his hand. He said, "Can you show us where you found this Samuel?"

Samuel canted his head.

Jed held up the rock with one hand and pointed at it with the other. He said, "Where?"

Samuel dropped the deer, turned and bounded away. Jedidiah hurried after him with the rest of the men following close behind.

Frank stopped and said, "Clyde! You stay here now boy and look after everyone."

"But pa!"

"You mind me, boy!"

•   •   •

They didn't have to travel far. On the fringes of their camp, Samuel took them down a steep incline into a ravine. The sun reflecting off the rocks burned their eyes and the group found themselves squinting and stumbling along the bottom, splashing through cold river water.

And then they were there.

Frank said, "Praise be to the Lord!"

Jedidiah said, "It wasn't the Lord. Samuel found this."

Frank said, "And the good Lord sent Samuel to us."

Jed studied Frank and turned back to what all the men had their eyes on. A large golden vein shined at them from the rock. Thick as a man's leg and as multiple as the branches of a tree, each man there knew they were now all rich.

•   •   •

In the evening, back at camp around the fire everyone was smiling and singing. Frank opened a bottle of whiskey he'd been hoarding and to everyone's surprise, he shared it with everyone. Even gave his son Clyde a shot. Everything was right with the world and God was clearly smiling upon them.

Jed knew hard and dangerous work was still ahead of them. That's fine that they found gold. They still had to mine it, they had to move it, and they would have to sell it. And that wasn't even the dangerous part. As soon as they sold even a small bit of the golden rock, people would be pestering them with questions. Where did they find it? How much was there? Who owned the land? Questions, questions, and more questions. People might even try to hurt them for the information. Finding this gold could bind their group together stronger than before. Greed and self-interest were powerful incentives to grow tighter. This could work out to Jed's advantage. This gold, strangely enough, could keep Samuel safe.

Jed said, "Before we go forward, we all need to be in agreement."

Robert said, "About what?"

"Once we bring any gold in, you know what's going to happen right? Questions. People will want to know where we got it and how we found it. People will want to take it from us. Gold can turn even the kindest man into a murderer."

Frank said, "That's true."

"So, we need to be in agreement about how we found this here gold. And one thing we can't be telling anyone about is Samuel. He found it, and with the way he seems to like shiny things, he could find us more. Now, I say Samuel here has fed us, got us furs to trade and now, has made us, every one of us, very rich men. If people find out about him, they'll try to take him, and if they can't take him, they'll kill him. And if we want more riches in the future, I say keeping him a secret would give us a better chance at that. What say you?"

Frank nodding, said, "He's our secret. He's part of our group. No one will breathe a word about him. You have all of our oaths on that."

Nobody could have known what the secret would cost them, their children, and their children's children.

· · ·

Lindsay was fourteen when she found out what that cost actually would be. She also learned she would be the next one to pay it. She was walking with Samuel and her father on their land in the woods on a walking trail made by the passing feet of her ancestors. It had been a summer day, the air sticky, but cooler in the shade under the branches of the trees. Even though she was young and homeschooled, she was aware Samuel was a secret member of their family. She learned that her family had the responsibility of looking after Samuel. He wouldn't go and live with any other members of the original community when they eventually did split up. Samuel had chosen Jed and Claire and after them, no one but their children would make him happy.

Her father said, "He made everyone rich, Samuel did. And that money trapped us as much as it freed us. We were rich and free in the ways money can liberate a person, but it also imprisoned us in this house and on this land. The other community members didn't have to be tied to one spot. They could move about the country or even out of the country if they had a mind to. They had two obligations. The first one was to keep quiet about Samuel. The second was deciding which family would have to sacrifice one of their children. You see, the real problem was keeping our family line going without, you know, inbreeding. The obvious way to prevent that was to mate with someone outside. Every once in a while, that is what would happen. An old-fashioned arranged marriage."

"An arranged marriage? Does that mean someone has already been picked out for me?"

Her dad stopped walking on the trail. He palmed a line of sweat at his hairline and wiped it on his pants. He sighed, and said, "Yes and no. There are a couple of boys to choose from, and there is no rush to do so, no rush at all. Who you choose will be up to you, but you will have to choose one of them... eventually."

"Huh." Her chin dipped toward her chest. She furrowed her brow. She said, "What do these other boys think about this... arrangement?"

"I don't know. It doesn't matter. It's part of the deal. They haven't a choice in the matter. Not if they want to stay rich. You see, we have all the gold, right here. Samuel wouldn't let anyone else take it. It had to stay with him or with us. We take all that gold, turn it into cash using gold shops all over the country, never trading too much in one store, and we funnel it out to the families. They'll stay rich if they toe the line. And I don't know of anyone who would choose poverty over wealth."

"I don't have a choice either, then. Do I Dad?"

"Well, I'd never force you to do anything you didn't want to do. And neither would your mother. We were arranged, and we turned out damn well, but that's not always the case. I did it for Samuel, and I think I got a hell of a bargain out of the whole deal. So, you have to ask yourself, is Samuel worth it to you?"

"Do I have to answer today?"

"No, no. You're fourteen. Marriage is a ways down the road. I wanted you to be prepared, is all. I wanted you to have the time to make up your mind. Samuel's not really a lot of work, but he does cause a lot of worry. He can't be seen by other people and if he is seen, it can't be near our land. That's why we have those tunnels. They surface far enough from our land so even if he is sighted, he wouldn't necessarily be associated to us. And he loves being down there in the caves, too, which is a bonus. I've always wondered if his kind were cave dwellers or something. Could be why he likes shiny things. Sparkles in the darkness or something. I don't know."

Samuel stiffened and twisted his head. He chuffed and ran toward something only he could sense. Silent, within seconds he disappeared.

Her father patted his pockets, and then snapped his fingers, "I forgot."

He'd recently quit smoking and was having a hard time of it. Lindsay wondered if she hadn't been with him this morning, would he have snuck out a pack?

"Samuel needs looking after. He may be the last of his kind. And it's always a sad thing when something disappears forever from this earth. It happens too often, in my opinion. He is dangerous, though. He's dangerous to anyone that steps foot on our land and not in the company of a Grayson. He knows not to kill people for the most part. He's never killed anyone off our land except for those who were trying to do us harm. But he will kill anyone stepping onto our land and that's a fact. I was younger than you the last time Samuel hunted people. Those people heard from someone, we still don't know who, that we had gold hidden here on the property. They thought they could take it from us. They were wrong.

I don't know if they knew we had Samuel or not. Who'd believe such a thing anyway? Still, greed has a way of swatting aside fears. But their sin hadn't been trying to get the gold. No. The real sin was stepping onto our land. No one can trespass on what Samuel must think of as his lair or his home and threatening the welfare of his family, us Grayson's. And there is nothing anyone can do that could stop him once one of those rules are broken. He turns it into a game, you see? Hunting the smartest prey. He gets off on their fear like maybe a lion or a bear does. It could be part of his DNA. Nature telling him to hunt us, needing to hunt us and maybe before old Jedidiah saved him from that pack of wolves, maybe it is what their kind did or had done for centuries. Could be where all those stories of werewolves and big foot actually come from. A tribe of Samuels. Imagine that? Monsters in the dark. And since they live so long, maybe the urge to reproduce isn't as strong which is why there are not so many of them running around that people know about them. Once again, I'm no scientist so I don't know. I do like to speculate, though."

Her father stuck his hands in the pockets of his pants and continued walking.

Her heart stuttered in her chest. She remembered her mouth being dry. She didn't want to tell him what she had to say, but in the interest of Samuel, it had to be done.

"Daddy?"

"Yeah?"

"I don't know, I don't think, I uh, don't like boys... not in that way."

Without turning to look at her, he said, "Yeah. I figured. So did your mother, by the way."

Lindsay stopped, mouth open and her eyes fixed on her father. He turned and said, "You're our only daughter. Our only child for that matter. We pay attention. Come on. It's a nice day. Let's keep going here."

They continued their meandering walk through the wooded area around their home. Her father tipped his head back with his eyes closed whenever a sunbeam penetrated the overhead trees. The sun highlighted his contented expression.

He said, "So. Do you like girls then?"

The question stopped her. Blushing, she said, "I don't know. I don't think that I do. I don't like boys or girls, not in that way." Her voice hitched, "What's wrong with me? I feel like, like a freak, like I'm unnatural." Her eyes welled.

Her father wrapped his arms around her. He said, "Unnatural? You're a being of nature. You can't be unnatural. And you can't help being you, so, the only thing I worry about, for you, is that you're safe and that you're happy. It'd break my heart to think you felt shame, or fear to talk to me or your mother. Especially about something other people have decided what is 'right' or 'good'. That's for you to decide and for you alone. You have to look at yourself. You have to judge yourself. And a good person rarely chooses wrong. You are a good person, Lindsay. And whether or not you like or don't like members of the opposite or the same sex has nothing to do with that. So, who cares?"

He rubbed her back, stepped away from her, winked, and said, "Let's go."

She wiped under her eyes and caught up to him.

"But Daddy? Doesn't that ruin the plans for Samuel?"

"Doesn't ruin anything. Just means we have to improvise, come up with a new plan, or figure out exactly what it is you're comfortable doing. We need to keep the Grayson line going, for Samuel's sake. But that doesn't mean you couldn't adopt or, be artificially inseminated, right? Science has provided people with options they never had before. Wait… you like kids, though right?"

Lindsay smiled and said, "Yes. I do. Kids are very interesting to me. I like reading about how they learn, how their brains absorb information, all that kind of stuff, is like, cool."

"Well, good. I am going to say that without your mother, all of this would have been very hard for me." He pointed to his temple, "You're strong. Right up here. Stronger than I ever was or ever will be, so that might not even be a problem for you, but you should think about that. I know this can be a burden and sometimes burdens are lighter when they are shared. And I'm sorry for that. I'm sorry you weren't born into a family with neighbors and other kids to play with or going to a real high school and maybe going to your first dance with your hair all done up and wearing clothes your parents wouldn't approve of. But you were born into this family. And we have a responsibility."

"I'm not sorry, dad. Samuel is… a miracle of nature. No one else knows of him, but I do. And besides… you and mom? You're okay. As far as parents go. I could have done worse, I guess."

"Oh yeah? I don't know if I can take such high praise."

"I know. You may work your way up to a 'good' rating, if, for my sixteenth birthday, I get a new car."

"Bribery will improve our score?"

"Of course."

"Well, I'll think on it. I'll bring it up to your mother, too."

"Cause you know, you just said we are rich. What's a new Range Rover to the rich?"

"Range Rover?"

"Yeah."

"Sheesh. Come on, now. Let's finish this lap and go fix your mother some lunch."

• • •

BOOM-BOOM-BOOM!

Shaken from her reverie, Lindsay turned the flashlight beam toward the sound. Someone was banging on one of the tunnel's steel door.

"Don't go over there, Lindsay. You have a job to do." She had never talked to herself this much before in her life.

She walked toward the sound. She bit her lower lip.

Standing at the top of a long-tunneled incline Lindsay flashed the light on the dark door. The door had been painted an earthy brown. There was no window in the solid steel. Her flashlight beam must have penetrated the seams of the door because the banging increased and the men's voices raised, battering at her.

BOOM-BOOM-BOOM!

"Help!"

"It's going to kill us!"

"Let us out!"

"Please!"

Lindsay's stomach twisted. She turned from the door and ran from the pounding and the pleas for help.

-60-

Lost… again." Kyle almost laughed, but his chest hitched instead.

How many times had he been lost since this whole nightmare started? Had he ever known where he was? All he wanted to do was to go home. One bad decision to stop at a bar and now look at the predicament he was in. In an underground tunnel, being hunted by a bona-fide monster and maybe (if they hadn't been killed yet) by the father of the woman he had killed and that asshole's remaining friends. If this was the cost of a beer, he'd never drink again. If he escaped from this, he may even follow through on that promise.

The corridors had dark rough walls with older and newer timber supports from the ground to the ceiling and then across. Tunnels branched off leading to more tunnels or sometimes, locked steel doors leading to who-knows-where. For all he knew, if he happened to get one of the doors open, he'd end up popping his head up in the middle of a police station floor with coppers leaning back in their chairs, reading the paper and sipping on coffee. Wouldn't that be a sight? His sought after head appearing in the midst of the police?

That woman said one tunnel would lead straight out of this place and only one. Had she even told them the truth? She wouldn't want anyone of them to get out of here. They might tell people what was really down here. Not that anyone would believe this happy horse-shit about a monster.

And he had no idea if this game was rigged. How would he know if the creature wasn't just hunkering by the exit waiting for him or anyone else to pass by? Was it really running around down here, tracking them? Seemed like a lot of work. He approached a dark spot on his left. Kyle shivered staring into the blackness. He didn't want to be stuffed into those jaws. No thanks. His teeth clacked in the silence. He put his palm against a support beam and leaning against it, frowned. There was something here, something lurking at the back of his mind, something he was missing. He straightened, and canted his neck from side to side, stretching the muscles out. *What is it?*

His fingers splayed against the wood of the support. The wood felt almost damp, newer, and not dried out like older timber. Now, wouldn't newer wood be supporting newer tunnels? If so, how does that help him? Hank said this place had history. Did he mean the family or the actual place? Kyle pictured the house from his approach before being crammed into a cage. The house had no driveway and no access for a car to get close to the house. How had he missed that the first time? Not that it would have stopped him from breaking in. He had been starving! And he still was but, stay on point here, Kyle.

So, how did they bring supplies in? It had to be through one of these tunnels. If that were true, would that tunnel be one of the older ones? Would it have the old timber instead of the newer? Most likely. Did that help him though? Maybe. If he avoided the tunnels with the newer wood, he might have a better chance of stumbling upon the one tunnel that would lead him out of here. Right? Unless the old wood had been replaced because it was crumbling or something. Damn.

He didn't have any better ideas. At least it was kind of a plan. Looking at the newer wood of this tunnel, he thought he'd have to backtrack. Kyle turned around. Those little spots of light in the ceiling did nothing to alleviate the menace of the tunnel. The light only accentuated the shadows and darkened them. Anything could be hiding in the blackness. A scream made the hairs on his arms pull his skin taut.

-61-

Hank said, "No one's going to let us out of here."

Jesse said, "I saw a light, from under the door!"

"So did I. Could have been the lights of a passing car for all we know."

"Out in the woods?"

"We don't know how far we've gone."

Jesse's lower lip protruded. He said, "No. It was someone. And they left us here."

Vern said, "Might have been that woman. And she wouldn't be letting us out. No way. Her pet needs its food."

"Goddamnit Vern! Shut up about that shit!"

"It's true ain't it?"

Hank said, "Come on. Let's get moving."

They entered the tunnel with Hank in the lead, Vern in the middle and Jesse in the rear. They stopped under a light at an intersection. Hank glanced in both directions. Left or right presented them with the same scenery. Dark spots, light spots, rock and timber. More of the same any way he looked.

"Which way looks best to you, Vern? Jesse?"

Jesse said, "Do you smell that?"

Sharp scent of fur, of an animal, and a musty, but lived-in den.

Jesse's eyes widened. Claws emerged from the dark behind him and grasped him by the shoulders.

Jesse said, "Hank!"

Hank moved toward Jesse, not knowing what he was going to do, only knowing he had to help his friend. Samuel's jaws and amber eyes entered the light. Samuel's mouth opened wide, impossibly wide, like a snake as it engulfs a rabbit. Jesse's eyes bulged as the top portion of Samuel's jaws descended.

"Hank!"

The jaws closed. Blood spurted. Bones crunched and with a violent shake, Jesse was decapitated. Hank screamed. Vern ran. And Samuel retreated into the darkness with his prize.

•　　•　　•

Cold. So cold. Tommy's teeth clacked. His upper body muscles twitched. He couldn't hear Dave breathing near him anymore. That couldn't be a good thing and Tommy turned his attention to rubbing his own chest and arms with his hands. What he wouldn't do for a smoke right now.

The door opened. Light blinded him. He raised a hand before his eyes. The creature strode into the freezer room with another body over its shoulder. Tommy flinched as it came near him, "No-no... please."

The creature dropped the body on the ground beside Tommy.

"Ahh!"

The body had no head.

Even in his fear and disgust, Tommy hoped it was Kyle. At least then, there'd be some sort of justice to this horrendous day. The creature turned from Tommy. He couldn't tell who the dead person was. After a quick glance he knew it wasn't Kyle. He had been wearing that bright pink shirt the last time he'd seen him. So, it had to be another one of his friends. The door closed. Darkness dropped before he could find out which one of his friends lay dead beside him.

With great difficulty, he removed the jacket from the body. The coat was wet and sticky. And warm. He wrapped it around his chest, shoulders and the lower half of his face to trap his warm exhalations. Tommy felt something hard in the jacket. His fingers explored it. He smiled. He knew what it was.

In the darkness of the freezer, surrounded by two dead friends, Tommy lit a cigarette and was almost, not quite, but almost happy.

-62-

Lindsay found the vehicles Hank and his friends arrived in. A car, a pickup truck, and two motorbikes parked in a neat row. She had found them quick enough. Although thinking about it, they couldn't have been anywhere else. They were parked on the closest road to their house. Lindsay was mildly surprised though. The road was hard to find. An obscure turn off the main road down a long lane of bumps and wheel ruts brought you to this area. Only her family had ever used the road to bring in supplies. They had a hidden garage underground where they parked their own vehicles. From there, they'd use a golf cart to run groceries and even furniture through the tunnels to the house. Finding the cars so quick didn't surprise her, but it did at the same time because the road itself was so hard to find. But most of all, finding the cars as fast as she had saddened her.

She wanted to spend more time out in the woods, away from the house and the security room and the monitors. There were cameras in the tunnel system. And she should check up on Samuel only she didn't want to rush back home to do that. The men's pleas had bothered her and were continuing to bother her. She didn't want Samuel killing anyone, but she also didn't want him getting hurt and needing help while she delayed getting back home for as long as she could just so she wouldn't have to deal with her own guilt. Her dad said the men were no match for Samuel and she believed that, but they could both be wrong. What if she did what her dad said and put it all out of her mind and ended falling asleep in her bed, clueless that her family friend needed help? It will be hard enough to live with the fact that Samuel was hunting those men. Almost like she was sacrificing them to a pagan god. Even still, it would be even harder to lose Samuel to those same men. He was her family after all.

Now, it would be very unlikely for any of those men to get the upper hand on Samuel. They had no guns or weapons of any kind. There was equipment down there they used for the tunneling itself. They had a tunnel-boring machine, what her dad affectionately called "the mole" and hand tools such as sledgehammers and pickaxes beside where "the mole" was parked. Her dad really loved that machine. Their family had purchased it when her dad had been a teenager. Before that, the tunnel had been dug by the family, and the extended family, by hand. They had used jackhammers mostly so not really by hand, but she still imagined that to be hard labor. Her father bragged that they had more than doubled the area tunneled with "the mole".

If those men found the tools by "the mole", they could be used as weapons. Would they be effective against Samuel? Probably not. Still, she worried. Harder than hurting Samuel with, well, anything was actually finding those tools in the underground tunnels. There were so many corridors, laneways and tunnels Lindsay always thought it was more accurate to call the subterranean realm a maze. And Samuel? If you were into Greek mythology, like Lindsay, then you could liken him to the Minotaur. All of those reasons were why her dad had told her to do her best to forget about Samuel and the men. And they were good reasons. Her dad told her to move the cars and forget about Samuel and what he would be doing to the men in the tunnels and for her sanity, it would be smart for her to take his advice.

She sighed and got to work. She opened the garage door (a sod and dirt covered gate) and brought each of the vehicles from outside into the garage and parked them tight against the wall. The large initial garage hadn't been designed to accommodate this many vehicles and their golf cart. She was glad her father had moved the golf cart deeper into the tunnel before he had left. Not that he knew she would need the space in the garage, but it worked out for her all the same. Even without the golf cart in the garage, the two motorcycles were tight against the door when she closed it. Once the vehicles were hidden inside behind the camouflaged door, she stepped out of the garage through a metal man-door hidden in a grassy recess.

The night air was redolent of pine. Through a gap in the overhead foliage, the moon shone bright silver. It appeared so big in the sky. It seemed to be the sky. A beautiful night. She wondered how many of the men were already dead. She shivered. She pushed off from the door and heading back to her home, she thought only of keeping the flashlight beam on the trail. To think of anything else made her want to cry.

-63-

The screams echoing in the tunnel behind him put some speed into Kyle's steps. Flitting from shadow to light to shadow, he completely threw away the idea about paying attention to the timber beam's age. He wasn't a timber expert, so what the hell did he know? He only thought of it because he didn't want to feel powerless. He didn't want his death to be definite. Huh. All death was definite. He didn't want it to imminent, then. Predetermined to end on this night. Not that it wouldn't be a perfect ending to the five-star craptacular day he'd been having. Kyle wanted to feel like he had a hand in shaping his own fate and fortune.

The lady had said no one ever made it out of here alive, but she also didn't say how many people had been in this situation before. Maybe there had been only one person in this same situation before him. Maybe even two. In that context, was it completely unbelievable for him to escape?

Kyle's hand touched a beam as he turned a corner. He stopped and glanced over his shoulder. No one behind him. No giant hairy monster either. Walking, the adrenaline leaving with his receding fear, his injured knee throbbed. He rubbed it and lifted his leg while moving his foot back and forth, trying to get more blood into the sore hinge. Being exhausted didn't help his balance any and his one-legged standing proved difficult. He tilted over, hopped a step and dropped his leg to the ground. He put his hand out where he thought the wall would be and met no resistance and staggered.

"What?"

The dark pocket swallowed his hand.

Kyle retraced his steps until he touched a wall. Placing his hand on the wall and walking forward, he found the spot where the wall ended. Another tunnel, but without lighting. Why? No reason to hide anything down here. The whole place was hidden.

Kyle really didn't want to walk into the darkness. That was where a monster lurked. A giant monster with scythe like teeth, clawed hands and amber eyes.

"Maybe this isn't a great idea."

Kyle's feet crunched on what? Glass. It felt like glass. A soft light, outlining the straight line of a wall, glowed not too far ahead.

"Nothing hidden, here Sherlock. A bulb broke is all. Maybe the monster's enormous head broke it."

Kyle stopped and stared at the soft glow ahead. He looked behind him at the light from the tunnel he had left. Was there any reason to return that way? He sighed and decided to investigate the new tunnel, the one hidden by darkness.

Walking forward, he crinkled his nose. Dirt and his own body odor. What he wouldn't do for a shower.

Turning the corner, he stopped just outside the cast of the light. His eyes bulged and his mouth opened. He forgot to breathe. On metal pallets, stacked as tall as Kyle, were bars of gold.

"Holy shit!"

On the floor in front of the pallet were canvas sacks. The canvass of one bag had deteriorated with age, or mice had gotten to it. Either way, a hole in the corner of the bag exposed the contents inside. Golden coins shone like mini suns in the dirt.

Kyle remembered what the lady had said, and thought Samuel does like shiny things. He grinned. His cheeks touched his ears.

He kneeled on the ground and his injured knee cracked. Kyle winced and said, "Jesus!"

He rubbed his knee and exhaled slowly through the thin slit of his mouth. As the pain receded, he eyed the gold coins. He picked one up and held it to the light. Man! Gold sure is beautiful. Not only for the riches it represented but also because the golden discs gleamed and shone like a sun you could look at and hold in your hand. No wonder people killed for it.

He kissed the coin and put it in the pocket of his jeans. Kyle picked up more coins with both hands and stuffed them into his pockets. It would be so much better if he had a backpack. Hell, it'd be freaking awesome to have a car to back up here and take all of it.

Kyle giggled. The coins jingled and sang. Like anyone doing something they shouldn't, Kyle glanced about to see if he was being watched. Twisting his head left, the wall, twisting his head right, he spied another side tunnel with a golf cart halfway down. Wait. A golf cart? Kyle frowned, stood and walked toward it. The coins jingled in his pocket. He put his hand on the cart and ran his hand on the surface. Keys dangled from the ignition. Charging cables ran to a battery. The green light flashed. Kyle had a fully charged golf cart at his disposal.

Now, to load up this golf cart, and get out of here, that would be one spectacular payday. With that type of money, he could disappear. Live somewhere warm all year round. No more suffering through Canadian winters. Yeah. Great plan, genius. That would only work if he could make it out of here alive with the gold.

The lady's words, "no one has ever made it out alive", sent a tremor through him.

Those words didn't instill in him a lot of confidence concerning his survival. Question was, did he want to die with nothing in his pockets? Or did he want to die trying to drive a golf cart loaded with gold out of this sick, underground playground for a human-eating monster?

He picked up two gold bars and grunting and bow-legged with the weight, he walked them over to the golf cart.

-64-

"What are we going to do Hank?"

"What do you mean what are we going to do? We are going to get out of here!"

Vern's bulging eyes explored the tunnel ahead, behind them and down every branching hallway. His head twitched every-which-way. His movements reminded Hank of Jeff Goldblum in The Fly when he recorded himself demonstrating how flies eat using a donut. His jerky movements irritated Hank. Hank's hands opened and closed at his side.

"You think so, Hank? You think we'll get out of here?"

The growing heat of anger in Hank's stomach cooled. He was getting mad at his friend for being scared. Hank was scared too. He knew the constant fear was making him irritable. He hated the feeling. Hated not being in control of himself. And this thing chasing them in the tunnel had reached into Hank's brain and wrestled his control from him. He pictured the creature's jaws closing on Jesse's head. A tremor ran through him.

"What? You see something Hank? What? Why you jerk like that?"

"Jesus Christ Vern! Will you shut it with all the questions? How am I supposed to hear anything with you blathering in my ear all the time?"

"Sorry, Hank. I'm just scared."

"I am too for crying out loud. But yipping about it doesn't help anything. All we can do is keep moving and hopefully find a way out of here."

"Against that thing we don't have a chance! Nobody has a chance! See what it did to Jesse? See what it did to Dave? What chance have we got, Hank?"

Hank put his left hand around Vern's neck and pushed him against the wall. A vein pulsed behind Vern's eye, drool spilled from the corner of his mouth and snot ran from his nostrils. Pathetic and useless. Hank resented having to look after him. It was hard enough looking after himself and running around in a maze being chased by a family pet that shouldn't even exist.

What's wrong with a dog? A cat, even? No. These people had to have a werewolf-bigfoot-Neanderthal monster patrolling their yard. And now most of his friends are dead and knowing they were dead because of him and his insistence that they look for that murderous shit-fuck Kyle, the guilt, the anger and the frustration made Hank crank back his right arm and think about how good it would feel to smash Vern's snot-covered face into the rock wall. Vern closed his eyes awaiting the fist. This acceptance of Hank's telegraphed violence doused the flames of his anger running like high-grade cocaine through his veins.

He dropped his right arm and let go of Vern's neck. He turned from him and walked away. His pulse pounding in his ears, it took a few steps for the rhythm to slow enough to hear Vern's scuffling footsteps following behind him. Always following.

Hank ground his teeth and scanned the paths branching off, not knowing what he is looking for, but thinking he'd know it when he saw it. Maybe there'd be a bright red EXIT sign glowing neon in the dark. He grunted. Fat chance of that.

"Hank?"

"What now, Vern?"

"What's that?"

Stopping, Hank turned. Vern was staring down a tunnel they had just passed. Had Hank missed something? He walked to Vern and stood beside him. Another rock hallway with intermittent lighting. Light, dark, light, dark and what is that?

"Huh."

A machine. From this angle, he saw a machine on treads, like tank-treads.

Hank walked toward the machine. Dust puffed under his boots and sweat ran down his spine. The machine's door drew closer. After a short pause, Vern hurried after him.

Stepping into the room with the metal contraption, Hank tilted his head back. This room has a higher ceiling. He examined the rest of the room. Against one wall stood a metal tool rack. Pickaxes, sledgehammers and one of those tools that shake the wielder's arms, what's the name of that tool? A jackhammer?

Behind him, Vern said, "Look. A jackhammer."

Hank ran a hand along the treads of the machine. Short, boxy, with a large drill head for the nose, Hank knew this was how they had built this underground maze. Even with this machine, it would have been hard work. But, if you had a trained monster to help, the heavy lifting work wouldn't be so heavy now, would it?

Hank opened the door of the machine. Inside was a metal dashboard, a steering wheel and a shifter with a black cue ball for a handle. In the floor were three pedals; the gas, the brake, and the clutch. There was no key in the ignition.

"Shit."

Vern said, "What?"

"See if you can find a key or something. On that tool board over there. We could drive this sucker right through a wall and out of here."

"Alright."

Hank thought Vern sounded calmer now. Maybe because he had something to do, something to think about other than being eaten. Hank closed the machine's door. Holding his right hand out in front of him, fingers splayed, it shook. He wasn't consciously shaking it. The control of his hand didn't belong to him right now. Hank closed his fingers into a fist. Still shaking, he stuffed his hand into his pocket. He hadn't been this afraid before. But no previous experience scaled with this craziness. Death was stalking them in these tunnels. A thing of nightmares with bone-crunching teeth, eviscerating claws, and incalculable strength. Vern was right. They had no chance against that thing.

Hank shook his head. They aren't dead yet. They needed to stay ahead of it.

"You find any keys?"

"No. Nothing."

"Ok then. Which one do you want?"

"Which what?"

"Weapon."

Vern's gaze scanned the tools.

"I'll take the pickaxe, I guess."

Hank said, "I'll grab the sledge."

"Yeah."

Hank picked up the sledgehammer in his left hand and rested it on his shoulder. On the tool board shone a long screwdriver. He picked it up by the handle and stabbed it into the board. It sunk in half an inch.

Hank said, "That'll do."

He put the screwdriver in his pocket.

Vern said, "Now what?"

"We get the hell out of here, that's what. And if that thing gets in our way, we'll move him."

Vern nodded. His Adam's apple danced in his neck.

-65-

Sitting on the back of the golf cart, sweating through his clothes, Kyle patted the gold bars piled beside him, thinking he would trade one of the gold bars for a bottle of cold water and a sandwich if the opportunity presented itself. He had plenty of gold to spare. Thinking about his parched throat, the water didn't have to be all that cold. It could be lukewarm for all he cared.

He ran his tongue around the inside of his mouth. He swallowed. He stood and stretched the tight and trembling muscles in his lower back. How long had he been loading this cart for? Seemed like forever. It was time to get going.

Kyle sank onto the vinyl cushion seat behind the steering wheel. He turned the key to the on position and stepped on the accelerator. The engine hummed electric. The pedal vibrated under his foot. All that noise and no forward movement.

"Fuck."

Kyle sighed and hit the steering wheel with the flat of his hand. He had put too many gold bars in the golf cart and now it was too heavy to move forward. He'd have to offload some. His forearms twitched with the thought. His quads trembled.

Or he could leave all the gold behind and zip out of here. He had taken some time to load up the gold. And time was something he didn't think he had a lot of.

He turned his head, glanced at the yellow bars and swallowed. What? Leave all of it behind? Hell no. He could take some, right? He deserved something after all he'd been through. Let's call it monster tax. Yeah.

Kyle turned the key to off and stepped out of the cart. He twisted his shoulders from side to side. The middle of his back cracked. He hissed through his teeth.

Stopping behind the golf cart, Kyle picked up each beautiful golden bar, turned and dropped them one at a time. They clanged to the dirt. He counted off ten (because that should be enough right?) exhaled and got into the golf cart. He turned it on, stomped on the gas and felt the machine humming underneath him. It didn't move forward.

"This sucks."

He removed five more. The golf cart lurched ahead four feet, whined, and stopped. Kyle pursed his lips. Doing it this way, pushing the golf cart like this, he could burn the motor out and then what? He wouldn't have the golf cart or the gold. It'd be better to have the golf cart and a little gold then neither.

Kyle plucked ten more bars off the golf cart. He returned to the driver's seat and wiped sweat from his brow with his forearm.

"Come on!"

Kyle depressed the accelerator. The golf cart moved forward, steady, without lurching and with no discernible strain on the motor.

"Yes!"

The wind fluttered his hair and cooled his sweaty skin. A pleasant feeling for once. He smiled.

-66-

Lindsay watched Hank and Vern turn a corner and walk away from the recessed camera in the ceiling. One held a pickaxe; the other a sledgehammer. She leaned forward. Her fingernails clicked against her teeth. She turned from the screen and glanced at the shotgun leaning against the wall. Samuel didn't need help, did he? And did she really want to be a part of these murders? She knew what she didn't want. She absolutely did not want Samuel to get hurt. To know that those men now had weapons to use against Samuel while she hid in the safety of this room didn't sit well with her. It turned her guts a bit to be honest.

On another screen, a golf cart sped past a camera. There were golden bars in the back.

"What the hell?"

This has got to be the strangest day she had ever experienced.

She glanced at the camera number and the direction the golf cart was moving in. It was heading the right way down the right tunnel. If it didn't make any more turns, the tunnel it was in will take it right to the garage with the other cars. Shit. On the table in front of her sat the pile of car keys. She nodded. At least he wouldn't be able to take one of the cars out of there. Would he drive that golf cart out, though? Down the dirt and gravel road into town to finally stop outside a gold shop while grinning all the way? Was there even a gold shop in town? A smile creased her cheek. Of course not. But still. No one was allowed to escape. If people suspected Samuel, or something like him existing, they might investigate. And if they came onto their land to do so, well then, there'd be nothing she could do to stop Samuel from bringing them down into the tunnels for another game. That would be way too many missing people to ignore and people would come looking for them. Samuel would eventually be found out. Their family would be ruined.

What should she do here? Take the shotgun and go get those weapons from the men or stop the golf cart guy from escaping? Which objective had priority here? She didn't want to think it, but there it was, shining and bright at the front of her mind: no one can escape. Not once a person has seen Samuel. And especially not once they've seen the gold. More than hunters would come here. Thieves would appear in droves. They had appeared before in the past and only because of a rumor. If people actually knew there was a cache of gold here, they would come again. She had to stop golf cart guy first. Then she could help her friend.

For now, Samuel would have to take care of himself. She knew him to be more than capable. She would bet on him every single time. Even if the men had their guns with them, she believed Samuel would come out on top. Samuel and the shadows were one. He moved through the tunnels without making a sound. But believing him triumphant versus knowing he'd be triumphant in any situation were two different things. A lucky swing with the pickaxe could debilitate him. And that sledgehammer could do real damage if it connected with any part of Samuel. They would have to hit him first though and that wasn't impossible. Improbable, yes. But not impossible.

Lyndsay stood. She cupped her elbows with her palms and squeezed her forearms to her stomach. She exhaled a slow breath through pursed lips. She examined the monitors, eyes flickering over the multiple screens, hoping to catch a glimpse of Samuel. Nothing. Even the cameras had a hard time capturing him.

"Good luck, Samuel. I don't think you'll need it. I hope you don't need it, but good luck all the same."

On another screen, the golf cart zoomed by.

Lyndsay stood and turned her back to the screens. Picking up the shotgun, she left the monitor room and for some reason, she closed the door. At the front door, she plucked a spring coat from the closet and put it on. Summer, but it was fast approaching early morning and what was once warm evening air had chilled considerably overnight.

Lifting the shotgun and opening the front door, she stepped outside. Crickets rubbed legs and an owl hooted. The night air refreshed her, and she inhaled a deep drought of it. She saw a light blue glow in the eastern portion of the sky. She stepped off the front stoop, said, "Knife," returned inside and attached a knife and sheath to the belt on her jeans. She checked the breech of the shotgun, saw a shell inside and nodded. Sweat trailed down her hairline and followed the line of her jaw. Nervous. And if truth be told, scared. She wished she didn't have to do this alone. It was so unfair. The one time her parents weren't here this crazy shit happens?

Lyndsay shook her head. Fair? What did that even mean? Life is life and fair has nothing to do with it. Bad situation? Sure. Does whining help? No. It never does.

"C'mon Lyndsay. Time to get to work."

She stepped out of the house and closed the door behind her. Her eyes sought the moon. She couldn't find it. Morning was a short earth-turn away. She needed to get moving. Needed to get this done. She didn't want golf cart guy escaping and getting far enough to wave someone down in a car on their way to work or something. The morning light revealed too much. The night hid dark deeds and Lyndsay had her family to protect.

-67-

The tunnel lights flashed overhead. Kyle drove from darkness into lightness into darkness and concentrated on the tunnel ahead. Passing other branching-off tunnels Kyle dismissed the old wood versus new wood theory. His new tactic was simpler. Drive straight. If he came to a dead end, reverse and find a new tunnel. Rinse and repeat. He hadn't been travelling for long when he entered a large cavern containing cars and motor bikes. He stomped on the brake and the gold shifted forward and pushed the cart ahead a few feet before it came to a stop. His teeth clacked together.

A dark sedan, two motorbikes and a pickup truck were crammed into the space close to a large garage door. Jesus H. Christ on a popsicle stick! He'd found the way out! His heart danced against his ribs. His hands trembled. His eyes turned to the pickup truck. He turned his head to take in the gold in the back of the cart. He could load the gold he has, go back, get some more and… wait, no, no, no. Not with that thing running around down here. He'd been lucky so far. Damn lucky. No one gets out alive, remember? That's what the woman said. And this gold behind him, he'd never seen so much money. To go back for more would be worse than his usual stupid.

Biting the nails on his right hand, he tasted blood. He'd ripped the nail too low worrying about the gold and thinking about what to do. He spit out the nail and drove the cart toward the pickup truck.

Stopping beside it, he stepped out, opened the door and climbed in. No keys. He scanned the dash, he opened the center console, and finding nothing but candy bar wrappers and gas receipts, reached over to the glove box. He popped it open. The owner's manual and a screwdriver. That was it. Certainly not any keys.

"C'mon! For real?"

Kyle stepped out of the truck and poked his head in so that he could see under the driver's seat. Dirt, stone pebbles, a nickel, plastic wrappers, but guess what? No keys. He walked around the nose of the truck and opened the passenger door. After searching the passenger side and not finding any keys, he slammed the door.

He checked the car next. Nothing. The motorbikes. Once again, no keys.

Shaking his head, he felt a madness laugh building in his chest. Would he have to drive the golf cart out of here? He hadn't expected to find cars in the first place. The gold had clouded his brain. Fine to spend all that time loading up the golf cart, but since he hadn't expected to find a car to take, what was his actual plan of getting out of here with all of the gold? Kyle hadn't formed one. He saw the gold and his brain fell out his ears. Loading it up, taking all that time like an idiot while the creature roamed the tunnels, searching, hunting him for food.

Still, if not for the gold, he wouldn't have found the cart. Without the cart, he wouldn't be here right now, standing a few feet from a garage door leading to freedom. He didn't have to take the gold, though. That was just greed and stupidity. He could've taken the cart and he'd be in the same situation as he is in now only a lot faster. How much time had he wasted? But money did something to people and Kyle wasn't immune to what the golden blocks promised. Even now, he loathed leaving the gold behind.

He slapped the cart. What should he do? His eyebrows climbed his forehead. He walked over to the pickup truck, pulled open the door, peered behind the driver's seat, and, yup, a backpack. He'd have to leave more gold behind but at least he wouldn't be leaving this crazy place completely empty handed. Smiling, he picked the bag up by the straps, closed the door, turned, and faced the business end of a shotgun.

-68-

Hank stopped at the next intersection of tunnels. His fingers tightened on the handle of the sledgehammer. Vern stood a few feet behind him where he always has been since this whole thing started. Not in front. Not beside him. Always behind him. And Hank knew why. Vern expected the thing to be waiting for them in the darkness of a tunnel ahead. Hank had been checking each tunnel they passed. And if the thing was there, the thing would see Hank first. Vern stayed behind Hank hoping that if the thing did attack, it would go after Hank before him. A logical precaution and Hank was mildly annoyed and a little impressed that Vern, in his seemingly perpetual terror-state, had thought that far ahead. Because it was a logical assumption. Every time Hank neared a new tunnel offshoot, his body shone with sweat and his breathing rate increased.

The darkness of the next tunnel entrance loomed ahead on the left, a dark mouth with the promise of a sinister monster hiding in its depths. It could be waiting for them, drool spilling from its open mouth, impatient for the walking meat meals approaching it. Right there ahead of him the-thing-that-shouldn't-be could be waiting for him. After seeing what it was capable of, Hank had no trouble imagining it ripping his arms and legs off and leaving him as a bleeding torso on the floor.

Hank's legs stopped moving on their own. He gave no conscious command to stop. His knees trembled. The muscles in his forearms holding the sledgehammer ached. All of his senses had magnified in proportion with his fear. The hot breath in his mouth, the smell of dirt mingling with sweat, seeing the tiny holes in the rock wall, the swirls in the wooden timbers. He'd had enough. This day, this night, this whatever, he's had enough of it.

Hank said, "Vern? Why don't you take point for a change?"

No answer. Figures. Don't want to deal with something? Just ignore it. Vern's classic answer for anything bothering him. He pulled this same shit when he had no good reason for coming up short on money owed on a drug deal. He'd avoided Hank for three whole weeks once. Didn't answer his phone. He didn't even answer his front door when Hank came knocking. Vern wouldn't ignore him this time. Fuck that. It felt good to have someone to be annoyed with. It made him forget for a time how scared he was. He turned around to tell Vern what's what and the thing was holding Vern by his head.

The creature's one clawed hand was wrapped around Vern's skull cupping his chin and covering his mouth. Vern's eyes protruded. It lifted Vern off the ground and hugged him to its chest. Vern's feet kicked at the air and still clutching the pickaxe in his hands. The amber eyes of the beast locked onto Hank.

Hank prepped the sledgehammer to swing and in the space of a breath, the creature stepped forward and with his free hand, pushed Hank in the chest. Hank's feet left the ground. A ceiling light burned into his retina and he closed his eyes. He hit the ground on the upper part of his back, and it knocked the wind from him. The wooden handle of the sledgehammer in his hands clacked into his chin and his teeth crunched through the skin on the inside of his cheek. Blood flooded his mouth leaving a salty coating on his tongue. He blinked. Bright, dancing motes obscured his vision. He was going to die. Validating this thought was the creature's easy decimation of his friends. They were in its home. It had moved through these tunnels in complete silence, knowing every turn, probably knowing where he and his clumsy friends were at all times. And when it moved! A lightning strike appeared slow in comparison. Hank hadn't even seen the hand slamming into his chest that sent him flying. Vern had been right. What could they do against a creature like this? They were dead men. Their brains just didn't know it yet.

Hank sucked in a lungful of air, got a mouthful of the dust his body hitting the ground had raised, and coughed. He rolled onto his hands and knees with the sledgehammer grip end held loose in one hand. Warm pink drool fell from his mouth onto the knuckles of his right hand. His eyes drifted to the thing.

The animal held Vern out with one arm by his neck. Vern still had the pickaxe, but he was frozen. His feet aren't even kicking anymore. Sweat streamed down his face. His mouth opened and closed.

With his other hand, the thing plucked the pickaxe from Vern's hands as easily as an adult taking a toy from a toddler. The creature tossed the pickaxe and it landed two feet in front of Hank's feet. It didn't care what weapons they had. That's why it tossed the pickaxe near Hank, where he could reach it. It wasn't afraid of them armed or unarmed. Weapons were useless to them.

Vern's face, caught in half-light and half-shadow, purpled with blood. With his free hand, the creature dug and twisted his claws into Vern's abdomen. A squeal erupted from Vern, a high-pitched noise sounding as though it was being pushed through a straw. His legs danced on the air and blood pattered the dirt below him.

Hank stood, hefted the sledgehammer, gritted his teeth and said, "Fuck you!"

Hank ran at the creature, lifting the sledgehammer, intent on hitting a homerun with the shaggy head of the beast and envisioning knocking the cranium off its neck.

Hank only had to travel fifteen feet. In his first few steps, the creature removed its gore coated hand from Vern's stomach. Entrails slipped out and fell to the ground. Grey, red and slimy and Hank thought, *I hope I don't slip in those*, and then his head connected with what felt like a wall. His body was still moving forward with the momentum of his running. His feet left the dirt again and for a moment his body was parallel to the ground, as though he had decided to take a nap mid-air.

The back of his head struck the ground first. Sharp pieces of rock and debris scraped the skin off the top of his shoulders, his neck and his head. The world disappeared into darkness. He opened and closed his hands. No sledgehammer. Where did that go? The missing sledgehammer failed to startle him. His thoughts felt anchored in muck and floating through fog. In this state, time had a different feel to it, like watching a film in slow speed, frame by frame. He moaned, blinked and the tunnel roof materialized out of the blackness. The roof moved as though it breathed. He blinked again and the roof stilled. His face stung. It was warm and sticky. His ears rung. He opened and closed his jaw, trying to dispel it.

Hank lifted his head. The monster stared at him with those amber, reflective eyes. It raised its gory hand and extended its index finger. It wagged the dripping digit back and forth.

It turned its large, hairy head to Vern. Vern's eyelids fluttered. Blood coated his mouth. Vern's kicking legs stilled.

The creature pointed its snout at Vern. Its chest expanded and deflated. Its tongue darted out between teeth. It reached down and grabbed Vern's ankles and squeezed them together. One hand held Vern by the neck and the other hand was holding the ankles securely together. It turned Vern so he was horizontal. It glanced at Hank, maybe to make sure he was sitting still like a good boy or to make sure Hank was still watching. Hank didn't know and it didn't matter. He couldn't look away. Not now.

It chuffed at Hank and then it buried its snout inside Vern's stomach and started eating.

Hank clamped his hands over his ears. The sounds! Those terrible, wet, meaty sounds! For some reason unknown to him, Hank remembered a line from a National Geographic show on predators. While a lion tore open the stomach of an antelope and was eating it alive the narrator said in a robotic, calm voice, *Predators, to avoid injury, always go for the soft spots first.*

Hank turned his head to the side and vomited his partially digested Subway sandwich.

-69-

Kyle said, "Oh. Hey."

The barrel didn't waver. Her eyes were locked onto his. They were not as steady as the shotgun. She blinked repeatedly. She bit her lower lip. Dots of sweat beaded her brow. She was afraid and instead of relief at the realization, he felt fear. People did weird shit when they were scared. He would know. He was pretty much an expert on weird shit. He raised his hands, palms up, to shoulder height. He smiled and failing, produced a sneer instead. Her gaze hardened.

Kyle said, "Hey, uh, take it easy."

"Stop talking!"

"Alright! Alright! It's cool. I'm cool-"

"Why are you still talking?"

"I-"

"Shut up!"

Kyle closed his mouth and lowered his chin to his chest. His mouth dried. His mind experienced two simultaneous thoughts, *She is going to shoot me* and *How many times has a gun been pointed at me over the past day?*

She said, "You weren't supposed to make it this far! Samuel was supposed to get you! Not me! It shouldn't be up to me! How in the hell do you always seem to get away? The cops couldn't get you, those men couldn't get you, and Samuel, he couldn't get you before you made it here! Now, I have to deal with you. No one can get out alive! Don't you get it? No one! It's not allowed!"

Kyle heard her sob. He glared at her, and she poked the barrel toward him.

She said, "You're not getting away this time. Your luck has run out."

Luck? Kyle laughed. He couldn't help himself. Waking up with a decapitated human head in his lap. That's lucky is it? Getting chased around the woods, getting lost, and running around scared for hours on end? Lucky again, right? And the kid, wait, no, no, don't think of that, don't think about him. And then getting caught, being put in an actual cage swinging on a chain from a ceiling only to be released so that some mythical monster could chase him around in an underground tunnel intent on eating him? Lucky too?

Once Kyle started laughing, he couldn't stop. Absurd. To call him lucky. Stupidest idea ever.

His shoulders shook with his laughter. Tears squeezed out between his eyes.

"What are you laughing at?"

The question made him laugh harder. He put his hands on his knees. The laughter hurt his stomach, and he thought laughing like this might give him an actual six-pack. He pictured a DVD box with his own smiling face on it with a title, *Laugh Your Way To A Washboard Stomach!* and he laughed harder.

"What is so goddamn funny, huh? This shotgun funny to you? Why are you making this so hard?"

He was making this hard? The question brought on another bout of sidesplitting laughter.

"Shut up!"

There was anger in her voice now. Gone was the self-doubting, questioning tone. Her anger dried up his laughter. Hard things are easier to do when you're angry. Anger gives you that extra juice. She was one yell away from pulling the trigger and Kyle was one more chuckle away from oblivion.

"Sorry. Sorry for laughing," Kyle wiped his eyes, "it's just," a giggle threatened, "you called me lucky. This past day is not what I would call lucky."

She blinked. Her eyes shone even in the dim light. Could he talk his way out of this? Or would she just keep him here until Samuel caught up to him so she wouldn't have to do the dirty work she clearly had a problem with? Would she actually shoot him if it came down to that? The shotgun barrel didn't move. It didn't shake or tremble. She had it in control. A solid piece of death dealing metal locked to her shoulder. He could probably balance a dinner tray on the barrel and eat a meal. But did that equal her resolve to kill him? She didn't seem like a killer, not at first glance, but what did he know? He didn't think of himself as a killer, either. More like a person put in unfortunate circumstances.

Kyle said, "So what's the plan here?"

"Stop talking!" She sniffed and said, "And put your hands back up!"

Kyle raised his hands, palms toward her. He smelled his own breath, and it wasn't good. Her scent carried to him. Her smell made him think of a hot shower and a thick, body-covering lather of soap. When was the last time he'd had a shower? Stupid thoughts. Always with the stupid thoughts. What did that matter now?

Scared and indecisive, he didn't want to piss her off. Kyle had difficulty sitting still, staying quiet and being told what to do. He had an impulse to disobey. Those attributes had garnered him a lot of trouble over the years and he knew it. If he could, he would change those aspects of himself. To him, those behaviors were in his DNA. Might as well try to change his eye color or make himself taller. Those characteristics, bad and annoying as they were, he knew there was nothing he could do about them.

Kyle shifted his feet.

"Stop moving!"

Kyle wiggled his nose. Suddenly itchy, a mad desire to scratch it infused him. He closed his eyes and shook his head. Still there. The itch needled him.

"Can I scratch my nose?"

"Shut up!"

He rocked from side to side, palms up, the itching too much to take.

"Sorry! Gotta do it!"

Kyle scratched the side of his nose with his left hand. Instant relief! A smile formed.

"Put your hands back up!"

"Ok! Ok!"

He raised his hands. He had been holding them up for some time now and his shoulders were beginning to ache with the rest of his body. Some parts of his body were worse off than others, like his right knee and other parts ached from a multitude of diverse exercises such as his constant running from the police and others. His shoulders burned. His hands shook, then his forearms and then his biceps.

"I can't hold my hands up forever! My shoulders are killing me!"

"You're a goddamn pest, aren't you?"

"That's not the first time I've been called that." A pause, "Can I put my hands down or what?"

"Fine. Fine."

"How long you plan on keeping me here."

"No one gets out."

"Yeah. You've said that. But listen for a second. I am being hunted by the police and they will never stop looking for me. And maybe, just maybe, one of them might think that I came here. Or they just might check here anyway, because why the hell not? And then what will that thing do to them?"

"Samuel. His name is Samuel."

"Ok. Samuel. Anyway, if there is anyone to be the first to make it out alive, I'm the perfect person to let go from here. It'd be actually helpful. To you. I'd lead the cops away from here. They won't come knocking at your door and they won't come onto your precious land."

"They'll catch you. You'll talk."

"No, no. I may be a lot of things, but a rat is not one of them. But let's say that I do get caught and I squeal my face off. So what if I do? All they want me to say is 'I'm guilty.' You think they'll take the time to listen to me talk about anything else? You think they'd even believe me about Samuel? That I found a murdering Bigfoot in the woods? Not only that, but that I also found blocks of gold in an underground tunnel system any gopher would be proud of? They'd be sending me to a shrink if I told them all that."

Her eyes tightened over the barrel. She shook her head, "No. No one can get out of here. Not after what you have seen. It's too risky."

"More risky than when the cops show up on your land looking for me?"

"I uh, I have to think. I can't make this choice. I don't want to."

"You gonna shoot me, then? I don't think so."

She stared at him. Her nostrils flared. Sweat cut a line down her forehead.

She said, "Maybe I don't have too."

Kyle suppressed his smile. Had he just talked her out of shooting him? Is she thinking of letting him go? He didn't want to push her. Not now that he is so close.

Keeping the barrel of the shotgun pointed at his chest, she inhaled a chest expanding breath and yelled, "Samuel! Help!"

Kyle's lower jaw dropped. He said, "You fucking bitch."

-70-

Hank spat out the remaining chunks of vomit in his mouth. The noises of the creature feeding on Vern filled the space.

Putting his hands over his ears, he closed his eyes and said, "Stop it, stop it, stop, stop, stop it you fucking fuck!"

The ground shook. Something heavy had fallen.

He opened one eye. The monster had tossed Vern close to Hank. Hollowed out and looking like an empty banana skin, Vern's eyes found Hank. His mouth opened. His hands twitched. Still alive. How the hell was he still alive?

"Vern."

Vern turned his face up to the ceiling light. His mouth moved. He said something. Hank couldn't hear the words. He heard a broken exhalation of breath. Vern twitched. Once. Twice. Then stillness.

The monster stood watching Hank, always watching. Its head brushed the ceiling. Blood and bits of Vern slow-dropped from its chin. The furry hands were shiny and dark with blood. What a thing to see as your last sight on earth. A friend eaten and dumped on the ground the way Hank would toss a chicken bone once he'd stripped the meat from it. Thrown aside without a thought. Hank didn't want to die on his back with vomit coating his chin. If he is going to die, and it sure seemed like a foregone conclusion at this point, then he is going to do so on his feet.

"Alright. Let's get this done."

Hank rolled to his stomach, careful to avoid the puke for some reason, like it mattered, and he pushed himself to his feet. He faced the thing. Its hands were at its side, legs spread, chest expanding and deflating with each breath. Hank turned his head. A pickaxe on the ground and a sledgehammer four feet to his right. His eyes returned to the beast. It was crouched now like a sprinter at the starting blocks. Muscles rippled under the coat, along its chest and under the jeans, its quads flexed.

Hank thought in other times, on the occasions when he mused on the possibility of his own death, that it would be better to go quick. Best even to go in your sleep if you could manage it. Facing this thing from fifteen feet away, he thought the opposite. He wanted to go out fighting this beast. He wanted to hurt it. He wanted it to feel fear. He wanted it to experience the pain and terror it had subjected him and his friends to. Why should it get to rip through them all without even getting a scratch? Why should it have Hank and his friends pay such a price for stepping over an invisible line in the dirt? That's what this was about, right? Dirt? Strange, even though Hank understood the logic. He employed such logic himself when other drug dealers tried to test him by selling on his turf. Someone steps into your home? You put them down. And you do it fast. Even though Hank understood it, that didn't mean he would quit at the end and let this thing have a happy ending for free. No. Hank will hurt it. And he knew he would die in the attempt and right now, he was okay with that. He grinned at the thing. Hank said, "C'mon, then, you freaky fuck! You're going to have to earn this meal. Yeah. I'm going to make you pay for it in blood.

It growled. Hank assumed a grappler's stance. Bent knees, balanced and with his hands out in front of him.

The amber eyes shone.

"Come on!"

It stood. Hank gasped. It moved so quick. One second it was crouched low, ready to pounce and in a movement his eye didn't catch, the thing was standing. Hank swallowed, and waiting, studied the creature.

Its posture had turned from aggressive to... not. It reminded Hank of a prairie dog in the field with its head up and looking in the distance at something.

Hank glanced behind him. More tunnel. Nothing to see. Nothing that Hank could see, or sense, anyway. Back to the creature, Hank saw it sniff the air while its ears rotated forward. It growled again and shot towards Hank. By the time Hank raised his hands to his head, the creature had moved past him, and in a few strides, was out of Hank's sight. Dust settled to the ground in its wake.

What was that about? Hank's whole body started to shake. When his trembling stopped, he muttered, "You're not getting away that easy you bastard."

Studying the ground, Hank saw the distinctive print the creature had left. Hank picked up the sledgehammer and followed. It had moved that way for a purpose. Even if following the creature wouldn't lead him out, he would at least know where the creature was. And if the creature came back for him, it wouldn't catch Hank off guard again. He white-knuckled the handle of the sledgehammer. Besides, he had a score to settle.

-71-

Kyle pushed the barrel of the shotgun to left side of his body with the back of his hand. The shotgun boomed. He felt the heat of the slug pass under his armpit and saw her eyes widen. He punched her in the nose with his right hand. It crunched under his fist and he didn't think he'd ever experienced a more satisfying feeling in his life. Her knees wobbled, her eyes rolled up and before she could fall back and away from him, Kyle snatched her arm holding the shotgun by the wrist and he hit her again above the left eye. Her skin exploded along the eyebrow. Kyle lost his grip on her arm. She hit the ground still holding the shotgun. She fell in a star pattern. Blood flowed from her nose and eyebrow. He stepped to her and kicked her in the ribs. She cried out. He stomped on her hand holding the gun and felt her bones crack under the sole of his shoe. He yelled. He heard himself yelling. He knew he wasn't making sense with his yells, but it didn't matter. He was in the moment now.

"Fucking! Stupid cow! You think! Fucking shotgun? Tired! Getting shot at! Fucking bitch!"

The toe of his shoe sank into her middle. Kyle lost his balance and fell onto his injured knee.

"Oof!"

Breathing heavy with spittle coating his lower lip in foam, Kyle rubbed his knee to survey what he had done. The woman's chest rose and fell. She was still alive, but she wasn't moving. She moaned. He reached for the shotgun. When he started kicking her, she had pulled it into her middle and did her best to turn away from his kicking foot. Even half-conscious, she cleaved to the gun. He yanked at it. Her arms were wrapped tight around it and they were not letting go.

"Give-me-the-damn-gun!"

Kyle punched her in the face. Her one eye had already swollen shut and the other one rolled up white when he hit her again. She turned her head and spit. Kyle saw teeth in the blood. Tough lady. She wouldn't let go of that gun. He grudgingly had some respect for her, taking a beating like that and still holding onto the shotgun.

A roar echoed down the tunnel toward him. The hair along his body stood. He felt cold, as though he had swallowed a bowling ball of ice and it rested in his stomach. The noise sounded far away but who knew how sound travelled in these maze-like tunnels? Samuel could be right around the corner for all he knew. Forget the gun. Time to go.

He scrambled to his feet. Coins jingled in his pocket. The gold. He paused, considering the gold bars left on the golf cart. Another roar. Was the sound closer or farther?

Now, where had she come from? She had surprised him, that's for sure. How did she do that? Was she already here and waiting around just in case one of them made it this far?

Scanning the dirt floor, he saw her hard-to-see footprints. An imprint there. A rounded portion there. He backtracked her steps, attacked by mini-heart attacks when he lost sight of them, knowing Samuel is coming, is on his way and when he finds her on the ground in the shape she's in it won't go well for Kyle, no sir.

Sweat fell from his forehead, plopping on the dirt. His breath burned his mouth. Indented in the wall, hidden initially by the angle of the rock, was a steel door. He rushed to it and yanked on the handle. Locked.

"Fuck! Of course! Goddamnit!"

He sprinted back to the woman and patted her pants. He found a bulge of keys in her front right pocket. With shaking hands, he pulled the keys out of the pocket.

A roar sounded. Closer this time. Definitely closer.

Kyle ran back to the door and yanked on it. Why won't it open? He sobbed and raised his hand to run it through his hair as he normally did when stressed and raked metal across his hairline.

"Ahh! What?"

He stared at the keys in his hand. How did he forget about them? This stress was going to kill him if the creature doesn't. He wanted to laugh at the thought and instead had to stuff down another sob.

On the fourth key, the door opened. Kyle stepped outside into the morning air.

-72-

The Chief couldn't sleep. He had gone home after speaking to the Inspector and slid into bed beside Natalie. He turned off the police portable and left it with his uniform on a chair by the dresser. He put his phone on the nightstand beside his head. The dispatchers knew to call him if something was to come up.

As he settled in, the bedsprings complained of his weight. Natalie's hand rubbed his back when he positioned himself comfortably. It was something she did every night. Something he took for granted. A simple gesture, but on this night in particular, her touch meant all the world. Ruby's smiling face floated in the ether of his mind. Had he failed her? His nostrils burned. The pillow dampened under his cheek. His brain turned.

Had he missed anything? Could he have done more? Would someone else die in the night because of him?

The Chief's brain drew circles around questions without answers. He gave up the attempt at sleep when the dark sky wasn't so dark anymore. He swung his feet to the floor.

Natalie said, "Did you sleep?"

"A little."

"You want breakfast?"

"I'll get it. You go back to sleep."

"I was hoping you'd make it for me, actually."

"I can, but I was going to grab McDonald's for breakfast."

"In a rush to get back at it, huh?"

"Yeah. I guess. I feel useless sitting here."

"Driving around in circles won't make you any more useful."

"I know. But I'll feel like I'm doing something."

"Well, be careful. That man isn't very particular about who he kills."

The Chief tilted his head from side to side until his neck cracked.

"I'm worried about some of my people. I've been hearing some rumors. They don't want to arrest him. They want to kill him. Execute him. I don't know if anyone of them would follow through with it or not. Saying you're going to do something like that and actually doing it are two different things. Still, I worry about it because what if one of them does kill him? That'd be a world of trouble."

"I don't want any of your people getting in trouble either. That is something to worry about."

"The worst part is, if one of them does find Kyle, and Kyle is killed, it could be it was in self-defense, that Kyle had attacked them because that would be perfectly reasonable, given what he has done so far, but because of all the talk, I'd always suspect it was murder. Cause that's what it would be, right? Murder?"

"So, even if they could get away with it, make it appear lawful so there'd be no backlash or trouble down the road, that would still bother you?"

"If I suspected murder?"

"Yeah."

"I uh, well, I think it should bother me. It's not our job to murder people. It's not our job to judge people. It's our job to protect everyone. No matter who they are and that's supposed to include Kyle. What bothers me more is that in my head, I think it should bother me, for all of those reasons I just said, only I'm kind of scared that right now that it wouldn't bother me. I'd almost feel relief and, I don't know, but I'd feel like justice was done and taxpayer money was saved from housing that animal. And that's wrong, isn't it?"

She rubbed his back and he heard her adjust in the bed behind him. Natalie is sitting upright in the bed with her back against the headboard.

She said, "Look, in 99.9 percent of circumstances, I agree with you. No cop should ever be judge and executioner. That's too much power for anyone and it would be abused. No doubt. But sometimes, and I know this doesn't sound like my usual liberal self, but sometimes, the world is better off without some people in it. And Kyle, this man who kills everyone he runs into, even children, he's like a rabid dog. And the only way to protect people from a rabid dog is to put the animal down."

"Ah, jeez, Natalie-"

"Look, I'm not saying you should go hunting him like some of your friends might want to. I'm just saying, if someone does take him out, and on the surface it looks, I don't know, lawful? Then don't dig too deep into it."

"What if that person is me?"

She sighed and rubbed her face with her hands. She said, "I don't know. I guess I'd say you've done your job. Sometimes the right thing to do is the wrong thing to do, you know? Or the line is so blurred the choice kind of hovers in the grey area. The law is not always right. The laws were written by people after all."

Rubes' face appeared. The boy's face floated. He closed his eyes.

"Yeah. No. Hell, I don't know. I don't want to have to kill anyone Nat."

"I know you don't. Just be careful, okay?"

"Yeah."

He stood.

• • •

The Chief picked up a coffee, a breakfast sandwich and a hash brown from McDonald's. He drove out toward the Grayson's, interested in the little laneway he'd seen on Google maps. The sun crested the horizon. It backlit the trees, turning them into dark sticks. Mornings could be beautiful if you had a mind to notice them. The Chief took a bite of the hash brown and followed the dry potato cake with a sip of hot coffee heavy with cream and sugar.

"Damnit!"

The liquid burned his tongue, and he spilled a bit down the front of his vest. He pulled over, his tires crunching over the gravel. Every good cop had napkins in their cruiser and the Chief was no exception. He wiped the outside of the coffee cup with the napkin, shoved the used napkin in the empty cup holder and since he was parked, he turned on his iPad. He brought up the Grayson home again and pinched the screen to zoom in. He shook his head. He could see an open laneway, a dirt one, in between a break in the trees. It looked like a road, but he couldn't see how to get to it.

The Chief spread his fingers on the screen to zoom out. The best course of action that he could see would be to follow the road around the property and see what he could see. He'd be able to see more in the daylight. At least he'd be able to write the Grayson place off as somewhere he had checked.

• • •

He spotted the break in the trees a short time later. He stopped on the paved road and rolled the window down a crack. A smooth dirt road continued through a narrow gap in the trees. Should he tell someone where he was and what he was about to do? He might be told to stay away from the Grayson place. Not that anyone could tell him to do that. He was the Chief after all. Still, that was their land and going onto it uninvited, he was technically trespassing. And he, like everyone else in town, had heard stories about the Grayson's over the years. And although his adult police brain dismissed the most fanciful of the tales, the kid in him felt a little tremor of unease glancing through the trees to the almost hidden road beyond.

No. He'd keep this little jaunt to himself. If he needed any help, he'd call in then. Besides, this is a long shot. There are miles of woods out here to get lost in. For Kyle to run into the only home for miles is, all things considered, very unlikely.

Leaving the road, the Chief drove onto the Grayson land. The morning light had brightened the scenery fast. The emerald leaves, the dark browns and the piercing shafts of light breaking through the overhead canopy brought the woods into clear detail. The Chief reached the area where the trees no longer covered the road, the place he believed he had seen on Google maps. He looked out his window and up at the sky, picturing the satellite orbiting, maybe capturing his tilted head staring right back at it. He brought his attention back to the road. It ended or rather, the road turned around and back on itself. From high up, it would appear as an outline of a lightbulb.

"There's nothin here."

More trees, more leaves, more dirt, more rocks, more… of nothing helpful, really.

He didn't know if he should feel relieved or disappointed. There was a hole in his chest, where his feelings should be. This could be a good thing. Kyle could be wandering the woods, without food and without water, and if he's out here long enough, the problem of Kyle would take care of itself. That would be an ideal resolution to the problem. He hadn't thought so at the beginning, but now, yeah, that would do very nicely.

He lifted his foot from the brake.

"Help! Hey, help me!"

And there he was. The devil himself. The Chief blinked a few times, not sure if what he was seeing was real. Kyle was running toward him on the driver side, emerging from the tree-line, waving his arms, and yelling at him, his mouth a round, black hole.

The Chief blinked. Still there. He was even getting closer. Even though the sight of Kyle defied credulity, it was the thing chasing him that caused the Chief's breath to stop while his heart jumped in his chest.

The Chief had heard the tale as a kid that there was a beast roaming the Grayson land. People went missing if they went too close to the lonely house in the woods. Only they weren't missing. Not really. They had become food for the monster of the land. A rumor, a tale the Chief had believed in with his whole heart when he was a child. He outgrew the story as most people do when any story involves monsters in the woods. Because monsters aren't real. Of course not. The only monsters on this earth are other people. And Kyle represented those monsters parading as people. Grotesque and cruel, he was still only a person.

The thing behind him, catching up to Kyle, was a monster out of nightmares. A creature with a lupine head, fur covered body, a gaping jaw with large, scythe-like teeth and claws that could eviscerate a person with a swipe while wearing the dark coat and jeans of a man.

Kyle was maybe thirty feet ahead of the predator. The creature gained five feet with every bound. Then Kyle was at the Chief's SUV, pulling on the handle of the back door. It'd be so easy to unlock it and let Kyle scramble in and drive off away from the creature. A simple push of a button. He could catch this man without even having to get out of his cruiser or even draw his handgun. Wasn't that what the Chief wanted? Wasn't that an ideal arrest?

"Hey! Let me in! Arrest me! Arrest me!"

The Chief's finger hovered above the unlock button. He still had time to unlock it and let Kyle in before the creature arrived. So, why was he hesitating? Rubes' face. The boy's face. Grace's decapitated head. And Kyle, the rabid dog at his door, pleading for help.

He pulled his hand away from the door's unlock button. He turned his face away from Kyle and fixed his gaze straight ahead. The Chief took his foot off the brake. The SUV rolled forward.

"Hey! What are you-"

The Chief pressed down on the accelerator.

"Ahhhhh! No, no, no, no!"

A look in the side view mirror. The creature now had Kyle. It picked him up and tossed Kyle over its shoulder. Its amber eyes fastened onto the Chief's.

An arctic chill vibrated through him and the steering wheel jerked under his hand. He dropped his eyes and accelerated away.

Leaving the dirt road, breaking through the gap of trees to join the paved road off the Grayson land, the Chief said, "A rabid dog."

He turned on the radio and tapping the wheel with his palm, hummed along with the song as tears coated his cheeks.

-73-

The last time Lyndsay remembered experiencing physical pain was when she was a child and had been learning how to ride a bike. She thought she had the hang of it, the whole balance on two-wheels thing. The front wheel didn't wobble under her grip anymore and she had stopped looking at her handlebars and kept her gaze straight ahead toward where she wanted to go. She felt comfortable with her skills. While self-congratulating herself on navigating the trail running around her home with professional adeptness, her back tire clipped a rock sending a jarring jolt through the frame. When she opened her eyes, she was staring up through the branches overhead. She felt a stabbing pain in her lower back and started to panic about not being able to breathe. She had recovered from the experience and was riding the trails again the next day but with more respect to how hard the ground could hit when you weren't paying attention. That day, in comparison to today on the pain meter, well, that day on the bike was more like a lower back massage to how Kyle had worked her over.

Samuel crouched over her, his hands hesitating over her body, not knowing where it would be safe to touch her or even if he should. He mewled.

She could only see him out of one eye. Her other eye had swollen shut. Half of her world was black. She spit blood out and felt the sharp edge of a tooth slip out from between her lips. She must look a sight. No wonder Samuel was thrumming with worry.

She said, "You have to get him Samuel. No one can get out." The words cost effort. Her mashed and split lips didn't work the way they normally did. Samuel understood her, though. After she finished the last sentence, his head turned, and he sniffed at the air. He growled.

"Bring him back, Samuel."

He stood. She could see the hesitation in his stance. He didn't want to leave her, but he didn't want the man who did this to her to get away, either.

"Get him!"

Samuel bounded off.

Lyndsay placed the shotgun on the ground and rolled to her stomach. She had held onto it the entire time. Even when he was beating her, she knew to keep a hold of the gun. If she didn't, he'd turn the barrel on her and that would be the end of her. She grimaced. Blood spilled from her open mouth. Her ribs! Her hand! Her face!

She gathered her breath and doing a terrible imitation of a push-up, she rolled herself so she ended up sitting on her heels. She wondered what her dad would think of all this. She shook her head and a sharp pain lanced behind her closed eye. She calmed her breath. The inhales were inflating her lungs and moving her ribs and that also hurt. All those kicks to her middle. He had probably broken something inside her. To minimize the pain, she breathed in short, small inhalations.

She heard Kyle yell, "Fucking stupid, thing!"

Through her one eye, she saw Samuel carrying Kyle over his shoulder. He stopped in front of her. He held a hand to her.

She said, "No, no. I'll catch up to you. I'll, uh, take the golf cart, I think. You do what you have to with him."

"With me? Fuck that! I got out! I beat your game!"

She smiled a bloody lipped smile and said, "It doesn't look that way."

Samuel walked away and Kyle used his hands to push against the back of Samuel so he could lift his head. He said, "There was a cop out there! And more of them will be coming! Everything you have here? It's gone! They'll be coming and there's nothing you can do to stop them! You and your fucking pet! It's all over! I beat you, bitch!"

She reached for the shotgun and stopped. Reaching hurt. She knew the ribs were connected with almost all of the large muscle groups. She'll be hurting for a while. She put her hands on her knees and thought maybe she'd leave the shotgun here. What did she need it for now anyway? She picked it up anyway. With how this night has been going, be better to have it than not.

-74-

Following the monster-prints in the dirt and the roars echoing in the tunnels, although he didn't know it, while in pursuit of the creature, Hank was approaching the exit. He held the sledgehammer in a two-handed death grip. He had it cocked over his right shoulder, ready to swing. Sweating, he repeatedly used the right sleeve of his shirt to clear the stinging liquid from his eyes. He had a headache from continually clenching his jaw. His back still ached from the last contact with the creature and every so often, Hank would stop and attempt to stretch it out by arching his back and twisting from side to side. It was exhausting being scared all the time. Hank knew he hadn't been in the tunnels all that long but now, walking around with this sledgehammer, a killer headache and an aching back, he almost couldn't remember a time when he was not down here and running and hiding for his life. He wanted this night to be over. He wanted all of this to be over. He didn't want to be scared anymore.

Hank stopped, body tense and his eyes squinting into the darkness of the tunnel. He had heard something. Voices.

"With me? Fuck that! I got out! I beat your game!"

A lighter, murmuring voice followed. Must be the woman. All of his friends were dead, so it wasn't one of them. But there was something wrong with her words. Did the tunnels do that with sounds? Then why did he hear the man so well? Hank straightened. A frown pulled his brow low. Who was that man? It could only be one person. Kyle.

Shaking his head, Hank muttered, "Motherfucker."

There followed more yelling, but he wasn't paying attention to the content. Hank was creeping closer to the voices and he pressed his back tight to the wall while remaining deep in the shadows.

Heavy footfalls approached. Kyle's complaining got louder and then the creature was there, the dark coat right in front of him and now passing him. He hadn't been seen! Now was the time. He wouldn't get another chance at this. All of his friends were dead because of this evil, hateful thing. Hank's anger and his fear surged energy into his body.

"Ahhhh!"

Hank swung the sledgehammer. It connected with the creature's leg, right about where the knee would be, with a satisfying crack. The creature howled and Kyle fell to the ground away from Hank.

The creature rolled onto its back and raised an arm as Hank was swinging and -crack!- connected and smashed the thing's wrist. The creature wailed and tucked the injured hand tight to its belly and Hank was already swinging again and -crack!- on the shin of the monster. Hank shimmied to the side, eyeing the head of the creature for the next swing. Smiling now, all the terror forgotten, all the aches and pains not even a background annoyance to this triumphant moment. He raised the sledgehammer, his teeth a grinning half-moon in his face and a shotgun blast hit him in the ribs. He staggered to the side and dropped the sledgehammer. He fell to his knees. Blood gushed from his side, coating the injured side of his body with warm wetness.

He said, "Not fair..."

The creature reached for him with his good hand and pulled him close. It growled as it opened its mouth. Hank could see down its throat. The rows of teeth punched through the crown of Hank's head.

●   ●   ●

After shooting Hank, Lyndsay crawled on her hands and knees to the golf cart. It had been a risky shot. She was in a lot of pain and had to go prone on her stomach to aim the shotgun. She knew the gun had slugs in it so she wasn't worried about the spread like she would have been if it had been loaded with birdshot. Still a tough shot though. The ground had compressed her ribs and she hissed with pain while trying to keep her sights on Hank. He danced around Samuel swinging that sledgehammer like a man possessed and the barrel bounced and jerked following him. He paused to lift the sledgehammer for a swing, and she took the shot. Hank dropped and Samuel finished him off. Lyndsay closed her eyes and waited for the waves of pain to subside long enough or her to be able to move again.

Two painful minutes later, she was in the driver's seat of the golf cart and rolling over to Samuel. He didn't look so good. Neither did the man she had shot.

She wouldn't be able to move Samuel. She'd have to attach something to the cart (maybe the trolley they used to bring in heavier items like furniture and appliances) and get him into that and drive him over to his food freezer. He healed fast provided he had enough food to fuel his recovery. Samuel was already at work consuming the man, and maybe, by the time she returned with the cart, he'd be done with most of him and that'd be one less heavy body to worry about. Wait. She glanced around, frowning. Where was Kyle?

-75-

Kyle ran. When the creature dropped him after being struck by Hank, he skulked close to the walls, and making himself as small and unnoticeable as he possibly could, he scurried out of there. He was almost by the exit when he heard the shotgun boom. He tucked his head into his shoulders, expecting another boom, and he shoulder-charged open the steel door and fell back and hit the ground. Locked. He stood, rotating his shoulder and patted his pockets and yup, he still had the keys. He started shaking and he ignored the burning need to look behind him to see if the creature was making its way toward him while he fucked around with the keys. On the third try, the door clicked open.

He ran. His legs pumped, his heartbeat against the bones in his chest, his lungs burned, and he continued running. He stumbled, tripped and fell to the ground and tore the skin from his palms when he tried to brace his fall. He hugged the earth with his body and the dirt he breathed against became mud in his mouth.

He rolled to his back, sucking in that wonderful oxygen, blinking at the bright morning sky. He should get up and get going only he was too tired right now and all and all, he was in a good position. The bikers chasing him are dead. The cops, one of them anyway, thought Kyle was dead. The creature was hurt and hopefully, wouldn't be coming for him anytime soon. And because of the monster, that lady wouldn't be calling anyone about him escaping. Right now, he is a non-entity. And that was an excellent position to be in, wasn't it?

He smiled and after rubbing his face with his hands, he dropped them to his thighs. The hard metal of gold coins in his pockets startled him. The gold. He had plenty of gold still in his pockets. He had crammed them into the front and back pockets. He must have felt them when he was scrambling for the keys but at the time, that hadn't been his focus. A smile spread across his face. A short bark of a laugh startled a bird from a branch. A giggle bubbled up and the giggle became unrestrained laughter that he could not stop.

Not for a long time.

ABOUT THE AUTHOR

A busy father of four with a cat, John Hunt lives and works in the City of Guelph. He is a member of the Horror Writers Association and has had nine short stories published in various anthologies.

He is the best-selling author of *Doll House*, the award-winning *The Tracker*, and the well-reviewed *Off The Grid*. He is the author of the apocalyptic novella *Balance* and a book of short stories titled *Four Shots of Horror*.

John Hunt is a co-host on the Movies of the Damned!! podcast where he discusses horror films with his friend, Kyle Grant.

NOTE FROM THE AUTHOR

Word-of-mouth is crucial for any author to succeed. If you enjoyed *Murder Run*, please leave a review online—anywhere you are able. Even if it's just a sentence or two. It would make all the difference and would be very much appreciated.

Thanks!
John Hunt

Thank you so much for reading one of **John Hunt's** Novels.

If you enjoyed our book, please check out our recommended title for your next great read!

The Tracker by John Hunt

"A dark thriller that draws the reader in." *–Morning Bulletin*

"I never want to hear mention of bolt-cutters, a live rat and a bucket in the same sentence again. EVER."
–Ginger Nuts of Horror